The Duke Who Lied

(THE 1797 CLUB BOOK 8)

By

USA Today Bestseller
Jess Michaels

THE DUKE WHO LIED

The 1797 Club Book 8

www.1797Club.com

Copyright © Jess Michaels, 2018
ISBN-13: 978-1721515417
ISBN-10: 1721515410

All rights reserved. This book or any portion thereof may not be reproduced or used in any manner whatsoever without the express written permission of the publisher except for the use of brief quotations in a book review.

For more information, contact Jess Michaels
www.AuthorJessMichaels.com

To contact the author:
Email: Jess@AuthorJessMichaels.com
Twitter www.twitter.com/JessMichaelsbks
Facebook: www.facebook.com/JessMichaelsBks

Jess Michaels raffles a gift certificate EVERY month to members of her newsletter, so sign up on her website:
http://www.authorjessmichaels.com/

DEDICATION

For Michael, who helps with all the solutions but was especially patient listening to me scream about this book. Thanks babe.

PROLOGUE

Spring 1811

Hugh Margolis, Duke of Brighthollow, dug his heels harder into his stallion's sides, urging the animal to fly faster through the almost moonless night. It was reckless to push himself and the beast so hard, especially in his current emotional state, which was pure rage. It was hot and red and rough, and he knew that it limited his ability to be rational, something he'd always prided in himself.

Tonight he was not rational, and with very good reason. He was riding through the night, desperation heavy in his chest, for one reason and one reason only: his younger sister Lizzie.

She had been a mere child when their parents died, just eight. He'd been twenty-one and inherited her guardianship along with the dukedom and all the responsibility that entailed. He'd become her father in every sense of the word.

And for so long, they'd gone along together, affectionate and close. He was so very proud of her, for she was an accomplished young lady. And she was always obedient and sweet natured.

Until a few months ago. At sixteen, she had become a little secretive, a little furtive. He'd ignored it. After all, most children hit a difficult phase, or so friends told him.

He should have been more involved. He would hate himself forever for that. Especially if he could not reach her in time. Hugh was almost to the border now, Scotland was less than a league up this winding, wild road. Scotland was where *he* was taking her.

Aaron Walters…the man Hugh wanted to kill at this moment.

His heart leapt as he saw a cottage looming just ahead. He'd been following Lizzie and *him* for three days now, always just a step behind them, always getting information too late. But his last source had said they planned to stop at this cottage before riding on to Gretna Green in the morning.

Hugh's stomach turned at the thought of it.

He pulled the horse up short before the house and swung down. It was a tiny place, rundown, certainly not fit for his sister. But then, the man who had taken her was not thinking of her comfort or her heart or her future.

He was thinking of her enormous fortune.

Hugh didn't knock. He hit the door with his shoulder and the lock broke, allowing him to tumble into the room without preamble. As he did so, he heard a little scream and looked up to find Lizzie, just as his source had claimed.

She was standing before a fire, before a bed, in the arms of the man who had taken her. Walters' shirt was half-undone, Lizzie's bright honey hair was down around her shoulders. She looked at Hugh with shame and pain, her blue eyes darting away.

Walters, on the other hand, stared straight at him. He smiled. The bastard *smiled* as he said, "Brighthollow, we did not expect you. Come to witness our wedding, have you?"

What Hugh wanted to do was stride across the room, put his hands around Walters' throat and squeeze until he went limp. He wanted to put a bullet between his eyes. But Lizzie was standing there, Lizzie was watching, and her eyes were now filled with tears.

"Hugh," she whispered, almost imperceptible in the tiny room.

He pushed away the irrational, uncontrollable rage and sank back into the deep control he had mastered over himself since he'd become duke eight years before. With great effort, he extended his hand and said, "Lizzie, come."

His voice was gentle, and for that he was happy. He was not angry with her. No, he chose to put all his anger on the bastard who was still holding her. Walters' fingers tightened on her arms for a moment, but as Lizzie let out a shuddering sigh and moved toward Hugh, he did let her go. Hugh nearly collapsed with relief and gently pulled her behind him. Her hands shook as she clung to his.

"She is sixteen," he managed to growl through clenched teeth.

Walters arched a brow and shrugged one shoulder. "It hardly matters now."

Hugh snorted in a deep breath through his nose. "Lizzie, go outside. I'll join you in a moment."

"No!" She tightened her grip on his hand. "Please, please, no Hugh. Please don't. We—we care for each other."

Hugh jerked his gaze down at her. There was hesitation in her voice. Like she had determined the truth before he arrived but felt she had no escape from it. Tears gathered in her eyes, and one slid down her cheek.

He shook his head as he wiped it away gently. "He does not care for you," he whispered, and hated how she flinched.

"One way or another, I get what I wanted, don't I?" Walters said, and his smug tone drew Hugh's attention back. His eyes were lit up and a smile settled on his face. Handsome, yes. Young, yes. Kind? Oh no. There was nothing kind about this man. He was a swindler who had lured in Lizzie, taken advantage of her innocence of spirit as much as her body.

And now she saw it, perhaps more clearly than ever before. Her lips parted and her expression twisted in pain. "What—what do you mean by that, Aaron?"

He looked past Hugh to her. "My dear, I would have married you, and engaged in all those pleasures you and I had just begun to explore."

Hugh could not stand it anymore—he lunged for Walters, but Lizzie held fast to his arm and kept him from exacting the

3

kind of revenge this bastard deserved.

"But as you can see, Brighthollow will never allow it," Walters continued, apparently unmoved by Hugh's rage or Lizzie's pain.

"I will not," Hugh managed through clenched teeth.

"So you remember that when you look at him. *He* took your future from you, not me."

"Don't you dare act like a gentleman thwarted by my cruelty. You are only interested in my sister's inheritance," Hugh spat.

Walters did not deny the charge, and Hugh felt Lizzie shrinking into herself with every barb exchanged between them. How he wished he could shield her from the truth, from the pain.

But he couldn't.

"It *is* a very nice inheritance," Walters said with a nod. "But I won't need it now."

"Aaron," Lizzie whispered, her voice so broken that it was like shards of glass slashing through Hugh's skin.

Hugh stared at Walters, stared at his smug, untroubled expression, and a sick feeling began to grow in the pit of his stomach. "What do you mean you won't need it?"

"My driver, the woman who owns this home, my friends…everyone knows that we snuck away under your very nose. And that we have been alone for several nights."

"But—" Lizzie began, her voice shaking.

"Hush now, Elizabeth, your brother and I are negotiating," Walters said, never looking at her, never seeing how the sharpness and dismissiveness of his actions and words cut to her very spirit. "You don't want all this to be unleashed into Society, do you? This thing that will ruin all her chances at a future?"

Hugh released Lizzie's hand. He did not move forward, he didn't move at all. Somehow he remained in place as he said, "I will kill you."

For a moment, a flicker of fear moved over Walter's face, but then he managed it. He smiled once more. "Do it, go ahead. If you do, it will only make this scandal all the larger and drag down your entire legacy…along with her."

Hugh's nostrils flared, for of course the bastard was right. If he said a word against this man, if he laid a hand on him with the rage that boiled so deeply inside of him, he would be exposing Lizzie's indiscretion. She would be humiliated and shunned if he were imprudent.

"What do you want?" he asked.

"For you to do what any loving brother would do in this situation. You will pay me handsomely to cover up your sister's foolish, youthful mistake."

Hugh was too stunned to speak, but Lizzie staggered forward, her hands shaking as she stared at Walters. Hugh could see all her heartbreak on her face. She had truly cared for him, been convinced by him that this was their only future, their only path. And now…now to have all her hopes and dreams shattered, to have her humiliation used as a bartering tool…

A piece of her innocence was dying right before his eyes, and that had nothing to do with whatever she had allowed Walters to take from her body.

It killed Hugh to see it, and to know he could do nothing except hand over everything this bastard requested.

"How could you?" she whispered. "How?"

Walters looked her up and down, leering. Then he shrugged. "You wouldn't understand. You've always had everything you ever wanted."

"Get out," Hugh said, his hand shaking as he pointed toward the door behind them.

Walters grinned. "I'll come to your solicitor's in London in…shall we say two days? I will assume my very generous payment will be waiting for me there. Good evening, Your Grace," he said as he strode past them. At the door, he paused and turned back. "Oh, and Lizzie?"

She had been staring at the floor, tears streaming down her cheeks. She lifted her gaze toward this man she had apparently cared so deeply for. "Yes?"

"It's been a pleasure," he said, and walked out, laughing the whole way.

The moment he'd gone and shut the door behind himself, Lizzie tipped forward, dropping to her knees on the floor beside the bed. She buried her head in her hands and began to weep, the sobs wracking her entire body.

Hugh rushed to her, his heart aching as he dropped down beside her and gathered her into his arms, rocking her as he had so many times when she was a little girl, woken by nightmares. Only this time the terror was real—he could not hush it away with soft words.

She would feel it, because he had not been aware enough to protect her from it.

"I'm sorry," she finally hiccupped against his shirt. "I shouldn't have thought he could truly love me. I was such a fool!"

He slid a finger beneath her chin and tilted her tear-streaked face toward his. "No. Sweetest Lizzie, if you believed he cared for you and he took advantage, it is he who is the fool, not you." He cleared his throat. "But I do wonder why you thought you could not tell me about him."

She squeezed her eyes shut. "He encouraged me to sneak out. Said he'd tried to talk to you and that you were uncertain based on his lack of title."

Hugh pursed his lips. Lies. But ones his sister had somehow believed. "You thought I would be so cruel as to separate you from someone you truly loved, even if I believed he had your best interests at heart?"

She worried her lip, and that was his answer. "You are protective. I know you wish for me to be safe. To be settled well."

He sighed. He'd had his part in this, it seemed. By not watching closely enough. By not pursuing the trouble he sensed when Lizzie withdrew. By not behaving in a way that made her feel she could speak to him about anything.

"Oh, and now I've ruined everything," she said, putting her head back into her hands and returning to the sobs. "And after you've taken care of me for so long."

He wrapped his arms more tightly around her and smoothed a hand over her hair. "You've ruined nothing. I adore you, and being your older brother and your guardian has been one of the greatest joys of my life. Even if I have made a muck of it, it seems."

Her sobs slowed and then ceased. She rested her head on his chest and let out her breath in a long sigh. "You haven't made a muck of it. I thought he loved me. But he didn't. So what will happen now?"

Hugh let out his own long sigh. He was pushed into a corner, a position he did not allow himself to take. Not ever. But for the first time since his parents' deaths, his power could not save him. Or her. In fact, his power was an element in their demise if he wielded it too swiftly or strongly or harshly.

"I will pay him a handsome sum," he said, trying to sound cheerful about the prospect.

"Take it from my inheritance," she suggested as she pushed from his arms and used the edge of the bed to get back to her feet.

"I shall do no such thing." He followed her up and shook his head. "I have more than enough money. Once he is paid, we will...move on. If you think you can do that."

She lifted her chin ever so slightly, and he smiled, for he saw in her the strength of their mother, long buried in a cold grave beside her husband. When he caught her likeness in Lizzie's face, it always lifted his spirits.

"Yes," she said.

He watched her fix her hair swiftly, shoving pins from the bedside table in here and there until it was a messy bun. He hated that it reminded him of what had been happening when he entered. He didn't know if she had truly surrendered her innocence to the man. In the end, it wouldn't matter to the gossips. Ruin was ruin in these cases. The particulars were only fodder for the height of the flames of the destruction.

She faced him and swallowed hard. "I will do my best,

Hugh. And I promise I will never do anything ever again that will force you into such a situation. I will look for respectability. I shall never seek out love. I promise."

With that, she turned toward the door and moved outside to his horse. He watched her go, but her declaration gave him no pleasure. In the past year, he had watched several of his best friends find the deepest love. The idea that Lizzie would never seek it due to this unfortunate incident broke his heart.

And made him more determined than ever to fix it. He had to fix this. For her sake. For his own. And for whatever future both of them had laid out before them.

CHAPTER ONE

Late Summer 1812

Hugh swung down from his horse, jerking out a nod at the servant who rushed down to take the animal. With a long sigh, he looked up at the fine estate before him. His London estate, though it had never fully felt like his. None of the estates felt like they were, no matter how long he had been duke. It still felt like he was living a stolen life. A fraud who would be discovered at any moment when his own father returned from the dead.

How disappointed he would be in his son. Hugh knew that more than he knew anything in the world.

The door to the house opened and his longtime butler, Murphy, stepped out. Hugh forced himself out of the melancholy that had tracked his every move for over a year and climbed the steps two at a time to reach his servant.

"Welcome home, Your Grace," Murphy intoned as he took Hugh's hat and gloves. "I hope your trip to Brighthollow was most excellent."

Hugh barely contained his flinch at the benign words. He'd been at his country estate in Brighthollow for the past fortnight, tending to a bit of business and checking in on Lizzie. He'd begged her to come to London with him. She had refused.

After her ordeal the previous spring, she had not been the same. It felt like she was folding up into herself and there seemed to be nothing at all he could do about it.

"Uneventful," he choked out, since Murphy was awaiting the barest politeness of a response. "Is there anything to report here?"

He began to walk toward his study, the butler keeping up with him at his heels. "You've several invitations from the members of your club, Your Grace."

Hugh nodded. Of course he would. Since he was a boy he'd been the best of friends with a small group of men all destined to be dukes. The 1797 Club, they called themselves. He adored them all, but he could see the concern on their collective faces when he called on them. They knew something was wrong—he just hadn't the heart yet to tell any of them the truth.

How could he? How could he reveal his sister's deepest shame, how could he tell these men of honor that he had done nothing to the bastard who had hurt her? They'd say they understood, of course. They would, on some level. And yet he would feel his failure all the more if he dared speak it out loud.

So he kept it to himself and ignored their questions when they asked why he brooded, why he'd let his hair grow out and only shaved when Society required it. Why he hid in his castle at Brighthollow or his chambers here in London like a wounded beast.

"I shall look at them. I assume you left them on my desk?" he asked as they entered the study together.

"Of course." Murphy indicated the small silver tray on the corner of Hugh's desk, the one now brimming with correspondence in a variety of hands he knew so well.

He ignored them and went around to his seat. As he took it, he glanced up at Murphy. "If there isn't anything else…"

Murphy cleared his throat. "Only two pressing matters, Your Grace."

Hugh arched a brow. "And what are those?"

"You told me to treat any messages from Mr. Kendall as urgent. One arrived for you yesterday."

Hugh pushed back from his desk, his chair making a screech on the wooden floor that caused his butler to turn his face in displeasure. "Kendall?" he repeated. "Where is it?"

He grabbed for the tray and began to sort through the letters there, shoving aside the ones from his friends in the search.

"Here, Your Grace," Murphy said, his tone suddenly hushed, concerned as he dug into his inside pocket and drew out a folded piece of vellum, sealed with red wax. "I-I held it aside for you."

Hugh snatched it and turned it over. His name was spelled incorrectly. But he hadn't hired the man for his letter writing skills. "That will be all," he said, his voice shaking as he turned it back and grabbed for his letter opener to break the seal.

"Your Grace, there is one other thing—"

"No!" Hugh waved him off impatiently. "It can wait. Thank you, Murphy."

The butler nodded and saw himself out, shutting the door firmly behind him. Once he had gone, Hugh rushed to the fire and took a seat there. It was a short message, thank God, for Kendall truly was a terrible writer. His handwriting was barely legible and his poor spelling made Hugh have to reread each sentence to pick out its meaning.

But there it was, in the end, in black and white. The nightmare Hugh had been waiting for the moment he hired Kendall over a year ago.

Aaron Walters found nother. He askt a lady to mary im. It aint publick yet. See Vycunt Quinton. His doter. —Kendall

His hands shook as he set the letter in his lap and reached up to cover his eyes. "Fuck," he muttered to no one in particular.

"Can't help you there, mate."

He jerked his head up to watch as one of those very dukes he had been musing over earlier, Lucas Vincent, Duke of Willowby, entered his study with Murphy at his heels.

"I'm sorry, Your Grace, I did try to tell you that His Grace was here to see you," Murphy sputtered.

Hugh nodded. "It—it's fine, Murphy. Thank you, that will be all."

As the servant departed, Hugh shoved the letter into his

pocket and got to his feet. "Lucas," he said, coming forward with his hand outstretched.

Lucas rolled his eyes and tugged him in for a brief hug. As he pounded Hugh on the back, he said, "Don't pretend I'm not your best friend."

"How could you not be?" Hugh said, finding some way to fall back into old habits as he crossed to pour them each a scotch from the sideboard. "The youngest member of the club and the youngest man to become duke. We were bound to be best friends, even if you *didn't* write to me all those years you were running around as a spy."

Lucas smiled slightly. "Holding that against me even still, I see. You know you would have guessed what I was doing. I feared you would figure out why."

Hugh bent his head. Lucas had been gone from their circles for many years, with no word, no news. He'd worried about his friend very much. Since Lucas's return a year before, the two men had renewed their friendship. And Lucas's secrets, the ones that had caused him to run from his life, had come out. They had changed nothing, of course, except that Hugh wished he'd been able to help his friend in his pain.

"Why are you here?" Hugh asked as he handed over the drink.

Lucas sprawled himself into one of Hugh's chairs and stared at him far too intently. "I knew you were returning today and I wanted to see you."

"Oh yes?" Hugh said as he took a place beside his friend. "Why is that?"

"Because you haven't been yourself in a long time. Everyone says it over and over again. They whisper about it at the duke meetings, you know."

"We don't have duke meetings," Hugh said with a dry smile.

Lucas shrugged. "Perhaps you aren't invited."

"It would be awkward if you are, indeed, talking about me." He shook his head.

Lucas's smiled faded. "I'm tired of the subterfuge and the avoidance. I came here because I think it's time we addressed this directly."

Hugh wrinkled his brow. Lucas was not the first to approach him on this subject. He was usually able to put off the others. But Lucas looked determined.

"That isn't very spy-like," Hugh tried as a means of distraction. "To just come out and confront me."

"I'm not a spy anymore," Lucas said softly.

Hugh nodded. That was true. His friend had been badly injured eighteen months before, had nearly died and had been brought back to life by his now-wife, Diana. He did not work for the War Department any longer, at least not in any official capacity, though Hugh did suspect he and Diana occasionally provided some kind of consultation in that world.

"Aren't you?" he asked.

Lucas's lips pressed together, and he leaned back in his chair. "Very well, if you want to play it that way, I will behave in a way more befitting whatever you think my position is. An interrogation is really more about observation, so let me share mine with you."

"This is an interrogation now?" Hugh said with a rusty laugh.

Lucas did not join in on it. "You would not allow a friendly conversation and I will not leave here without the truth, so this is what it is." He ticked off one finger. "First, I know you were recently in Brighthollow with your sister. You adore her, you are more her father than a brother, in truth. And yet there are shadows beneath your eyes, which means you did not sleep well over the last fortnight."

Hugh blinked those same bleary eyes his friend had just observed and said, "Perhaps I was enjoying myself in the country."

"No, you weren't," Lucas said, and this time he did laugh. "There is a difference between the expression of a man tired because he's been indulging himself in pleasure and a man who cannot sleep for the demons that plague him. If you'd like to observe that difference, look yourself in the mirror for the latter and look at any of your married friends for the former."

"Not all of us can walk away from our dukedoms as you did," Hugh snapped, regretting the words the moment he said them, for they were harsh and ignored the pain his friend had endured in the not-so-distant past.

But Lucas looked anything but offended. "No, I suppose not. And yet it isn't your duties that trouble you, either. You have never shied away in discussing your problems with your estate and title with the others, even with me. But you refuse, which means you have problems of a more personal nature."

Hugh pushed to his feet and heard the letter in his pocket crinkle. He set his hand on the outline of it as he muttered, "You are being ridiculous."

"Am I?" Lucas ticked off a second finger. "My next observation is that Lizzie is now seventeen, is she not?"

"Yes," Hugh managed through gritted teeth. "Seventeen this February last."

"That means she is of an age where you might present her to court, bring her into Society here in London, even if you had no desire to drive her into a match at such a young age. And yet she is not here. She's hidden away in Brighthollow. My sources say she has not come to Town at all, not for any reason, in over a year."

Hugh stiffened. Lucas was too close to the truth now. And his own pain was rising with every word he spoke. "Don't you have something better to do, Willowby?" he snapped. "A wife to spend time with, for example?"

Lucas smiled. "If you think Diana wasn't the one who helped me prepare this interrogation, you do not understand my wife."

Hugh pivoted on him. "So you've corrupted that lovely woman entirely."

Lucas's grin grew. "*Entirely*," he said with another laugh. "And I shall not be distracted, so stop trying."

"Lizzie will come out next year," Hugh grunted, folding his arms as he did so.

"You don't sound certain."

Hugh threw up his hands and paced away. Of course he was not certain. Lizzie was entirely against coming out. She refused to even discuss it now. And while no one would talk if she made her debut at eighteen versus seventeen, if the time stretched to nineteen, to twenty and beyond? The talk she was so terrified of creating would begin without her.

Already, it seemed it had, at least amongst his friends.

Lucas moved toward him, and now his expression was gentler. Like he was beginning to understand just the kind of pain Hugh was struggling with. "I shall move on to my third observation," he said softly.

"Do. I am on the edge of my seat."

"I watched you shove a letter into your pocket the moment I arrived here, and since you keep touching that same pocket every time I mention Lizzie, I have to assume that you have received some kind of news since your arrival. Would you like to read it?"

"I already have."

"But you want to again." Lucas said it as fact, not a guess. And of course, the bastard was right. Hugh desperately wanted to read the letter again. To start making plans on how to deal with what was within those few lines.

"I can wait," he ground out through clenched teeth.

Lucas folded his arms. "So can I."

They held gazes, and for a moment Hugh was transported back to so many years ago. When he had run through fields with this man and all the others, when he had believed anything was possible. When they had cried together and laughed together and he'd known he could depend on them for anything. Especially Lucas.

He found his hand moving to his pocket and withdrew the now-crumpled letter. He stared at it a moment. He wanted the help his friend offered. Not just the emotional kind, but Lucas's connections could perhaps do even more for him. Could find out more about Walters. About this woman he had apparently pursued and won, very likely under false pretenses.

"Hugh, you are my best friend," Lucas whispered. "You were thrust into responsibility at far too young an age. And unlike me, you didn't run. A year or so ago, you talked to Baldwin, at least, about trouble with Lizzie, and you have never been the same since. I look at you and I see you buckling under the weight of whatever this secret is. Let me take some of it from your shoulders."

With a shuddering sigh, he handed over the note to his friend and watched as he read it. Lucas's face was impassive as he looked over the lines a few times, then handed it back.

"It's meaningless to me. Written in a hand of someone who obviously isn't of your rank, referring to names of people I do not have a relationship to, though I think I met this…I assume he means viscount…at some party I was dragged to. But it clearly means a great deal to you. So explain it. And let me help you."

Hugh stared at him, and it felt like a lifetime passed before he could find his voice. "If I tell one of you, I know it is telling all. This is too…sensitive to do that."

Lucas's brow wrinkled. "I will not breathe a word to anyone. Diana, I suppose, but it will go no further than the two of us. I have an enormous capacity to keep secrets—it used to keep me alive, remember?"

Hugh bent his head. The weight Lucas had observed upon his shoulders felt so devilishly heavy in that moment. The lifeline his dearest friend offered was tempting beyond measure.

"More than a year ago, right before Baldwin met Helena, Lizzie was…*seduced*." He said that word and his stomach turned. "She was seduced by a man."

Lucas's eyes went wide. "No."

He nodded. "Yes. I was…distracted. I saw the signs that there was some trouble in her world, but I did not act swiftly enough. He convinced her to run away to Scotland to marry.

When I found out, I raced after them. He was a fortune hunter, a rogue of the worst description. But I was too…I was too—"

Lucas caught his arm and squeezed. "I understand. She did not marry him, did she?"

"No. That, at least, I thwarted," Hugh said with a shuddering sigh. "Not that it mattered. Her reputation would be in tatters if the story came out. They'd been alone more than one night while on the road. I paid that bastard to keep his mouth shut in the hopes I could still provide her with a future."

Lucas straightened. "Is he blackmailing you?"

"No." Hugh snorted out a humorless laugh. "I gave him so much money, he would not have to come after me again for a very long time. I did so in the hopes that Lizzie would find her happiness in the interim and then whatever he said would matter little. It isn't blackmail that has troubled me."

Lucas frowned and glanced at the letter in his hand. "This man, it's the Walters this person refers to, isn't it?"

Hugh nodded, and he was certain his misery was plain on his face. "Yes. And as you can see, he has found another lady to pursue. This time I assume he has been more conventional in his engagement plans, but I have no doubt he has used the money he wrung from me in desperation to convince this woman he is not a fortune hunter. And yet he is."

"You didn't stop him in order to protect your sister from a reckless act," Lucas breathed. "And so you have lived the last year regretting that you did not thwart him as he deserved."

"And fearing he would do exactly what it appears he's done and find another victim," Hugh finished. "My source says their engagement is not public yet, but how long before they begin the announcements? A week or two to arrange some kind of sparkling ball? And then it will be too late to escape him without damaging this new woman's reputation just as he would have destroyed Lizzie."

"I'm certain that is his intent. To be sure that if his true motives are discovered, it will be too late to get out of the arrangement," Lucas muttered as he paced away. "And if he was willing to take advantage of Lizzie's sweet nature, I cannot give him the benefit of the doubt that he would have changed since then or truly loved this new woman."

Hugh barely maintained control over the anger that still burned inside his chest. "He *mocked* my sister after he ripped her world to pieces. There is nothing decent or good in his heart."

Lucas looked at him. "How is she?"

Hugh stared out the window in the distance. "Brokenhearted still. At first it was because she had truly cared for the man and she mourned whatever future she had hoped to have. But as time has passed, I've watched her turn her loathing away from him and toward herself. No matter what I say, she sees herself as a fool with no ability to know what is true and what is not. She only wants to stay in the country, locked away from everyone. She barely receives visitors, and only at my insistence. He broke her spirit. I wish I had killed him when I had the chance."

"Doing so only would have hurt her more," Lucas reminded him. "Which you know, or else I assume you would have done just that."

Hugh jerked out a nod. "Yes. And here we are. This new woman is just as endangered by Walters as Lizzie was. I doubt she or her family have any idea the snake they are letting into their home."

Lucas tilted his head. "That is not your responsibility, Hugh."

"Isn't it?" Hugh let out his breath slowly. "I have power and I could have destroyed him. It was my pride that kept me from it."

"Perhaps your pride had some part, but it was the love you feel for your sister that kept you from publicly flaying him. Her well-being and reputation were your main concerns."

He shrugged. "Either way, I have a responsibility to ensure this man never repeats his actions. So I must do something to stop him now."

Lucas took a long step closer. "What?"

"I don't know," Hugh breathed. "But I will find a way. I *will* stop him, by any means necessary."

CHAPTER TWO

Miss Amelia Quinton watched in the mirror's reflection as her maid, Theresa, swept her dark hair up in a pretty style. She smiled at her face, seeing all her happiness reflected there, then reached up to pinch her cheeks and make them even more pink.

"What are you on about, miss?" Theresa asked with a laugh as she continued at her work. "Staring at yourself like you've never seen a mirror before."

"I'm just trying to see if I look different now that I am an engaged lady," Amelia said.

Theresa's smile was kind even as she shook her head. "You are lovely, just as you have always been lovely. No man or future could ever change that."

Amelia rolled her eyes at her maid.

"But Aaron has changed my future, and so very romantically," she argued.

"So you've said." Theresa's tone was dry as she slipped a few pins between her lips and mumbled, "I assume you'd very much like to tell the story again."

Amelia tried to keep from bouncing, but it was nearly impossible. "I know it bores you right to tears, but you must understand how difficult it is not to be able to share with my friends. Papa is very firm that we keep the news private until we make the formal announcements next week."

"Go ahead then," Theresa said with a wave of her hand. "I will pretend to listen."

Amelia laughed at her teasing and then shut her eyes so she

might relive every moment of the story she would tell in her mind. "We were out for a walk in the garden," she said. "The weather had been positively putrid for days, but that morning bright, happy sunshine had pushed through the clouds and was shining so warmly on us."

"Practically providence," Theresa said, and gently slipped a pin into Amelia's locks.

Amelia opened one eye and shot her a look. "It could have been. I was pondering the daisies when I turned to say something and there he was, on bended knee just like the paintings of knights of old." She clasped her hands together. "He asked for my hand after reciting a...frankly very long piece of poetry, and of course I said yes."

Theresa nodded. "He knows your sense of romance, that much is clear. I assume your marriage will be only sunshine, flowers and butterflies for the rest of your days."

Amelia smiled at the apt description of how she pictured a romantic marriage to a man who seemed to understand her very soul. He liked all the same things she did, he shared almost all her opinions—in every way he had fashioned himself to be the man she had dreamed of since she was a little girl.

And yet...

"There was only one thing missing, I suppose," she mused, almost more to herself than to Theresa.

The maid hesitated. "Something missing? Whatever could it be? You have not mentioned it before."

Amelia worried her lip and caught Theresa's eyes in the mirror's image. "I was trying not to be greedy. Trying not to look for where the moment lacked."

"And where did it?" Theresa asked, and her face was lined with concern as she moved around to look at Amelia directly.

"A kiss," Amelia whispered, and bent her head as heat flooded her cheeks.

"Miss Amelia!" Theresa burst out in surprise. "A lady ought not—"

Amelia got to her feet and fled across the room to escape

the words coming from Theresa's lips. "I know, I know what I ought not to want. And I suppose I'd rather he be proper with me. And yet I did want him to do it regardless. When else would a stolen kiss be more expected than when making such a proposal?"

Theresa sighed, and Amelia turned to find a still-troubled look on her face. She shook her head. "There will be plenty of time for kissing after. I'm certain he must want the same things you do. You'll have your whole life to...learn what those things are."

Theresa was blushing quite as dark as Amelia knew she herself was. She lifted her cold hands to her cheeks with a nervous laugh. "Oh, I'm sorry."

"You shouldn't be," Theresa insisted, and looked her up and down. "Now, you look lovely and ready to join your father for tea."

"Thank you," Amelia said. "I'll go to him now."

Theresa waved her off and turned to tidy up her dressing table. Amelia took her leave, heading into the hallway and down the long back stair that would take her to the parlor where her father likely awaited her arrival. He would be cross if she was late, so she scurried through the dim hallways. She was just turning down the last one and could see the parlor door when she came to a stop.

Their family butler, Fielding, was coming her way down the long hallway from the direction of the foyer. And he was not alone. Following him was a very tall, broad-shouldered man. His hair was bound back in a queue and his dark eyes were focused. He had a grim line to his mouth and did not seem to notice her as he followed the butler right into the parlor where her father waited.

She stared as they disappeared. She didn't know the man. Not that she knew every person her father had a reason to interact with. But she had played hostess in this house for several years and she would have remembered the dark, very handsome stranger who had intruded in their halls.

She turned away from the door at that thought. She was engaged. It was not right to be calling him handsome. Thinking that he was. Noticing it…that was a betrayal, was it not? Certainly she would not want to hear of Aaron ogling some young lady who had come to call on his family.

Not that she had met his family or knew much about them. She pushed all those jumbled thoughts away and approached the parlor as Fielding exited the room. He met her gaze as he shut the door.

"Good afternoon, Fielding," she said softly. "Who was that man?"

He glanced over his shoulder, and for a moment she saw a nervous expression cross over the normally implacable butler's face. "The Duke of Brighthollow, miss," he said. "He arrived unexpectedly to see your father."

"A duke?" Amelia repeated as she stared at the shut door. "How curious."

Of course her father knew dukes—he'd taken her to plenty of balls and gatherings where those of rank were in attendance. But there was a marked difference between a lesser viscount and a man of such status. Normally they didn't call.

"Quite, my lady," Fielding said.

"Well, I assume that means my father will be busy for tea."

"I believe so, Miss Amelia. I shall have a tray sent to the blue parlor if you'd like."

She nodded. "Thank you, that would be perfect."

The butler executed a smart bow and then hustled off to take care of his business. Amelia stared at the door. It was too thick to hear anything that was going on inside, of course. Not that it was a ladylike thing to eavesdrop. She sighed and turned to take herself to the other parlor for her tea.

Whatever this duke wanted with her father, certainly she would hear about it soon enough. And in the end, it probably wasn't a visit of any consequence anyway. Nothing to do with her and nothing that would make any kind of difference in her already planned out life.

Hugh sat in a comfortable chair across from Lord Quinton, watching as the man poured them each a drink. He was having a hard time reading the man he had come to call upon. All he could truly tell about Quinton was that he was surprised to be visited by a man addressed as Your Grace.

And why wouldn't he be? Hugh had spent the day since he discovered Aaron Walters' engagement researching the family of the lady in question. Lord Quinton's line was not a very important one and it was attached to only a modest fortune. He was part of Society, of course, but he tended to mix mostly with those of a slightly lower rank.

Perhaps that was why Walters had chosen them. To marry the viscount's daughter was certainly an elevation for him, but not one that would cause too much of a stir as he began his pretended courtship of the lady.

Hugh swallowed back the bile that rose in his throat every time he thought of that bastard and forced a smile as Quinton brought him sherry.

"I thought you might want something a bit stronger than tea," Quinton explained as he settled into the seat near Hugh's. He looked confused, but not particularly nervous at present. He wasn't a large man. In fact, he was rather thin and hawkish in his appearance.

A short bit of silence thickened the air between them. "While I am honored at your unexpected arrival, Your Grace, and welcome you wholeheartedly to my home, I do admit I wonder what you could want," Quinton said at last.

Hugh felt the corner of his lips quirk slightly. "So you are a direct man. Certainly I appreciate that. I shall be as direct." He cleared his throat. "Recently I have heard rumors that your daughter…Amelia is her name, yes?"

Quinton's brow wrinkled in deeper confusion. "Yes,

Amelia is my only child."

Hugh jerked out a curt nod. "Very good. I have heard rumors of her recent engagement to a—" He broke off for he was not about to call her fiancé a gentleman. "—a *person* named Aaron Walters."

Quinton's face faltered and annoyance flared in his eyes. "That girl. I give her one directive, to keep quiet, and she chatters incessantly like a foolish romantic. Where did you hear this rumor?"

Hugh narrowed his eyes at the dismissive way the man referred to his daughter. There was little affection there, it seemed. Could that mean this Amelia was even less protected than his own sister had been? After all, Hugh adored Lizzie—he was quick to protect her.

It did not seem Quinton was of the same mind.

"I did not hear this news because of anything your daughter said or did, I assure you," he said softly. "As for where I came by the knowledge, it doesn't really matter at this point. I know they are engaged."

Quinton examined him closely and then threw up his hands. "Well, soon it will all be announced, so I suppose this murmuring you've heard matters little. I cannot imagine why it interests you, though, Your Grace. I am not exactly in your sphere, nor is the gentleman in question."

"Quite," Hugh said, still trying not to physically recoil at the concept that Walters was a gentleman of any quality. "I am here to discourage the match."

All the color drained from Quinton's face and he rose to his feet slowly. "I beg your pardon?"

Hugh stayed seated, allowing the other man to have the higher ground in his upset. There was no reason to be challenging, at least not yet. Quinton simply didn't understand the gravity of the situation.

"The engagement must be ended," Hugh said, keeping his tone neutral. Calm. As if it meant nothing to him, when it most certainly did. "And before the public announcement in order to reduce the impact on your daughter's reputation."

Quinton shook his head. "You must be in jest, Your Grace. This man has made a reasonable offer for my daughter. She seems to care for him, as is in fashion at present. Why would I end it? And once again, why would you care? Do you have some kind of *tendre* for my daughter?"

Hugh pressed his lips together. "No, of course not. If I wished to press my own suit, I would have done so. As for why..."

He trailed off. The why of this situation was still devilishly sensitive. To tell it was to expose his own sister to gossip, rumor, innuendo. He had no desire to do this, even if he was driven to protect this unknown woman from a predator he had not stopped when he had a chance.

"Go on," Quinton said, folding his arms. "Give me a good reason."

"I have had dealings with Walters," Hugh said carefully. "And I can assure you that he is not a good...person. I guarantee he does not have your daughter's best interest at heart."

The viscount's gaze flicked over Hugh, and a shrewdness entered his gaze. "You and I have shaken hands at parties probably three times in the last decade. I doubt we've shared more than a minute's conversation until today. And yet you want me to throw over the intentions of a man who has made himself known to us nearly every day for two months. You wish me to cast him aside as ungentlemanly based upon the most vague of accusations."

"I can be no more specific," Hugh said, and now he did rise, towering over the other man. "But my word is my bond—you may ask anyone who knows me. I am not a man to slander another lightly. What else can I say to convince you that this is not the best match for your daughter?"

Quinton observed him, and then he smiled just slightly. "You are not married, Your Grace."

Hugh shifted as his meaning became clear. "I am not," he admitted.

"Losing this match will cause me…troubles," Quinton said with a scowl. "Are you willing to offer me a better option to consider?"

Hugh jerked back and staggered away. "What are you asking me?"

Quinton shrugged. "I need to marry my daughter away. This year is best. Trading an engagement to an unranked man for one to a duke seems quite beneficial to me."

Hugh could not mask the shock from his face, no matter how hard he tried. "I have come here to warn you that your daughter is in danger and you try to…bargain with me?" he managed to grind out.

"Why shouldn't I?" Quinton asked. "I have no idea if what you imply about Walters is true. You ask me to go on faith and destroy whatever arrangements I've already made with the man. And my daughter will be miserable if I do not allow her this marriage. Why should I not benefit and be able to present her with some kind of boon for herself to soften the blow?"

Hugh glared at the man as he tried to picture how he would have reacted if someone had come to him before Lizzie ran away with Walters. What he would have done and said in reaction if he could have shielded her from harm long before the damage was done.

And this man had none of those responses. He looked at Hugh only in terms of profit versus disadvantage to himself. Just as he must look at Walters, though Hugh could not picture what Quinton believed he was buying with his daughter's dowry.

This woman—*Amelia*—she was in just as much peril at the hands of her father as she was with Walters, it seemed. But the idea of marrying her, a stranger…how could Hugh agree to it? Even the idea of placing a scandal on Walters' doorstep, making it clear Hugh had stolen her away from him…even *that* did not lessen his hesitation. Though the idea of it was comforting, indeed.

"Let me meet her," Hugh said softly. It was really the only way to know what to do next. And if he had a chance to speak with the young woman, perhaps he could convince her to break the engagement herself and that would end all this foolishness.

Quinton stroked his chin as he seemed to ponder that request. "You may *see* her," he said, and stepped to the bell. He rang for the butler, who arrived shortly. Quinton shot Hugh a look before he said, "Fielding, ask Amelia to go pick some flowers for the hall."

The butler glanced at Hugh with confusion. "Miss Amelia is having her tea in the—"

"Tell her to do it now," Quinton insisted.

Fielding nodded and left the room. Slowly Quinton turned to Hugh, a smug expression on his face. Hugh stared. "You will not let me speak to the young lady. The woman you wish me to agree to wed."

"Once you see her you will not need to talk to her, I think." Quinton left the room, calling after himself. "It's now or never, Your Grace. Let's have this done."

Hugh clenched his fists at his sides and followed the man from the room, his rage bubbling up in him with every step. He was steered down the winding halls of the viscount's estate and out through a parlor that led to the veranda behind the house. As they exited the room, Quinton caught up a spyglass and strode to the edge of the terrace.

Hugh stepped up next to him and looked down into the garden. A young woman was strolling through the flowers, basket in hand, plucking a rose here, a daisy there. She had dark hair and a lovely figure, but she was too far away to make out any other features.

Quinton smiled and handed over the spyglass. Hugh took a deep breath and stared down at her. She had turned, and he caught his breath. Amelia Quinton was...stunning. That was the only way he could describe her. She was the kind of woman men would turn to look at if she passed them in the park. Her dark hair framed a pale face with full, pink lips that were naturally quirked into a half-smile. But what stood out, above all else, were her eyes. He had never seen such a blue before.

There was a stir of desire in his stomach that he had not felt in a very long time. A need that reared its head and made him want to get closer to this woman.

He lowered the glass and glared at her father, who had a mightily smug expression on his face. "She favors her late mother," Quinton said at last.

Hugh handed over the glass and shook his head. "She is lovely, which of course you know since you are trading on that fact. But you cannot truly expect me to make an offer for her without knowing her. Without her consent."

"She'll give it," Quinton said as he motioned Hugh back toward the parlor. When they stepped inside, Quinton turned toward him. "*If* we handle this situation very carefully."

Hugh stared. "Handle it? What do you mean by that? You've told me she fancies herself in love with Walters."

He flinched as he thought of Lizzie's broken expression that night he'd found her with the bastard. Some version of that heartbreak had never gone away. It was always with her now. And he would do something similar to the woman outside.

"She also loves me," Quinton said. "She's always seeking my approval. Tell the right lie and she'll come to heel quickly enough."

Hugh's stomach turned. "You are as bad as her fiancé."

Quinton didn't seem offended by that accusation. "You're a man of the world, Your Grace. I'm surprised you do not understand how it works. We trade on relationships, we trade on what we can. If you do not like how you think Walters will treat her or how I treat her, you can save her."

Hugh walked away, pinching his lips together. If he married this woman, it would do just that. *Save* her, even if she wouldn't see it that way. And it would buy Hugh some time to expose Walters without revealing Lizzie. To keep that bastard from ever having the power to do this again.

But marry? A stranger? Under these circumstances? Everything in him chafed at the idea.

"She has a fine dowry," Quinton said, and there was

something harsh in his tone. "Her mother's family made certain of it. You would lose nothing by marrying her. My name is respectable. It would be no different than if we arranged the union in a more traditional way."

Hugh turned his face. He'd watched seven of his best friends fall madly, passionately and permanently in love with their wives in the past two years. He'd almost forgotten that wasn't the way of the world, in truth. That arranged marriages unfilled by affection or passion, perhaps troubled by resentment and regret, were more common than love matches.

Not that he'd been looking for a love match to begin with.

"Let me think about it," he said, his voice odd as it said those words almost against his very will.

Quinton threw up his hands in frustration. "You must think quickly, Your Grace. I have no reason not to carry on with arrangements just as they have been made. Amelia's engagement will be announced in less than a week. Once that happens, your chance may be lost."

Hugh stared at this man's expression, and for a moment he felt incredibly sorry for the young woman in the garden. Did she know how little her father cared for her welfare? Did she know who her fiancé truly was at his core?

"Good day," he growled as he pivoted on his heel and strode from the parlor toward the foyer. But as he walked away from Lord Quinton, he couldn't help but let his mind wander back to images of Amelia Quinton. And wonder what the hell he should do now that the choices before him were so jumbled and so uncertain.

CHAPTER THREE

Amelia did not know the Duchess of Willowby, at least not beyond the rumors that circulated in Society about the lady and her husband. *He* had resurfaced in good company after a long and mysterious absence just a year before and had swiftly married her. As for the lady, well, everyone knew she had not come from a house with a title or even a link to the nobility. Amelia's father had grumbled a bit about that at the time.

Amelia had seen the lady once at a party, and she thought the duchess quite beautiful. She and the duke were also very clearly in love, which warmed Amelia to her even further. Now she smiled just thinking about it. Marrying for love certainly looked like a very good endeavor from the outside, and here she would soon do so herself.

The door to the parlor opened and the duchess stepped inside. Up close, she was even prettier, with thick, auburn hair, stunning green eyes and a mischievous tilt to her lips. Amelia smiled at her and watched as the lady's gaze flitted over her from head to toe. She suddenly felt as though she was being sized up, and she shifted with discomfort at the idea.

But then the duchess smiled and crossed to Amelia with her hand extended. "Miss Quinton, welcome. Thank you for coming to share tea with me. I greatly appreciate it."

"Thank you for inviting me, Your Grace," Amelia said as the two women shook hands. "Your home is lovely."

"As are you. And you must call me Diana." With that

stunning request made, the duchess turned away and moved to the sideboard where she began preparing the tea.

Amelia blinked at her hostess. "D-Diana? Your Grace, I do not think that would be—"

"Appropriate?" Diana finished with a laugh. "I'm certain not, but I care little about that. I did not come up in Society, and I think so many of their rules so silly. If we're to be friends, why wouldn't we call each other by our given names? Anyway, when someone addresses me as Your Grace, it puts me to mind of my mother-in-law, and she is not a very nice person. Let her have the formality, for she revels in it."

Amelia was just staring at the lady, and then she lifted her hand to her mouth to stifle a giggle at the unexpected and rather blunt assessment of their situation. It was decided now. She liked the duchess...*Diana*. Even if she still had no idea why the woman wanted to be friends.

"Come and sit," Diana said, motioning to a pair of chairs before the fire. "We can get to know each other."

Amelia nodded, and soon they were warming themselves by the fire, chatting like old friends. Diana was a quick wit, sincere and kind, and she liked many of the same authors that Amelia did. She was growing more comfortable by the moment and her worries about why the lady had invited her here were beginning to fade.

Suddenly Diana glanced at the clock on the mantel and her smile fell. "Goodness," she said. "I have lost track entirely chatting with you. I needed to speak to my cook about supper. Would you excuse me just a moment?"

Amelia wrinkled her brow at the odd pretext but nodded. "Of course. Though if you are busy, I can go."

Diana reached out to catch her hand as she stood. "Don't be silly. Stay and I'll be back in an instant."

Amelia let out a sigh as her new friend exited the parlor. She got to her feet and crossed the room toward a portrait that hung on the opposite wall. It was of the duke and duchess. It was a good likeness of them both, and though it was formal, it captured the twinkle in Diana's eye and the rugged handsomeness of the duke. From the way their hands were clasped, it was clear their hearts were bound, and she tilted her head to look a little closer at their expressions.

She heard the movement behind her as she did and turned, expecting to find Diana returning after her errand. But it was not her new friend. Instead, the same man who had called on her father the day before now stood just inside the parlor. The Duke of Brighthollow—that was what Fielding had said.

His long hair was bound back again, but a lock had fallen away, curling around finely cut cheekbones and framing his full lips almost as if he'd meant it to.

Her own lips parted, and suddenly it felt as though all the air had been sucked from the room. He stood there, staring at her, his dark eyes holding hers far too firmly, his hands clenched at his sides. The door was open behind him—there was nothing improper about them being together, aside from the fact that they had never been formally introduced.

And yet everything about the unexpected moment felt very improper. The man filled all the space around her, and even though he was at least five long paces away, she felt crowded by his mere presence.

She swallowed hard. "G-good afternoon," she managed to squeak out.

He inclined his head slightly. "Good afternoon, Miss Quinton."

She blinked. Why did he know her name? Why did he act like they were already acquainted? "I—" she stammered, uncertain what she should say next. Even more uncertain why the wildly twisting feeling in her stomach was telling her to run away from this man. From the odd sensations he created in her.

"I apologize," he said, taking a step closer and raising the riot in her body even higher. His voice was very…soothing. No, that wasn't the word for it. Mesmerizing. "We have not been introduced. I am the Duke of Brighthollow. I'm a friend of the Duke of Willowby."

She nodded, mostly out of habit. And what else could she do? She was staring at him like a ninny already—if she didn't respond in some way she would look like an utter dolt.

"I—yes," she said. "I remember you. You came to call on my father yesterday, did you not?"

His eyes went wide. "You saw me there."

The strength of his reaction surprised her, and she wrinkled her brow. "Yes, in the hallway. I was about to meet him for tea when you arrived."

"Ah." Some of the tension went out of his face.

She waited for him to speak further. To say anything, but he didn't. He just continued to watch her. It wasn't lecherous at all, not like many men looked at her. There wasn't anything threatening about it. But his expression was so very focused. Almost intimate. Like they knew each other, though they didn't. Her stomach fluttered and she hated herself for that.

Her stomach was only supposed to flutter for one man. It wasn't this one.

"Did you…did you need something?" she burst out, if only to break the tension.

He blinked, almost as if he didn't realize he'd been simply staring at her. "No," he said. "I was just passing by the room. My apologies for the intrusion, my lady. A very good day to you."

With that, he executed a formal bow and turned on his heel to walk away. She stared after him, her hands shaking and her breath short. What was it about that man that set her on her heels so completely?

And how could she make that stop?

"I do not approve of this foolishness," Lucas said as Hugh returned to his friend's study.

Hugh glared at him as he shut the door behind himself and

leaned back into it with all his weight. "Yes, that was what you said before I went to meet Miss Quinton," he growled. "I did not think your mind had changed in the time I was away—you do not need to keep reminding me of it."

"I think I do," Lucas snapped as he pushed up from his desk. "So, you have met the girl now. Please tell me this puts an end to any consideration you have of this ridiculous notion of marrying her in some attempt to save her."

Hugh flinched as he strode to the sideboard and poured himself a stiff drink. He downed the entire tumbler in one breathless gulp and thought of his encounter with Amelia. She was even more beautiful up close, if that were possible. She had an intelligence to her eyes, a brightness that he had not had in his life for a very long time. And she smelled of vanilla and something spicy, heady. Something a man could drown himself in.

If he married her, there would be no difficulty with wanting her. Of course, she would despise him. But plenty of people despised their spouses. Lucas's parents, for example, had hated each other. And that had...ended terribly.

Hugh shook his head. "It isn't a ridiculous notion."

Lucas came approached him and grabbed his arm, giving him a solid shake. "Are you telling me that or yourself?"

Hugh stared into the concerned gaze of one of his best friends. He dropped his head in defeat, for there was no hiding his true heart from this man. "I'm not sure. But I don't think it is a ridiculous notion."

"To consider marrying a stranger for revenge? For some sense of self-flagellant duty?"

Hugh shook off Lucas's arm and glared at him. "Plenty of people have married for far worse reasons."

"Not *our* people." Both men turned to find Diana at the door. Her lips were pressed together in a thin white line that told him she didn't approve of his plans any more than her husband did.

"Did the young lady leave?" Hugh asked, his throat

suddenly dry.

Diana nodded slowly. "She seemed a bit…off kilter when I returned. I have no idea what you said to her, but her expression was positively bloodless. She made some excuse and departed abruptly."

He frowned. He hadn't been trying to frighten her. That was a very bad start considering what he was pondering could come next.

"Well played, Brighthollow," Lucas muttered.

Diana gave Lucas a look, and he threw up his hands and walked away like he was surrendering to her.

Of course he would. She was his everything.

Diana stepped to Hugh, and she smiled at him with kindness and understanding. In that moment, he didn't care that she knew the truth about his sister and what she'd been through. He knew she would keep that secret to her grave. She was incapable of any cruelty.

"Hugh, your friends have all married for love. None of us would want to see you settle for any less than the happiness we've found." She touched his hand gently, the touch of a healer, seeking a way to fix him.

He shook his head slowly. "Love is not the destiny of every man."

"So seven of your friends have said before you, and foolishly so!" Lucas barked out from his desk.

"Not helpful, my love," Diana said without looking at him. She smiled at Hugh. "Though not entirely without merit. Think of what you would give up."

Hugh looked at her, and then he closed his eyes. Through his mind he saw images of his married friends, easily brought up. Stolen kisses and meaningful glances, joyous celebrations of children and laughter. He saw their struggles and their pleasures and all the things they had earned through their love. He saw it and he knew he would never have that. Not if he forced this young woman's hand.

"Perhaps I don't *deserve* what my friends have found," he

said softly.

Her eyes grew wide and pained. "Hugh," she breathed.

He stepped away from her. "I knew my sister was...struggling and I didn't pursue it. I thought it was a phase that would pass."

"How could you have known what was really going on?" Lucas asked, all the heat gone from his voice now. "We were all that age once—I remember acting out. No one could have assumed Lizzie was pondering something so wild as to run away."

Hugh clenched his fist at his side. "But when she was wronged by this...this thing...this man, I did nothing. I said nothing. I paid him his devil's price and I let him walk away. And now someone else will suffer. Someone else will become his prey because of my pride. I do not deserve happiness or love or anything else. It's my duty to do all in my power to prevent him from damaging another person."

Diana moved toward him. "Then tell her the truth! I spent an hour with Amelia before I left to allow you your meeting. I like her a great deal. She seems kind and clever, witty and bright. If you were pursuing her for any other reason beyond this foolishness, I would say she was a good match for you." She caught Hugh's hand and squeezed. "At least give her the chance to make up her own mind about this man."

He shook his head slowly. "She is in love with him."

Diana cast a quick glance at Lucas. "She *thinks* herself in love with him because of the lies he's told her, the image he's presented. Many a lady makes a foolish mistake based on those things. It doesn't mean it's real or lasting."

Lucas cleared his throat and moved toward her. Hugh watched, mesmerized, as Diana stepped away from him and into the circle of her husband's arm. Lucas leaned down and pressed a kiss to her temple, and in that moment they were in their own world. It had a language Hugh didn't understand, a history he could not study. And he envied it. Down to the core of his soul.

"I'm sure you're right that she has been taken in, just as

Lizzie was," Hugh croaked out. "But that doesn't mean that what she thinks she feels isn't real in this moment. My sister ran away with this man when they felt their relationship was threatened. What if I tell Miss Quinton the truth and she…she goes to him with my accusations? God knows how much worse it could be then."

Lucas's jaw set. "You think he might hurt her?"

"I have no idea what he is capable of," Hugh whispered as he thought of Walters' cruel laughter. That sound that echoed in his head and his dreams nearly a year later. "Besides, what would I tell this woman even if I could? Give her the truth about my sister? What if she spread that gossip all over Society? Then everything I've done for Lizzie will have been for nothing at all."

Diana shook her head. "You must try, Hugh. Try *something*. Respect this woman enough to try."

He ground his teeth. Those words were enough to stop him in his tracks. Here he'd been judging her father for not telling her or protecting her, but he was not giving her any options either if he didn't make the attempt Lucas and Diana were pushing for.

"How?" he asked.

"Just like today," Diana said. "Meg and Simon are holding a soiree tomorrow night. I'll be sure the young lady and her father have an invitation. We can distract the viscount and you find a way to speak to her alone for a moment."

Hugh moved to the window and stared out into the garden behind Lucas and Diana's home. It had begun to rain, and the weather reflected his heart so perfectly that he almost laughed.

"Fine," he said. "You are correct that she deserves the chance to make her own decision. If her father won't allow her that, I must. Talk to Meg, if you would. Arrange it and I will do my part."

Only as he looked out at that dreary day, he wasn't certain what his part was. Was he savior or demon to this woman? And would their futures converge the way her father demanded they should to save her?

More to the point, why was he so warmed by the idea of spending a moment alone with her again?

CHAPTER FOUR

Amelia couldn't help the flutter of nervousness in her stomach as their carriage rounded another corner and took them closer to the ball at the Duke and Duchess of Crestwood's estate. There were many reasons why her heart had taken to pounding so loudly. One was that this was the second invitation she'd had from a person of such stature in as many days, and it confused her.

Another was that every time she thought of dukes, she thought of the Duke of Brighthollow. Since the previous day when he had entered the parlor, she had found herself thinking of him many times. *So* many times and hating herself whenever it happened. She was engaged to Aaron! How could she think of another man's stern, handsome face? Or recall every vibration of his deep voice?

How could she dream of another man? It was a wanton thing, a desperate thing, a thing that marked her even if no one else ever knew it. Heavens, when Aaron had come to call just that morning, she'd found herself having a hard time looking him in the eye. Their interaction had been brief and for the first time, she'd been happy for him to go.

She tried to shake those thoughts away, but her anxiety did not fade, for the third reason for her nervousness was sitting across from her, glaring at her as if he knew she'd done something wrong. Her father shifted and said, "I still don't understand why you have suddenly garnered the interest of such lofty company."

"Trust me, Papa, I have no more idea than you do," she said, wishing her voice didn't squeak so.

"First the Duchess of Willowby invites you, then Crestwood. That is two dukes in two days."

"Three, actually," she mused, hating how her mind could so easily spin an image of the third. "The Duke of Brighthollow is a friend of Willowby. He was calling when I was there yesterday. I think you know him."

Her father's mouth grew hard. "Just in passing. He was at the Willowby estate, was he? And did he speak to you?"

Amelia hesitated. She almost didn't want to tell him about the strange encounter with the man. Somehow, she wanted to keep it just for herself. A secret no one else had to know.

He didn't seem to care that she didn't answer, though. He shook his head. "It is too bad you could not aspire to this before you engaged yourself to someone of lesser value."

Her lips parted. "Just because Aaron is not the rank of duke does not mean he has lesser value."

"Of course he has!" Her father waved toward the bright, big house in the distance. "This circle of dukes, this little club of them, is filled with comfort and riches. With title and pomp and circumstance."

Amelia thought of Brighthollow's dark eyes, the way they'd bore into her with an intensity that made her entire body tingle. That was so different from the soft, sweet glances that Aaron shared with her. She *felt* different.

"I don't want what is in this world," she whispered, almost more to herself than to Quinton.

His gaze flitted over her, and then he turned his face. "Do you truly love Walters?"

"I said I would marry him. Of course, I care for him."

"But what do we know of him, really?" he pressed. "He appeared so suddenly and such a short time ago. Perhaps we should put this engagement off a while."

Her eyes went wide. "We have so much in common, Papa.

He is kind and gentle. He likes all the same books as I do. My favorite songs and dances are also his. He even likes to take walks on the same paths in the park as I do."

The carriage began to slow, and her father let out a harrumph of breath. "Well, we can speak about it later."

As the door opened and he headed from the carriage, she stared at his retreating back. Talk about it later? She had no idea what in the world he could mean to talk to her about. Everything was decided, it simply hadn't been announced. There was nothing left to talk about.

She followed him into the foyer, and they were led down a long, bright hallway toward the ballroom. Amelia tried to calm herself with every step. After all, there would be no Brighthollow tonight. Or if he was in attendance, he certainly would have nothing to do with her. Whatever had brought him to her father's parlor wasn't her concern, and his odd behavior in the Willowby parlor had to be an anomaly.

To consider it anything else was to court folly more than she already had.

Hugh sipped his drink and watched from a distance as Amelia was all but surrounded by the duchesses, that collective group of his best friends' wives who swept up anyone they liked into their wake. He had no idea what Diana had told them about Amelia, but clearly they were sweeping *her* up at that moment.

"Watching anyone in particular? Or just observing the storm that is the wives?"

Hugh turned and couldn't help but grin. Christopher Collins, the Earl of Idlewood, had approached him. As Hugh stuck out a hand in greeting, Kit tugged him in for a hug and pounded his back briefly.

"I had no idea you were in Town," Hugh said as they parted. "How is your father?"

He watched as Kit's face fell and felt a pit in his own stomach. Kit was the last of their little club of dukes who had not yet taken his title. His father, the Duke of Kingsacre, was the best of men. But he was failing. Dying.

And he saw the strain of it on Kit's face.

"He has good days and bad," Kit said. "Diana has come to see him several times and her medicines actually seem to help, which is comforting. Still…"

He didn't finish the sentence, and Hugh didn't push him. "So, he drove you to go to London, did he?"

"You know him. He insists that I go on with my life. He even says it's practice." Kit turned his face.

"And how is Phoebe?"

Kit smiled ever so slightly. "Very well. My sister is a happy little girl who adores her father. But she is so young. She doesn't understand his illness, though she does notice the change in him. Before I left, she very solemnly asked me why Papa was so tired now."

Hugh caught his breath. "I know a little about playing father to a younger sister."

"I know." Kit's voice cracked. "And when the time comes, I will need your help in exactly how to manage that feat." He shook his head. "But enough about that. What is it across the room that interests you so deeply?"

"Just watching the duchess cloud, you know," Hugh said, glancing back at the group of them. Amelia was laughing with them now, and that smile. Great God, but she was beautiful.

"Who is the girl?" Kit asked.

Hugh jerked his face toward his friend. "That obvious, am I?"

"I know you aren't the kind of man to covet a friend's bride," Kit said. "And you have a very…*covetous* look on your face. Since the young lady is the only unknown in the group, I must assume she is what draws your attention."

Hugh continued looking at Amelia without responding. What was he to say? Kit had such a deep sense of right and wrong. He didn't want this friend to judge Lizzie or try to talk him out of correcting what he'd done. And Kit had enough on his shoulders anyway.

"I have an interest," he said at last. "What man would not?"

"She is very pretty," Kit conceded. "Has an interesting light to her, doesn't she? And she seems to fit into the group. That's always a consideration, I suppose, now that so many of our friends are married."

Hugh nodded but said nothing to commit. If he did end up marrying Amelia, as her father required to break the prior engagement, it would be a good thing that she fit into the group of duchesses. But that left him no less troubled about the idea.

He didn't even know her.

"Why are you so disturbed?" Kit pressed. "I see it all over your face."

Hugh sighed. "It's a very long story and not one I'll bore you with. I appreciate the concern, though." He clapped a hand on Kit's shoulder and began to walk away.

"Where are you going?" Kit asked.

Hugh forced a smile over his shoulder. "To dance with the young lady. That's what men do in these situations, isn't it?"

Kit smiled at him, but as Hugh put his attention back on Amelia, his own expression fell. He felt no joy in what he was about to do. Not to the young lady, not to himself. But it was time to get it over with.

Amelia stood beside the dance floor. Thus far it had truly been a wonderful night. The Duchess of Crestwood was a wonderful woman, filled with warmth and welcome. She had swiftly been introduced to the group of Meg's friends, ladies who laughingly referred to themselves as "The Duchesses," for they were all married to dukes.

At first she'd been intimidated, but they were all so kind.

They insisted they be referred to by their first names, and within moments she had felt quite part of their circle. All her fears about this night had faded away, and she was left with a sense of peace instead. Of belonging, like she was an old friend returned to their little flock of beautiful swans.

But now they had all scattered, some to the dancefloor to swing in time to the music with their handsome husbands. Others were joined in conversation with other guests. All that was left now was Isabel, the wife of the Duke of Tyndale. They were very recently married, and the duchess still had a glow of newlywed bliss about her.

Amelia could only hope she would have the same joy when she was wed. Though it was a funny thing that she had not found herself thinking of Aaron all that often during the night. Not even when the ladies talked of husbands and weddings and implied scandals associated with it all.

"Look at James and Emma," Isabel said, motioning to the crowd. "I swear they make us all look so untalented when they dance together."

Amelia followed her friend's indication and smiled. Emma was the Duchess of Abernathe, and at present she was in the arms of her husband. The two moved in perfect accord together, perhaps a bit too close, but as if they had been built to waltz together.

"So lovely," Amelia mused.

"Ladies."

She jerked around at the deep voice that suddenly intruded on her fairytale thoughts. She knew that voice, though she'd only heard it once before. And there was its owner, the Duke of Brighthollow, standing behind them, dark eyes boring into hers just as they had in the parlor the day before.

"Brighthollow," Isabel said, reaching out to squeeze his arm with a smile. "I didn't see you arrive. Do you know Miss Amelia Quentin?"

Amelia swallowed. "We—we met," she stammered.

He inclined his head. "We have indeed. In fact, I came to

find out if Miss Quinton would favor me for a dance. The waltz has just begun, and I think we could still find a place in the crowd."

Amelia stared at him. He wanted to dance with *her*? This man of dark stares and full lips and strong arms and…what in the world was she thinking? Had she answered? No, and now Brighthollow and Isabel were both staring at her expectantly. There was no way to refuse.

"Yes!" she blurted out, far too loudly. "Er, I would be delighted."

Brighthollow held out an elbow, and she drew a deep breath before she put out a hand and slid it into the crook. Immediately she was met with a shock of unexpected awareness. His arm was very strong and very warm, and now he was staring down at her, far too close, and she could not remember how to breathe.

"Have fun, you two!" Isabel called out after them as he led her to the dancefloor.

Somehow Amelia managed to nod at her new friend, but then everything else was swept away as Brighthollow twirled her into a space on the dancefloor and they began to move in time together.

He was very graceful. She would not have expected that since he was so very tall and broad-shouldered. Yet he led her effortlessly. She almost felt like she was gliding on air and that the only people on the dancefloor were the two of them.

She stared up into his face as they moved. As always, he was looking right back at her. His expression was unreadable and so very focused. That same odd tingling she'd felt with him before began again in her stomach. Like a root unfurling through her body, fingers reaching to every part of her until she trembled with the power of the reaction.

"You seem to have become a fast friend of the duchesses," he said when it felt like an eternity of silence had stretched between them.

She blinked, trying to find some kind of focus through the fog he created around her. "I-I don't know. I've only just met most of them. They are wonderfully kind. So welcoming. I'm sure it has nothing to do with me, though. They must be like that with everyone they meet."

"Hm." His lips thinned a little and his gaze darted from her face. It was odd. When he looked at her, she felt uncomfortably exposed. But when he looked away, she didn't like that either. "I think the duchesses *are* very kind and would likely be lovely to anyone they met. But it's more than that."

"More?" she croaked out. That brought his attention back to her face and her knees almost buckled.

"Yes," he said. "I think you would...you would belong in their circle."

"Only if I were a duchess," she said with a nervous laugh. "Certainly, I would never be that."

He shrugged. "But if you were, do you think you would be happy in their company?"

The music slowed and then came to a stop. He stepped back and executed a formal bow. She was meant to curtsey but didn't. Instead she just stared at him, utterly confused by his questions and his looks and just...him in general.

The others on the dancefloor began to filter away, but she stayed in her place. "Why would you ask me such a question?"

He did not reach for her, nor make a gesture to move her along. "I'm curious."

She pursed her lips. "But...why? I'm sorry, I realize I'm being entirely impertinent and my father would rage at me if he knew, but I have no choice."

"None?" he asked, and there was a lightness to the question, even if he didn't smile.

She had no idea if he was gently teasing her or mocking her. "No," she insisted. "You and I have seen each other all of, what...twice? Three times if you count my catching a glimpse of you in my father's hall. You...stare at me but you hardly speak to me. When you do, it is to ask the strangest questions. I feel like you are trying to determine something, but I have no idea what in the world it could be."

She clenched her fists at her sides and tried to slow the wild beating of her heart. She had never confronted a stranger before. A gentleman. A duke, for heaven's sake! It wasn't done, certainly not by someone in her position.

And yet this duke did not seem offended. If anything, his stern expression softened a bit, and he nodded. "You are correct. I've been odd with you and that isn't fair. I would like to discuss it, but not here."

She drew back. "Not here?"

He smiled. "Unless you want to do it in the middle of the quadrille while the entire room gossips about us dancing two in a row together."

She looked around with a gasp. She had honestly all but forgotten where they were. Still on the dancefloor with couples returning to share the next. And they were staring at her and Brighthollow, probably utterly confused as to why they were standing in the way.

"Fine," she said, grasping for his arm. "Where can we go?"

"The terrace?" he suggested. "It is private…or more so. And not inappropriate."

"Yes," she said. "Fine. The terrace is fine. I could use some air anyway."

He said nothing as he took her through the crowd and out the doors that led to the terrace beyond the ballroom. The moment they had exited, she broke away from him and paced to the edge of the wall to stare out at the garden below. The moon was only a sliver of light above them, but the lights from the house made it bright enough.

She heard the doors close and caught her breath. It was only then she realized no other couples or groups were outside with them. She and this man who inspired such odd reactions in her were truly alone.

And though it wasn't entirely inappropriate, just as he had suggested inside, as she turned to watch him come across the terrace to her, it didn't feel very proper to her.

It felt dangerous. Thrilling. She'd never experienced this

kind of sensation when she spoke to another person. It was so very...wrong. That was the pivotal fact of it. She felt something *wrong* toward this man when she was engaged to another. Certainly if Aaron was feeling this way toward a lady Amelia would have been hurt, embarrassed.

Which was why she needed to end this conversation quickly and politely and be finished with the Duke of Brighthollow once and for all.

"I am engaged," she said as Brighthollow got within a few steps of her. That stopped him in his tracks, and that dark gaze settled on her once again. Heavy. Unreadable. Unsettling.

"Yes, I know," he replied at last, tension in his tone.

She drew back in confusion. "You know? How do you know? No one knows, not even my closest friends. My father insisted that we keep it a secret until it is announced in a few days."

Brighthollow shrugged. "I have my ways."

She glared at him. "You are a most frustrating person, Your Grace. Honestly, I do not understand you in the slightest."

He arched a brow at her impertinence, the second time she had displayed it that night. It should have shut her mouth, but instead, she took half a step closer.

"You are being purposefully vague about this subject, though what reason you have, I cannot guess. Nor can I guess why a man such as yourself, a duke with power and privilege, would have any interest in the marriage of the daughter of a minor viscount. One who he never met until one day ago."

He folded his arms. "I have no interest in who you marry, Miss Quinton."

She shut her mouth at that assertion and the flare of disappointment that followed it. "No? You certainly seem to when you are finding me all over London and searching out who I am secretly engaged to."

"I found you once," he said. "To be fair."

"Stop dancing around the subject!" she burst out. "You are playing games with me and I have no interest in them."

His jaw set hard and a muscle there fluttered before he ground out, "My interest, as I said, has nothing to do with you. My interest in is your fiancé, Aaron Walters."

She hesitated. "I…yes. That is him."

"I promise you I would not have sought you out at all if it weren't for the fact that he has entangled you in whatever his latest scheme is."

His face grew harder. There was anger there in it. Not below the surface, but right at it. It rippled over his features and she stepped back at the power of it. One never would have guessed it was there with how he controlled himself so well.

"S-scheme," she stammered, trying to remain focused on the subject at hand. "I resent that implication, Your Grace. My fiancé is certainly not involved in any scheme. He is a good man and does not deserve your…your interference."

"So, he has convinced you," Brighthollow said, running his hand through his hair. Some of the thick curls fell from his queue, and when he faced her his cheeks were framed by wild tendrils that she found herself wanting to smooth.

Just as she found herself wanting to slap that same cheek.

"You must be clearer," she insisted. "What is it you are accusing him of?"

For a moment he was silent. His mouth opened and shut, like he was trying to find words to say. Frustration and rage filtered across his face, but also something deeper. Pain. Regret.

"Your fiancé is not a good man," he said at last. "He has…done very wrong things in the past, and I have deep suspicions that he is up to no good again. With you."

She cocked her head. Brighthollow had stalked her across Town, found her in the ballroom, brought her out here for this big revelation, and that was all? This ambiguous accusation that Aaron was not decent?

"You are very vague," she said softly.

"I assure you, I am very honest," he said, just as quiet in the dim night.

"You *assure* me?" she repeated. "So I am to take you on,

what…your honor?"

"Yes," he said, seeming stunned she didn't simply accept that.

She shook her head. "I don't even *know* you, Your Grace. I have no idea of your motives or *your* schemes. Meanwhile, I have known Aaron for—"

"A few months," he completed for her as he folded his arms. "You think that is long enough to truly suss out a man's character? His intentions? Does it not bother you how swiftly he wooed and engaged himself to wed you?"

She stepped back. His words had two effects. The first stirred doubt in her, for she sometimes did feel as if Aaron had rather rushed their courtship. But he was a romantic. That was what she told herself, at any rate.

The second response was something she could handle more easily. She felt angry. At Brighthollow.

"You've been…are you *shadowing* him?" she asked. "And me? Tracking what he's been doing and seeing? And you claim *he* is to be doubted? Well, what do your actions say about *you*?"

Brighthollow let out his breath in a frustrated burst. "Your loyalty does you credit. I grant you that."

"Don't bother to grant me anything," she snapped. "I don't value your opinion of me, high or low."

He turned his face as if she had slapped him. When he turned back, his anger burned bright in his eyes. "If you knew what he was, you would fall to your knees and thank me for warning you off of him."

"I would never give you the pleasure of seeing me on my knees," she said.

"That's enough, Amelia."

Both of them jumped as the doors to the terrace snapped shut behind them. Her father stood at them, glaring at the couple.

She gave Brighthollow one last scowl and then strode past him toward her father. "I happen to agree, Papa. I've certainly had enough. Excuse me, I shall return to the ball."

She pushed the doors open and went inside, but the moment

she was away from Brighthollow, all her bravado faded. It was replaced by confusion, doubt and a continued draw to the man, despite what an ogre he was.

Despite what he was trying to do to the man she had vowed to marry.

CHAPTER FIVE

As Hugh watched Amelia stomp off into the house, leaving him alone with her father, he wasn't sure if he wanted to chase after her to shake her...or kiss her. Right now he wanted to do both. Especially when she'd conjured that image of her on her knees before him.

Now his body was as on edge as his mind, and he hated himself for how poorly he'd handled the whole night.

"You have violated my suggestion on how to handle this situation, and now look what you have done," Lord Quinton snapped as he strode past Hugh with a look of contempt.

Hugh pivoted to glare at him. "Mind your tone, my lord. You'd do well to remember to whom you are speaking."

Quinton cast a quick, nervous glance at him and then inclined his head. "My apologies, Your Grace. I overstepped. You must understand my frustration, though. I said you should not meet Amelia and then you did just that by arranging an invitation for her to the house of your friends."

Hugh pressed his lips together. "It is ludicrous to think that you would wish me to offer for her without speaking to her."

"Well, you've spoken to her twice now, and where did it get you? I came out too late to hear the entire scope of your conversation, but it was evident it was not going well. My daughter is in a huff."

"I thought I owed her the courtesy of allowing her to know the truth about her fiancé," he admitted, thrusting his shoulders back when Quinton gasped in horror. He was not going to be pushed around by this man who seemed to not even care about his daughter's well-being.

Quinton's expression calmed slightly. "If you were as vague in that explanation as you were with me, I assume she did not believe you and *that* is why you two quarreled."

"She is loyal. That is a fine quality under every circumstance but this one, when I need to shake her faith in Walters and force her to protect herself. I question why you would not be just as concerned about her future as I am."

"I am concerned," Quinton said, his frown deepening. "Although I do see her connection to him, there is no doubt that Walters has an interest in her dowry. But there are many men who marry with money in mind. It's the way of our world. He brings certain advantages to the match, himself."

"And what are those?" Hugh asked, unable to mask his disgust with either man.

"Connections," Quinton said softly.

Hugh stared at him. "I have made quite a study of Aaron Walters in the past year or so. He has no *good* connections, that is certain. Do you truly want to involve yourself in the kind of men he could bring to you?"

"Money is money, Your Grace," Quinton said. "Amelia's dowry was provided by her mother's family, in a way that I cannot touch."

Money. It was all about money.

Quinton let out his breath in a deep sigh before he continued, "But now that you've stirred her up, Amelia could very well run off to Gretna Green with the man, and then neither of us get what we want. I will have no promises and you no revenge for whatever wrong you accuse him of."

Hugh pushed his disgust about Quinton away at that thought. The viscount was right. After all, Lizzie had run with Walters when the man felt his future threatened. Why wouldn't Amelia do the same? And the pain that would follow would also be similar. He knew what it would be like. He certainly didn't wish it on the bright light that Amelia seemed to carry within her.

"You want me to offer for her," he said softly as his options faded down, whittled away to only one.

"Yes. If we could come to terms about money and connection, I would much rather see my daughter so elevated to your title." Quinton shrugged.

Hugh let out his breath slowly. "Fine. I will offer. But she despises me and she is engaged to another man. There is no way she won't spit in my face if I try to persuade her."

Quinton chuckled. "She would likely do that. She has fire in her that will have to be extinguished by whatever man takes her hand. And yet she can be manipulated, if the pressure points you apply are correct."

"What pressure points?" Hugh asked.

Once again, Quinton smiled, almost a look of pride on his thin face. "You'll see. Give her a night to settle down and come call on me tomorrow after lunch. Follow my lead and I assure you, you will have your prize." He turned toward the house. "For now, I shall escort her home and do what I can to smooth her ruffled feathers."

Hugh watched him go and bit back a curse. He did not like this, not one bit. But right now there seemed little choice. Not for him.

Not for her.

Amelia clenched her hands as she made her way through the ballroom and into the retiring room that was attached to the larger space. Inside, ladies could find smelling salts, cool water and a place to gather one's thoughts in the midst of the chaos of a ball.

Tonight she needed the latter. Desperately. And she was pleased when she found the small room devoid of other guests who might insist on chatting with her. She threw herself onto a fainting couch that was pressed against one wall and folded her arms. Her mind buzzed with everything that had happened between herself and the Duke of Brighthollow since he had asked her to dance.

And not just the horrible things he'd said about Aaron. No, she was just as turned upside down by the way his hands had held her so tightly as they danced, by the way he looked at her when he spoke to her on the terrace…by the way her own heart quickened when he did both.

She hated him. And she hated herself when she was with him. For making her forget Aaron. For making her…well, for a moment she had doubted her fiancé. What did that make her?

The door to the retiring room opened and Emma—the Duchess of Abernathe—entered, her cheeks flushed and a wide smile on her pretty face. When she saw Amelia sitting on the settee, that smile fell. "Oh, Amelia, is everything well?"

Amelia tried to force a smile of reassurance but could not muster it. She shook her head. "I'm sorry to be rude, Your Grace, but I must say that your friend is a terrible, horrible man."

Emma blinked, clearly in confusion and then gingerly sat on the opposite end of the fainting couch. "My friend? You'll have to be more specific."

"The Duke of Brighthollow," Amelia huffed.

Emma's expression softened slightly. "I noticed you two were dancing earlier. You do not like him?"

"I do not."

Emma let out her breath gently. "Hugh can be…hard. Though I think his history has earned him that. He did not have a happy relationship with his father, and when his parents died, he was forced into his title at a very young age, as well as guardianship of his much younger sister. A great deal of weight settled on those shoulders."

Amelia shifted. She did not know those things about the man. Heavens, a week ago she had never spent time with any dukes or duchesses. She knew her place in the world. It was on the periphery of those at the very top levels of the *ton*.

And now Emma said a handful of words, and suddenly some of Amelia's anger toward Brighthollow faded. "How old was he?"

Emma tilted her head. "Seventeen, I think? Eighteen? Just barely old enough to stake his claim at all. He leaned heavily on his friends, on their group." She smiled. "Their brotherhood has seen all of them through difficult times."

Amelia stared at her clenched hands. She did feel a little for Brighthollow now, but did that really change what he'd said about Aaron? Those vague accusations that the man she planned to marry was unworthy?

"Well, perhaps he has been elevated for so long that he does not remember humility," she muttered. "For he judges those beneath him quite harshly."

Emma looked truly surprised. "Really? I must say that shocks me. Rank has never seemed to matter as much to him as a goodness of character."

Amelia pushed to her feet. She liked Emma. Although they had only talked for a few moments in the ballroom, the duchess was kind, welcoming, intelligent. She was everything Amelia looked for in a friend.

But perhaps her sweetness made her blind to character flaws. Amelia had to believe that was it, because the alternative was that Brighthollow was talking to her about Aaron because he truly believed her fiancé to be untrue.

And that was not something Amelia wanted to face. Couldn't.

"I'm sure I was just overly warm," she lied. "And reacted badly to something that was not cruelly meant."

"Yes," Emma said, and got up to pour her a glass of water. "These events can be so very overwhelming! Hugh's gruffness can be easily mistaken by those who don't know him."

"At any rate, it isn't as though I really have to talk to the man again," Amelia reasoned, more to herself than to Emma. "We're only in the same circles by accident tonight. We do not click and we don't have to."

Emma shrugged. "You are correct. Though I hope we'll see you in our circles more often. All the duchesses like you a great deal."

Amelia smiled as the topic shifted to more benign ones. What Emma didn't know was that soon Amelia's engagement would be announced. And Aaron was not the kind of gentleman who would open doors to her to the Society Emma regularly kept.

So all this consternation about the handsome, horrible Duke of Brighthollow didn't matter one whit.

Hugh stood in the corner of Simon and Meg's ballroom, watching as the last of the guests staggered their way to the door. All that was left now were his friends. Members of their club. Only it had ceased to be a club and become a family.

And his family was giving him odd looks at present. As Simon and Meg returned from saying farewell to the last of their guests, it was Emma, James's wife, who approached him. Hugh was a little surprised by that. She was so soft and quiet, as bookish as she was beautiful. Normally she didn't start anything. In fact, she was the calming influence that often stopped any loud argument.

But at that moment she had an expression of concern on her face. One that was matched as the rest of their friends joined her.

"I spoke to Amelia Quinton tonight," Emma said softly.

He arched a brow. "I saw her with the duchesses. It seemed you all got along very well."

Meg glanced at the other ladies and nodded. "We all like her very much."

"Good," he said with relief. "That will make it easier."

When he said that, Lucas straightened, and Hugh saw Diana's fingers tighten on her husband's forearm. They were the only two who knew the truth.

"What are you saying?" Lucas asked, his voice tense. "What are you doing?"

"I'm offering for her tomorrow," he admitted, for there was no reason for him to keep that a secret. They'd all know soon enough.

That simple sentence set off a cacophony of reaction. Every face around him looked utterly shocked, some horrified, everyone confused. Except for Lucas and Diana. They just stared at him. Knowing. Pitying.

He hated it all to the pit of his soul.

"Why?" Graham finally asked, pushing his way to the front. "It's not that she isn't lovely. The duchesses all like her, which is a hearty recommendation, indeed. But you've barely spoken of the girl—I've never seen you interact with her at all until tonight."

"And she told me that interaction did not go well," Emma chimed in.

Hugh jerked his face to her, trying to determine how much she knew. "Did she?"

Emma nodded. "She was vague, but she seems to find you terribly heavy-handed and…unpleasant."

He pressed his lips together. That was a poor start, indeed, but what could he expect? He had made a bad attempt to crush every dream the young lady had. Why would she not despise him? And after tomorrow, she would hate him even more.

"Not everyone marries for the same reasons," he said, not meeting the eyes of all those happy couples. Not looking at what he would throw away because he had protected his sister's virtue and his own bloody pride.

"And what are yours?" Simon pressed, using that gentle tone that had come so naturally to him over the years. He was the peacekeeper of their group. The coaxer. The tamer of wild beasts.

Hugh let out his breath slowly. "There are advantages to the match for me. For her. She is very beautiful, of course.

Intelligent. It's a good match. And I'd be able to protect—"

Graham lifted his brows as Hugh cut that sentence off. "Protect her?" he repeated. "Is that what you were going to say?"

Hugh turned and walked away from them. Not far, but far enough that they couldn't see his face. He didn't want any of them to see his face.

"I know a great deal about protection," Graham said, crossing the distance Hugh had placed between them. "What do you need? How can we help so that you don't make some kind of well-intentioned mistake?"

Hugh shut his eyes. Held them there, like the dark could block out the truth. Block out the questions. Block out the future.

Then he opened them and speared first Graham and then the others with a stern look. "Just support me. And her."

He could see the arguments on the lips of all the others. See that the remainder of the night would consist of them wearing him down and demanding the truth and perhaps eventually prying it from him.

And then Diana stepped forward. She crossed to him and took his hand, her bright eyes holding his for a long moment. Then she leaned up and bussed his cheek. "Congratulations, Hugh. You have our support."

That silenced the murmurs. Quieted the questions. And his reluctant friends approached and gave him the same felicitations she had done. But it felt like a funeral rather than a celebration of his pending engagement.

And perhaps that was fitting, after all.

CHAPTER SIX

Hugh stood in the same parlor where he had first met Lord Quinton less than a week before. Today he faced the door, feet widely spread, hands clenched behind him. He was waiting for an executioner. Waiting for the inevitable.

It had been a sleepless night of pondering this decision. Trying to see if there was a way out of it. Only there was none. That became clearer by the moment. If he did not marry this young woman, she would be caught up in the snare set for her by Aaron Walters. He would take her dowry, he would turn away from whatever false costume he put on himself for her, and she would suffer.

Hugh would watch it. He would not be able to look away. And he would know it was his fault. He would know he had not done the right thing. The good thing.

Perhaps, given time, he could have convinced Amelia of the truth of the man she believed she loved. She was bright—she would see it. Only he was not being given that time. Her father had a purpose in mind: marry her off. And whether he received Hugh's good connections and money or Walters' poor connections didn't matter to him. He would have his announcement and his wedding, the good of his daughter be damned.

Now Hugh was left with this. Destroy her hopes. Kill her dreams. Steal her future. Marry himself to a lady he didn't know, one who apparently thought very little of him.

But it would save her. In the end, perhaps she would come to appreciate that.

The door to the parlor opened and Quinton stepped in. As Hugh moved forward, the viscount stepped aside and revealed his daughter. Hugh caught his breath. She wore a blue gown that matched the cornflower of her eyes to perfection. She lifted those eyes to him, and for a moment he saw a flare of heat. Of interest.

Then it was replaced by contempt and she folded her arms in frustration. But he had seen the first. Her fleeting desire called to his own. If he married her, he could slake that. Drown in it.

And introduce her to pleasures untold.

"Your Grace," Quinton said, his tone smug. "You've come. Very good. We can resolve this issue swiftly and move forward."

Hugh shook his head slightly. God's teeth, this man. He'd said Hugh was to follow his lead in convincing Amelia to wed him. He had no choice, but he hated it, for he didn't trust the viscount in any way.

"Yes, I look forward to handling this matter," he said. "Miss Quinton."

She met his eyes briefly. "Your Grace. I shall leave you and my father to whatever business you have to attend to."

She moved to go, but her father caught her elbow and kept her from exiting the room. Hugh looked at how his fingers dug into her forearm, and his heart lurched a little.

"Amelia, you shall stay," the viscount said. "This concerns you."

Her lips parted in surprise, and then she pivoted toward Hugh again. "Did you *dare* speak to my father about my engagement? You are a most impertinent man. You have no right to interfere in my life, especially since you hardly know me!"

A dozen retorts rose up in Hugh's body, threatened to spill out, but he held them back as Quinton said, "It is you who is being impertinent, child."

She faced him. "Unless he gave you a good reason, a *real* reason, for me not to marry Aaron Walters, I have no idea how I am not allowed to defend myself against his—"

"He did," Quinton interrupted, lifting his voice so it was louder than hers.

Hugh watched as a look of pure horror rolled over her face. The blood left her cheeks and her mouth dropped open in shock. "Wh-what?"

The viscount nodded, suddenly solemn. "Yes, my dear. The duke has given me a very compelling reason to keep your engagement to Mr. Walters from advancing."

"What could that be?" she burst out, her gaze darting from her father to Hugh and back again.

She was hurt. Brokenhearted. Hugh hated himself more than he ever had that he was a part of it. That he hadn't pushed aside his pride and found a way to turn Society against Walters before his duplicity went this far and involved another innocent young woman in his schemes.

"You will not marry Walters," her father said. "Because the Duke of Brighthollow seems to have purchased a great deal of my debt. And he will free me from that debt only if you marry him instead."

Hugh staggered. *This* was the way he would convince her to marry? To tell this vulgar, cruel lie? To use her love for her father against whatever love she felt for Walters? To make Hugh a deeper, darker villain than she believed him to be already?

She turned to him, her lips white, trembling, and stared. And in that moment he saw that she despised him. She would despise him for the rest of her days.

But he also saw that despite any fight she was about to put up, she would also ultimately surrender. She would marry him.

And he'd never felt sicker in his life.

Amelia couldn't breathe. She stared at Brighthollow, standing behind her father, face impassive, arms folded, dark eyes spearing her, and she couldn't breathe. She'd thought him wicked before, but now she saw how deep that went.

How far he would go to get what he wanted. He would lie. He would cheat. He would steal.

"You cannot mean this," she managed to push out past dry lips. She was speaking to her father, but she couldn't stop staring at Brighthollow. "I can't marry him."

Quinton cocked his head. "Not even to save your father? Do I mean so little to you, Amelia?"

Brighthollow flinched, turned his gaze away at last. It seemed he couldn't stomach his own cruelty. But when he looked away, she felt able to do the same and stared at her father.

"You are all I have left," she whispered. "You mean the world to me. But is there no other way?"

"I've found no way out," her father said. He sighed, but it didn't sound particularly sad. "This arrangement is all there is left. And look on the bright side, Amelia. You will be a duchess with power and money, far more elevated than a mere country gentleman could lift you. It is a good trade."

"A trade?" she whispered. "You trade my heart for comfort and you call it good?"

The viscount shook his head. "Gracious, Amelia, you are being ridiculous. I understand that marrying for the heart is all the rage in higher circles at present, but we must be pragmatic. Love or something like it fades with time. In five years or ten you would regret turning away a duke for a no one. One day you'll thank me."

She stared at her father, uncertain if he was trying to convince her or himself. She couldn't believe he was as laissez-faire about this bargain as he seemed. He had to know how much it cut her to think of walking away from the future she'd planned.

So she turned to Brighthollow. When she stepped up to him, he stiffened. His jaw tightened and he glanced down at her, holding her gaze with that entirely unreadable expression she now wanted to slap from his face.

"You cannot really want to marry me," she breathed. "You cannot really wish to trade my father's debts for...for me?"

He was silent for a beat. Two. Like he was struggling with the answer. His gaze flitted to Quinton, and then he jerked out a nod. "Yes."

Her heart sank. She would be forced to walk away from a man who showered her with romantic gestures, who declared their future loudly and proudly, to...this. To this silent ogre who would rip her from her happiness just to settle a score. Against her father, against her fiancé. She would be his tool, nothing else.

"I will *never* marry you," she hissed.

He arched a brow, and she waited for a storm to explode in him. Perhaps she wanted it, just to see that he was capable of *feeling*.

But he didn't. Instead, he bent his head. "I'm afraid you will, my dear," he said softly. "And quickly. It must...it must be this way. I'm sorry."

She heard those words come from his mouth. Perhaps meant to soothe her. Comfort her. Absolve himself. She wasn't certain. All she knew was that they inspired dark anger in her and desperation.

"If you are sorry..." she said, grabbing for his hand. When she touched him, that hateful awareness woke in her, defied her anger and pain. Still, she clung to him. "If you are sorry, then don't do it!"

She stared up at him, then to her father. They were equally immovable, and she saw that she had no cards to play here. No way out. And with a sob, she dropped his hand and ran from the room, away from the cruelty that had stolen the hopes and dreams she had so carefully crafted.

Hugh was shocked at his reaction when Amelia burst into

tears and ran from the room. The guilt of the action ripped through him, exposing all the nerves he normally protected and causing pain unlike any he'd felt in a very long time. He wanted, quite irrationally, to go to her. To comfort her. To help her somehow. Or at least to make her understand.

But he couldn't. Because he couldn't explain the reasons behind what she could only judge as his cruel actions. He couldn't tell her the stakes. Because of Lizzie. Because of his own pride.

"You'll take care of the special license," Lord Quinton said, his tone lacking any of the empathy Hugh currently felt for the man's daughter.

Hugh faced him. "*That* was your way of convincing her? To tell her that I'm blackmailing you? She now hates me more than ever."

"But she'll do it, won't she?" Quinton asked. "That's what you wanted, isn't it?"

"Not like this," Hugh said softly, staring off again at the place where she had run. He glanced at Quinton. "You'll watch her carefully during the next few days? To ensure she doesn't run in her desperation."

Quinton wrinkled his brow like he didn't understand. "You think she would let me be destroyed?"

Hugh huffed out his breath. In this man's mind, he was the center of the universe, certainly his daughter's universe. The concept that she might put her own desires above his, that she was owed the right to do so, was utterly foreign to him.

"Will you watch her?" Hugh ground out through clenched teeth.

"Yes, yes," Quinton said, waving his hand in a dismissive gesture.

Hugh shook his head. He certainly did not trust that answer, so he would have to take care of that himself. He strode to the door and out into the foyer, with Quinton trailing along behind him.

"I'll have the special license in a day or two," Hugh said.

"We will marry as soon as it is done."

"I'll be sure she is ready, whether she likes it or not." Quinton's tone had a touch of laughter to it, as if forcing this woman to do what she did not like was humorous.

Hugh pivoted and speared him with a dark glare. "Be kind to her, my lord. Be extra kind to her during the next few days. If I hear you have been anything but that, I will be very angry and you do not want to see that, I assure you."

Quinton drew back a fraction, and then he nodded. "Certainly, I can do that. Anything to have her in the right mindset, eh?"

Hugh rolled his eyes at the utterly selfish and stupid man who stood before him. One who had no understanding whatsoever at how to behave in a decent or loving manner.

So Amelia would come to Hugh with hate and desperation. With heartbreak and resistance.

And in that moment Hugh vowed, if only to himself, to do whatever it took to help her in that pain. To accept all her hate without reaction, and hope, one day, that she would no longer despise him.

CHAPTER SEVEN

Amelia hadn't slept, and her entire body ached as she paced her chamber in a cloud of utter despair. When the door opened, she hardly registered it and did not greet Theresa as she entered the room and clucked her tongue gently.

"Oh, miss," she said, and moved forward to fold Amelia into a brief hug.

Amelia sank into it, letting her emotions overwhelm her for the briefest of moments. They welled up, crashing over her like a wave from a stormy sea and she was going to drown in them. Which didn't seem the worst end when she considered the alternative.

"Come sit," Theresa said gently, helping Amelia to her dressing table where she began to brush her hair over and over in long, soothing strokes. "Did you sleep at all?"

"No," Amelia croaked, looking at herself in the reflection. A few days ago she had done this and seen all her hopes and dreams. Today she saw only sorrow. Betrayal. Uncertainty.

"Your father went out," Theresa said, her tone now thick with judgment. "He said there was much to do."

A bitter taste filled Amelia's mouth. "I'm certain there is. To rush me into this marriage, I have no doubt Brighthollow will obtain a special license within days. They will march me down the aisle at sword point just to be sure I do not thwart their little plan. I doubt I will be Miss Amelia Quinton by this time next week. I'll be...*his*."

She shivered as she said the last, and wished she could say that the reaction was out of pure disgust or horror. But deep in the heart of her, she knew it wasn't. Yes, she feared what was to come. Yes, she was hurt and angry, and she despised both the men who had so cavalierly put her in this position.

But part of her sleepless night was because of far less hateful thoughts of Brighthollow. Hugh, Emma had called him. That dark and dangerous man, so unlike Aaron Walters, did stir such strange feelings in her. And they weren't entirely unpleasant. Which was utterly confusing and terrifying in its own right.

"Your father said to be extra kind to you," Theresa mused, thankfully interrupting the wicked line of Amelia's thoughts. "He said that was your future husband's order."

Amelia's lips parted, and she pivoted to look at Theresa more fully. "*Brighthollow* directed him to this?"

"Apparently, though your father's suggestions on what that would entail were rather weak, indeed. Extra sugar in your tea, a chocolate biscuit? It took everything in me not to ask if extra kindness meant releasing you from the shackles he and this duke have thrown onto you."

Amelia bent her head. "I'm glad you didn't say it. I appreciate the sentiment, but we both know it only would have encouraged his rage. And I need you, Theresa. More than ever now."

"Well, I'll be there. Every step of the way. You know that." The maid folded her arms and her jaw set with a stubbornness that made Amelia's heart swell. Whatever unknown she would soon face, at least she would have a friend at her side.

"I suppose I should dress and face this day. It may be my last of freedom," Amelia sighed and looked at her mirror again.

Theresa bustled off to choose a gown, holding up one then another for Amelia's approval. When she pulled out a pretty pink silk with a gray overlay stitched in a swirling pattern, Amelia's heart sank. That gown had been Aaron's favorite. He had complimented her on it multiple times during a garden party just after they met a few months before.

"The rose," she said, indicating the gown. As she stood and let Theresa help her from her wrinkled night-rail and into the gown, her mind began to spin.

"You've always looked lovely in this one," Theresa mused.

"Thank you," Amelia said. "Did you tell me that my father had gone out for the day?"

"Mmmhmmm." Theresa's tone was distracted as she fastened the long line of fabric-covered buttons along Amelia's spine. "He didn't say where, just that it had to do with the upcoming wedding."

Amelia pursed her lips and sat when her gown was fastened. "Can you do that special twist?" she asked as Theresa lifted the brush again. Theresa nodded, and Amelia watched in the mirror as the maid spun and pinned her hair like a magician showing off a trick. Once again, she had picked a style that Aaron liked. They'd been walking in the park when he'd plucked a leaf from her hair and told her how lovely it was. Compared it to midnight, gone on and on about silk. Her heart had leapt with the romance of it.

After Theresa finished, Amelia stood and went to her full-length mirror across the room. There she looked at the girl with the hair and gown that Aaron Walters liked. And in that moment she knew exactly why she'd made these choices.

"I need to go see Aaron," she said softly.

Theresa had been folding the discarded nightgown, but at that declaration, she let the fabric swish back to the ground and jerked around to stare at Amelia.

"I beg your pardon?" she burst out.

Amelia pushed her shoulders back and set her jaw, for she knew what she'd said was exactly what she must do. "In a day or less, the entire city will know I am to marry the Duke of Brighthollow in what will surely be seen as a scandalous rush. That is not how I would have Aaron know that our engagement, secret or not, was broken. I must go to him." She caught her breath. "I-I must tell him myself."

Tears filled her eyes at the idea of seeing his broken expression. Perhaps he would argue with her, plead with her. And she would have to refuse him, even if her heart broke as she did it. The pain of that realization was enormous.

"Oh, miss," Theresa said. "That isn't a good idea. Your father..."

"Why would he have to know?" Amelia asked. "I could simply take my horse and sneak away. He wouldn't know a thing about it, nor would anyone else. If he discovered the truth, what could he do to me now? He's already forcing me to marry a stranger. He can take nothing more than has already been taken. And you will not be in trouble as long as you don't confess you knew."

Theresa worried her lip. "It's improper."

Amelia bent her head. "Excuse me for being coarse, but I say bugger propriety!"

"Miss Amelia!" Theresa burst out, her cheeks turning near purple.

"If one cannot curse when one is being marched to the altar against one's will, then when can one?" Amelia asked. "I don't care about unseemliness. I am about to lose it all. This is the one thing I can do to comfort myself in that loss. I'm going and I'm telling him myself. As I should. As he deserves."

Theresa let out her breath. "Well, I think I shall just turn my back then and go on to the folding. If you were to sneak out of the room when I wasn't looking, I would probably assume you'd gone to the library to find some relief and tell everyone to leave you alone for an hour or two."

"A good idea. I'm very upset." Amelia smiled at her, grateful for this one choice after all the others had been stolen from her. Theresa reached out and squeezed her arm, then turned to pick up the discarded dressing gown. She even began to whistle as she went about her work.

And Amelia slipped from the room and toward the last bit of freedom she feared she'd ever have.

Amelia had only seen Aaron's home once, when they had ridden by it in his rig during an afternoon excursion together. He'd pointed out the townhouse, one that faced the park, and she oohed and ahhed at the lovely location. Her father had cooed just as loudly later over the proof that Walters had money.

Now she rode her mare, Cherry, onto the drive in front of the house and shuddered. She'd somehow made it here uninterrupted and unmolested. Now she questioned her choice. She wasn't announced or expected. She didn't even know if Aaron would be home to greet her.

But it was too late to go back now. She owed the man this courtesy. She owed herself the chance to see him one last time before they were separated by these bitter circumstances.

She moved to the door and knocked. There was the sound of movement and then the door opened. She was surprised to find it was Aaron, himself, standing there. He had an apple in one hand, with a bite missing from it, and he wore no shoes or jacket. She blinked, unprepared as he stared down at her, almost as if he didn't recognize her.

His straw-colored hair was mussed, like he'd been running his fingers through it, and his dark blue eyes were a little bleary. His undone state was a shock to her, and she waited for that sense of awareness to fill her. The one that seemed to come with no trouble the moment she walked into a room with Brighthollow. But there was nothing but embarrassment that she had found him thus.

"Great God, Amelia!" he said at last as he cast a glance over his shoulder into the house. "I didn't expect you—what are you doing here?"

She swallowed hard. "Oh, Aaron, I know it's wrong, but I *had* to see you. Something has happened. Something terrible!"

He pursed his lips, and for a moment she thought perhaps he was annoyed. But then his expression softened. "You are overwrought. Will you…come in?"

He stepped aside at last and she entered. To her surprise, the foyer was quite plain despite the fine address. There were spaces where paintings had clearly once hung, but they were gone now. It was a rather cold and empty space.

"Come to the parlor." He led her there. "I'm sorry I cannot offer you tea. My servants have the morning off."

He opened the door, and she entered a small parlor. There were two shabby chairs in front of a fire and two half-filled wineglasses on the table between them. Since it was so early in the day, she wondered if they had been left over from last night. It seemed odd that his servants had not removed the items.

He muttered something beneath his breath and grabbed for them as she settled into a place.

"Let me just…I'll be back," he said, and then he left the room without another word. He shut the door and she heard him talking for a moment in the hall. A female voice answered, probably whatever maid was left while the other servants were out.

Amelia stood and paced the small room, her heart racing ever faster. What in the world could she say to his man? How could she find the words?

He returned a few moments later, and she smiled. He had fixed himself and was now wearing boots, so when he stepped into the room he seemed more the man who had courted her the last few months.

He left the door open to maintain some propriety and hustled to her, sitting down and taking both her hands in his. His gaze swept over her face as he said, "You are so very upset. What has happened?"

She drew a long breath and blinked at the tears that rushed to her eyes. His kindness didn't make this easier.

"I-I came here because I must tell you in person. It is only fair." She shook her head.

"Tell me what?" he asked, his brow knitting.

She swallowed hard and forced herself to be brave. "Aaron,

I cannot marry you as we planned."

The gentleness on his face departed in an instant, and he shook her hands away. "You are breaking our engagement?" he asked, his tone suddenly cold as an icy winter's day.

She bent her head. "Not because of my desires, I assure you. It turns out my father owes a debt to a very powerful man. And they've made an arrangement that my marriage to him will settle it. They're—" Her voice shook and she tried desperately to maintain control. "They're making preparations even as we speak. I will likely be forced to wed him before the week is out."

Aaron had been staring at her, his gaze even and cool and unreadable. Now he folded his arms. "Who?"

"The Duke of Brighthollow," she whispered.

His nostrils flared slightly, and then he got to his feet. He paced away, stopping the sideboard where he splashed a generous amount of scotch into a tumbler and downed it in one angry sip. He shook his head, and then he let out a humorless laugh.

"That bastard. Always thwarting the best laid plans," he said.

She stood and turned toward him, confused by the sudden shift in his demeanor. "What? What do you mean? Do you know the duke?"

He glanced at her, and then his expression grew sad as he set his glass away and sighed. "I'm afraid I do. I once lived in Brighthollow, myself. I certainly was not as elevated as the duke, but I knew of him. Talked to him in passing. He is a cold bastard, but what can you do when someone holds that much power? We had a disagreement over—"

He stopped and his mouth drew down deeply. She moved toward him. "Over what?"

"It hardly matters now," he said. "It would be unseemly to discuss him, especially since it seems you will be forced to wed him. I would not want to poison your opinion of the man."

She shook her head. "You could not. I already think him to be an ogre of the highest order. What he is doing to me is bad enough. But it seems he has some vendetta against you, as well."

He nodded. "He does. And I fear you may have been placed in the middle of it. He despises me and would do anything to destroy my happiness. It is possible he...no, I will not speculate."

She stared at him as the meaning of his truncated sentence became clear. "Do you think he bought my father's debt as merely a means to lord it over him and force this marriage? Just to thwart you?"

Aaron searched her face, and she saw just how emotional this situation made him. Still, he did not touch her as he sighed. "Perhaps. I would not put it past him."

Amelia lifted her cold hands to her suddenly hot face and shook her head in horror. "And I shall marry this man!"

"Is there no way out of it?" Aaron asked, his tone very soft.

"I cannot think of one that would be honorable," she whispered.

He opened his mouth as if he would speak, but before he could they were interrupted by a sudden and horrifying arrival. As if he had been conjured by their whispers, Brighthollow himself stepped into the room. Amelia saw him before Aaron did, and she skittered backward in surprise at his presence there.

He was staring not at Aaron, but at her. Those dark eyes were stormy clouds, hiding an explosion that was yet to come. Then his gaze flitted to Aaron and there was no mistaking his hatred for the person she cared so deeply for.

Aaron froze at her expression and slowly turned. Fear washed over his face as he stared at the intruder.

"B-Brighthollow," he stammered. "I didn't hear you knock."

"I *didn't* knock," Hugh said, his voice rough with emotion. It was the first time she'd heard such a thing in him. He was normally so controlled. He looked past him and toward her again. His tone was surprisingly gentle as he said, "Miss Quinton, go to my carriage. *Now*, please."

Her lips parted. "No, I will not leave you alone with him."

Aaron broke the stare between the men and gave her a reassuring smile. "It's all right, my dear. I'm certain the duke would not be so foolish as to hurt me when he knows you are a witness to his barging into my home uninvited. You may go to his carriage."

She jerked her gaze between them, once again stripped of any choice or power in this beastly situation. Then she did as she'd been told and left them alone. And feared what would happen once she was gone from the room.

Hugh's hands shook with rage as he watched Amelia slide past him from the chamber, her shoulders trembling and her mouth a thin, white line of displeasure. When she'd gone, he reached behind himself and yanked the door shut. Then he turned on this man he had hated for over a year.

All of Walters' false kindness and gentleness was gone now that his audience had departed, and he smirked at Hugh. "I can always depend on you to destroy my best plans, can't I?" he said with a laugh. Like they were equals. Like they were partners. Like they were friends.

"You bastard," Hugh growled, just barely containing himself.

Walters shrugged. "Not everyone has your advantages, Your Grace. You are quick to judge what you don't know. One must make a way in the world however one can."

Hugh glared at him. "You think your position in life can excuse your actions? You prey on decent women, you use them, ruin them and take what you want. All for a chance to earn their purse."

"Do you think I *ruined* your…I suppose she is your fiancée now, isn't she?" Walters smiled, and it was smug and ugly. "Do you think you're getting my seconds, Brighthollow?"

Hugh's stomach turned at the thought that this self-satisfied pig had laid so much as a hand on Amelia's body. It must have reflected on his face, for Walters let out a chuckle that grated along Hugh's spine. "You ask her."

It was enough. Too much. With a growl of feral anger, Hugh launched across the room and caught Walters by the lapels. He might have slammed him through the wall if the door behind them hadn't opened. They both turned as a half-dressed, bed-messed woman stepped inside. She was haggard-looking, tired. A lightskirt—Hugh would lay a bet on it and know he'd win.

She glanced at them, seemingly unworried about the two men fighting in the parlor. "Is she gone? Can I take my money and go now?"

Hugh glanced back at Walters, who shrugged. "I get what I want when I want it," he explained.

Hugh shook his head as he released him and backed away. "The circumstances of this situation keep me from destroying you. But I'm pleased to have bested you."

Walters' eyebrow arched. "Did you? You've disrupted me at most. And now you'll marry my leftovers and I will go on to find a better, richer heiress to woo. While *you* are forever locked in a trap of your own honor."

Hugh wanted to be the bigger man. The better man. But he couldn't. He swung on Walters and connected squarely against his cheek, sending him flying backward across the room and into the wall beside the fireplace. Walters grunted in pain as he reached up to touch his already swelling eye.

"Stay away from my sister," Hugh panted as he shook out his tingling hand. "And my...my wife."

He said nothing more, but pushed past the bored prostitute and out of the house. Toward his carriage, where he'd now have to deal with Amelia. And hope he could recover the calm than he had lost with Walters.

CHAPTER EIGHT

Amelia jumped as the carriage door opened and Hugh climbed inside. His face was drawn and grim as he settled in across from her and lightly tapped on the wall behind him to indicate that they should move.

She glared at him and folded her arms like a shield in front of her. One he could so easily pierce that it was almost a joke. "Where is Cherry?"

His brow knitted. "Cherry?"

"My horse," she explained.

He stared at her a beat, and some of the darkness bled away from his expression. "Of course you would worry about her. My man rode her back to your home," he said. "So that we might talk."

Relief flooded her, for at least she didn't have to worry about her animal. Just herself.

"What is there to talk about?" she asked, happy her voice sounded braver than her body felt. "You followed me."

Now his jaw set again, his dark eyes flashed with the anger he was controlling below the surface. "You dare be annoyed with *me* over that fact?"

"I'm angry with you for a great many things," Amelia snapped, losing her own control in the face of his.

He leaned in. The action was sudden and she had no moment to brace herself for it. He was just there, closer, bigger in the small carriage. She had searched for that heated awareness when she found Aaron half-dressed a short time before. Searched and not found.

But here Brighthollow was fully dressed, not even touching her, and that despicable, heated feeling flowed through her without any trouble at all. She hated herself for it. Hated him even more.

"I'm certain you are very angry. Would you like to go ahead and vent all that right now?" he asked.

She wrinkled her brow. "What?"

"You've been holding it back. Why not just say what you feel? It's better than keeping it in, I would say."

"You want me to rail at you?" she asked. "I suppose so you can lord it over me like you're lording my father's debts over me?"

He turned his head and his lips pursed. "I will not."

"And you think I believe any promise you make to me?" she asked, and the anger he demanded came right to the surface instantly. "After you lied to me about my fiancé, spreading scurrilous things about him. And when it didn't work, you then manipulated a situation with my father so that I would have all my hopes and dreams stolen out from under me?"

To her surprise, he did not react to her anger, but sat still, allowing her to pour it out. Now that she had started, it was difficult to stop.

"I despise you down to my very core," she continued. "I think you are a pompous, cruel person. Someone who would take whatever he liked with no thought for the consequences or damage he leaves behind. I *hate* you for forcing me to marry you. I hate how you make my stomach feel so odd when you just stare at me like you are. I hate…I hate you."

His gaze fluttered just a fraction and swept over her face before he said, "Anything else?"

She swallowed. In truth, she did feel better getting to rail at him. Only she knew he would likely punish her for it. She braced herself for that. "No."

He nodded slowly. "You are daring. It is not the worst

quality a person can have. But I must ask, did you come here to run away with Walters?"

She recoiled. "No!"

"No?" There was no mistaking the surprise in his question. "Then why?"

She folded her arms all the tighter. "You think me to have no honor because you have so little? My father made a bargain with you, Your Grace. I have no intention of breaking it, especially considering the circumstances. But I did think I owed my fiancé—" She broke off and dipped her head. "My—my former fiancé, the truth. Before you and my father make your devil's bargain public. Before our marriage takes place and he hears about it through Society whispers."

Hugh did not respond immediately, he just watched her. Her heart thudded with anxiety. She kept going too far and she waited for him to grow angry or defensive. But he didn't. His expression was neutral, unreadable, but he didn't lash out at her. Not verbally, certainly not physically.

Finally, he said, "Your honor recommends you, Amelia."

Her eyes went wide. That was the first time he had not addressed her formally as Miss Quinton. Truth be told, she liked Amelia better, but hearing him say it was still a shock.

And she reacted to the shock and the awareness and the interest she felt for this man by clinging to the anger and other darker feelings that boiled inside of her.

"And what of yours?" she asked, fighting to keep her tone as calm as his. "How can you dare speak to me of honor after what you're doing right at this very moment?"

Despair flashed through his gaze, and she jolted as she recognized it. It was deeply sad and seeing him lose control even that tiny bit made her long, quite powerfully, to reach out and take his hand. Even though she hated him.

She hated him, didn't she? She had to cling to that.

"Right now you despise me," he said. "I deserve that, though it is not how I would ever choose to begin a union with any woman. But I assure you, there is more to the story of how we got here then you know. And, I hope, more to me."

She held his gaze a long moment, then settled back against the carriage seat. "So who are you?"

He seemed surprised at the question. She was rather surprised she'd asked it. But since this marriage was happening, it behooved her to find out something about the man who would soon enough be her husband.

"I am Hugh Margolis, sixteenth of my line," he began, keeping his gaze locked with hers. "And fifty-third in line for the throne, or so I am told."

She shook her head. "Those things tell me nothing about *you*."

He hesitated, and then sighed. "What do you want to know?"

"What kind of man are you? What are your interests? Your pursuits? Your passions?"

He watched her, as he always watched her. "I am the older brother of one sister, Lizzie. I adore her beyond measure and would do...I would do *anything* to protect her. To ensure her future."

Amelia tilted her head. For the first time, something he said didn't seem measured or careful. He truly loved his sister, that was evident in everything about his countenance and tone. And for a brief moment, she felt an odd connection that wasn't like the physical draw she normally felt toward him.

"I hope I am a good friend," he continued. "I am part of a club of other dukes—we have known each other since we were boys. They're like my brothers."

"Family is important to you," she said.

He nodded, and it was clear he was uncomfortable with this kind of conversation. Still, he carried on. "I ride. I shoot. I read a great deal," he continued.

Amelia pursed her lips. She wanted him to be the monster who had stolen her away from a future with her prince. But right now Hugh Margolis, Duke of Brighthollow, seemed very...normal. Even a bit likeable.

"As for my passions," he said, and she jerked her head up at the thickness of his voice. The darkness that had entered into it and now called to the curling heat in her stomach that she had no concept of how to fight. "There are those, too."

She licked her lips without meaning to. Suddenly the carriage felt close, the air between them thick. Something was going to happen. Something...

But before it could, the carriage turned onto the drive of her father's estate and drew to a stop. As the rig rocked while the servants climbed down, the spell between them was broken. She turned her face, staring at her clenched hand on the seat. "I still strenuously object, Your Grace."

"To the marriage," he said.

She nodded and forced herself to look at him. "But I also acknowledge that this *is* the future for us both. And I promise you that I shall make the best of it."

He inclined his head. "I appreciate that, Amelia. And for my part, I promise to make your future as bright as I can, while I hope that some day you will forgive me the circumstances that forced this terrible situation."

Forgive him? Amelia stared into his handsome face and wondered...if he wanted to earn her forgiveness, why was he driving her so hard toward the altar? But there was no answering that question. Not yet.

Perhaps not ever.

"Good day," she said as a footman approached to escort her from the carriage.

"Good day," he repeated softly, and let her go without another word.

But as his carriage pulled away, she could not help but turn and watch him go. Whatever was happening here, whatever drove this man, it was not cruelty. At least not toward her. And right now she felt so many conflicting emotions that she feared she would never sort them all out.

CHAPTER NINE

Hugh tugged on his fitted waistcoat and smoothed the fabric reflexively before he turned on the room full of his friends and forced a smile. In a short time, the ball to announce and celebrate his engagement to Amelia and their sudden wedding the next day would begin. But for now he was alone with some of the people who mattered most to him.

His friends were clustered together in groups. The closest one contained Robert, the Duke of Roseford; Ewan, the Duke of Donburrow; and Lucas. Ewan's and Lucas's wives were off with the other duchesses. Robert, who was the rogue of their circle, was not married, and at present his face was drawn down and red with upset.

With a sigh, Hugh moved to that small circle and waited for the barrage. It didn't take even a breath to start.

"This is foolishness," Robert snapped, glaring at Hugh like he was doing something to personally offend him.

Ewan, who had been mute since birth, rolled his eyes and reached out to grasp Robert's arm gently. His message was clear, even without his writing on the silver notepad he always carried in his pocket.

But Robert shook off the hand and continued, "It is one thing to marry for love—" He waved his hand at the room at large. "Like all these other idiots have done. But *this*? This sudden *thing* that no one can explain?"

"Robert." It was Lucas who had spoken, soft but firm.

THE DUKE WHO LIED

"Everyone stop *Robert*ing me," Robert said with a glare for the two of them. "I want to hear Brighthollow explain himself."

Hugh cast a quick look at Lucas, the only one who knew the truth, and then sighed. "There are situations that crop up in a man's life that sometimes require...sacrifices."

He said that word, but the truth was that marrying Amelia was feeling less and less like a sacrifice the more he got to know her. Her beauty drew him in, of course. No man would look at her and not feel that attraction. But there was far more to it than that. He liked her loyalty, misplaced as it was. He liked her fire, the one her father insisted would have to be extinguished. Hugh didn't want to do that. He just wanted to turn it, have it burn in passion rather than anger.

He liked *her*, truth be told. The fact that she hated him in return was not easy for him. Not pleasant. Not what he wanted, though he didn't want to analyze what he wanted too deeply. Or else he might lose control of more than his emotional response.

Amelia seemed to inspire that in him.

"Sacrifice," Robert said, dragging Hugh back to the conversation. "I hate to watch you do this."

Hugh sighed. "I appreciate the concern, I do. But this is what it is. And it will happen tomorrow whether you rail at me about it or not. I can only hope that you all will not shun Amelia in some ill-conceived attempt to protect me from my own choices."

"The duchesses already like her," Charlotte, Ewan's wife, said as she approached and slipped her hand into the crook of her husband's arm. "And even if we didn't, we would never give her the cut direct. For your sake."

He glanced at his male friends and found them all nodding in agreement, even Robert. Relief flowed through him. "Good."

"Your Grace, the Viscount Quinton and Miss Quinton," Murphy announced from the door, then stepped back to allow the two to enter.

Hugh caught his breath as Amelia all but floated into the room on the arm of her father. She was stunning, just as she was always stunning. Tonight she wore a dark blue gown, three shades darker than her eyes. Her black hair was done in an elaborate style that accentuated her long, slender neck. The only thing missing from her lovely face was a smile.

He hated that she was so miserable, and that the lie he and her father had told had led her to despise him. It was a mighty hurdle to overcome. Perhaps he never truly would.

He blinked as he realized he'd just been staring at her for far too long, then came forward to greet his new guests. "My lord," he said, shaking her father's hand. "Amelia."

She swallowed, and her gaze darted away from his face. "Your Grace," she murmured.

"I believe you know some of the party," he said, motioning to the room before he did a quick reintroduction of his friends. He noted how welcoming they were to her. Even Robert did not show his displeasure in the match, though Hugh caught him watching Amelia even when she stepped away from him. He wasn't sure why that inspired such a swell of jealousy, but there it was.

Finally, the party began to break up, moving toward the ballroom where the rest of the guests had already begun to arrive. Amelia and her father stood behind, her shifting in her place, Quinton's jaw set.

Robert cast a glance at Hugh and then approached the man. "Lord Quinton, I think I recall that your father fought in the Seven Years' War. He was quite the hero, if I am remembering my facts correctly."

Quinton's eyes lit up and he stepped toward Robert. "Indeed, he was, Your Grace."

"I would love to hear the tales," Robert said, and motioned toward the door. The two men left together, with Quinton talking loudly as they departed.

Hugh smiled. Robert was a rake of the highest order and his most outspoken friend, but he could be counted on. Just as they all could. Now he was alone with Amelia, allowed to be her escort without any interruption.

He moved toward her with a smile. "You look lovely."

"Thank you," she said softly, lifting her gaze to his. "You...well, you are very handsome, I'm sure you know it."

He stifled a laugh at the almost reluctant compliment she gave. It was some progress, of course, but small, indeed. "May I escort you to the ballroom?"

She hesitated, then nodded and took his arm. Hugh caught his breath at the electric current that seemed to snap through him at that benign touch. Yes, he was attracted to this woman. More, perhaps, than he'd allowed himself to admit.

"Will I meet your sister tonight?" she asked as they exited the parlor and began the stroll to his ballroom.

He frowned and the good feelings left him. "No," he said softly. "Lizzie is in Brighthollow. With the wedding tomorrow, it would be impossible to get her here in time. But I have written to her. I would very much like to join her at the estate after the wedding so you could meet her. If that would be agreeable to you."

She glanced up at him, and there was no mistaking the surprise on her face. "You are asking me?"

"I'm sure that is not what you expect, given the nature of our engagement," he said. "But I hope you'll soon learn that I have no intention of forcing you into a life you do not wish to lead. If you say you will not go, I'll make other arrangements. But my shire is...it's wonderful, Amelia. Beautiful and quiet. My sister will adore you, I'm sure."

She seemed to ponder the reasoning, and then she nodded. "I think that sounds lovely. I would be happy to join you there."

The ballroom was just a few steps away now, and he found himself sorry for that fact. This was the first time that anger and betrayal were not pulsing between them.

It seemed she had somewhat of the same thought, for she turned toward him, stopping their progress as she looked up into his face. "Brighthollow...Hugh," she whispered, and his stomach clenched as she said his name for the first time. "I-I don't like how this situation was created. But I was very rude to you in the carriage two days ago. I'm…I'm sorry."

He expelled a long breath and then shook his head. "You deserve every bit of emotion you feel, Amelia. I deserve it, too. So if it helps to pour it over me, I will not fight you. But I do hope you will leave the door open to the idea that I'm not the ogre you think I am. At least not completely."

"I hope you're not," she said, her blue gaze never wavering from his. "Or else we shall both be very unhappy."

He said nothing, for there was no response to be had. He just took her hand and led her into the ballroom, where their engagement would be announced and their future sealed.

For better or for worse.

Amelia stood beside the dance floor, the first time she had been alone all night. Her engagement to the Duke of Brighthollow and the surprise that the wedding would be the next day had been announced almost as soon as the ball began. Since then she had been surrounded by people, asking questions, sizing her up, making assumptions.

The duchesses had been wonderful, of course. One of them had always been at her side, as if they were on guard to keep people from being cruel. At least to her face. She had no doubt horrible things were being said behind her back.

But now she was alone, and for the first time she could consider her situation. When the announcement had been made, she had expected a cold fist of dread to make itself known in her stomach, but that hadn't been the case. If anything, she had stood there, positioned between her father and Hugh, and she had felt…well, it wasn't exactly excitement, but there was an anticipation that wasn't entirely unpleasant. She accepted this was her future. She was uncertain about Brighthollow, but she intended to make the best of it.

There was little else to do.

She turned slightly and caught her breath. Hugh was coming across the room toward her, with that dark focus drilling into her as it always did when he looked at her. Her stomach came alive and her breath grew short as he came near her.

"Brighthollow," she whispered as he reached her. She could not help but note that every eye in the room followed him, sizing up their interaction. Heat filled her cheeks at the focus of the crowd and the varying expressions on their watchful faces.

He glanced over his shoulder to where her eyes had strayed and frowned deeply. "I can offer you two options, Amelia."

She forced a weak smile. "And those are?"

"Dance with me, knowing that it will be a show for them, or take a walk with me in the garden. The moon is full and the lanterns are lit. It should be a bit of a respite from the exhibition we are meant to put on."

She stared up into that stern face. That achingly handsome face that sometimes didn't reflect emotion and made it easy for her to judge him as cold or cruel. Tonight, she saw just a flutter of something beneath the surface. He was offering the respite for her.

And that gave her a strange kind of hope.

"The garden sounds lovely," she said with hesitation, for being alone with Hugh was always…complicated. "I wouldn't mind the air."

"Excellent," he said, and smiled as he took her hand and tucked it in the crook of his elbow.

She stared. Had she ever seen his smile before? It certainly relaxed his face, made him infinitely more handsome. It made him…younger, somehow. More carefree.

He guided her from the room and out onto the terrace. A few couples were gathered here and there, enjoying the moonlight. She even caught a glimpse of the Duke and Duchess of Sheffield focused on the stars. She was pointing at a few and he smiled indulgently as he watched her.

Hugh guided her to the stairs that led down to the garden and steadied her as they made their way from the house, the party, the people and into the quiet and calm of his garden. *Her* garden, too, she supposed, once the vows were said tomorrow.

She drew in a breath as she stepped away from him and looked around. She did love a garden, and this one was lovely. The grass was well tended and the flowers taken care of.

She felt him watching her and shivered before she pivoted to face him. "Do you regret my choosing this over dancing?"

The corner of his mouth quirked up in another shadow of a smile, and with the moonlight on his face he looked a little...wicked.

"Not at all," he said. "Although had you chosen to dance, I would not have been sorry, either."

"That is a diplomatic answer," she said, laughing. "You are a wonderful dancer, though."

He shrugged. "A gentleman's purpose on the dance floor is to make the lady look even more elegant. If I succeed, it says more about my partner than me."

"Is it one of your passions?" She stepped closer.

His eyes widened a bit, the pupils dilating. "Passions?"

"In the carriage the other day," she clarified. "I asked you about your passions and you were vague at best. Since you are so good at dancing, I wondered if that was one of yours."

He swallowed, and she found herself fascinated by how his throat worked at the action. "Something like it." His voice was low, rough, and that tingle between her legs that he seemed to so easily inspire started up again in earnest.

"Well," she said, surprised that her own voice contained a similar timber. "You are light on your feet for such a...big man."

He chuckled, but as that laughter faded away, the silence grew heavy between them. She watched, fascinated, as he took a long step toward her. Suddenly he felt very close indeed. Close and big and hot. So very hot as he stepped into her personal space.

She stared up at him, aware that her heart was throbbing and her hands were shaking at her sides.

"This isn't what I planned, Amelia," he whispered, his

voice barely carrying despite his standing so close.

For the first time she believed him. That he hadn't meant to rip her life apart. It didn't stop him, of course, but the intention meant something at least.

"No?" she asked. "What was?"

He remained still for a moment. Quiet. But tonight he was not unreadable. Tonight she sensed a longing in him, something that sang to the longing she suddenly felt herself.

"I don't know," he admitted as he lifted his hand and cupped her cheek.

She caught her breath, and then there was no breath. There was no light, no sound, no other person or beast in the whole world. There was only him as he lowered his head slowly and brushed his lips to hers.

Hugh had not meant to kiss Amelia. He'd wanted to. Truth be told, he'd wanted to do just that since the first moment he'd watched her pick flowers in her father's garden. What man wouldn't? She was exquisite and her full lips were like a beacon, begging for his mouth on hers.

But tonight he'd truly only meant to give her a break from the watchful eyes of the ball. And now it had escalated and his arms were around her and his mouth was on hers.

Her lips parted beneath his on a shaky sigh of pleasure, and he couldn't resist. He glided his tongue inside and was nearly unmanned by the sweet, sultry flavor of her. His hands strayed to her lower back and molded her to him as the kiss spiraled into something dark and passionate that bordered on out of control.

He wanted her. To stake his claim in the most physical way possible. Here and now, propriety and consequences be damned. He wanted to make her forget that she loved someone else. He wanted to make himself forget the sting of that fact.

But if he drove any further, those animal desires would take over, and he couldn't let that happen. She already believed him an ogre—taking her in his garden would do nothing to mitigate that.

With great difficulty, he pulled away. She remained in his arms, staring up at him with bleary, unblinking eyes. "Hugh—" she began, her voice shaking and her fingers tightening on his forearms.

God's teeth, but she tested a man. He was ready to claim her mouth once more when he heard someone clear their throat.

He released her and she paced away, her hand lifting to her lips as she stared off at some far-away place across his garden. He turned and glared as one of the footmen stood at the path, staring at anything but his master.

"What is it?" Hugh snapped, more sharply than he had intended.

"I'm sorry, Your Grace. Murphy requested that I ask for your assistance. It seems there is some kind of trouble with Lady Brookfield and—"

Hugh pressed his lips together hard. "Murphy knows how to handle these things. Tell him—"

Amelia stepped up, and her gentle hand on his silenced his snappish reply. "Hugh, why don't you go take care of it? Murphy doesn't seem the kind of man who would send for you without cause. I'll...I'll gather myself and come back to the ball in a moment."

He stared down at her, seeing his desire reflected in her eyes, though in a much more innocent and slightly confused way. That she wanted him set his soul on fire, but he tamped down the reaction and inclined his head slightly. "Are you certain?"

"Yes. Very."

He looked at their hands, now intertwined. She followed his gaze and snatched hers away, her cheeks turning bright pink as she did so. "If you are certain, then I will do so. I will look for you later."

She nodded, and then she walked to a bench a few steps

away. He watched her settle into place there, the moonlight falling over her like she had intended it to do so.

He shook his head as he motioned for the servant to take him to wherever the trouble was back up at the house. And yet he couldn't stop thinking of Amelia. He couldn't stop thinking about the kiss.

And he couldn't stop thinking about the fact that in less than twenty-four hours, he would be married to the woman and then everything he wanted to do with her, to her, would be out of the realm of fantasy and into the reality of his bed.

Amelia sat on the bench in the garden just three feet from where Hugh had kissed her so thoroughly and passionately. She set her head in her shaking hands and tried not to relive that moment for the tenth time since he'd walked away from her.

Tried and failed, for the feel of his hands on her, his mouth on her, his tongue touching hers, was alive in her body. Like he was still standing right there, filling her with an emotion she could not rightly name and a desire she didn't fully understand.

"Amelia?"

She jumped and lowered her hands. The Duchess of Willowby was coming across the grass toward her, pretty face lined with concern as she adjusted her wrap.

"Your Grace," Amelia whispered. "Hello."

Diana tilted her head, examining Amelia like she was reading her. Then she sat down on the bench next to Amelia and smiled. "I have always thought Hugh's garden very fine. In the moonlight it is even better."

"Yes," Amelia mused, staring at the spot in that garden where he had ravished her mouth so thoroughly. "It is…something."

Diana glanced at her. "Are you escaping the party or the man?"

Amelia worried her lip. "The party initially. Now I have a strong desire to run from all of it. Or...or to it? I don't know, I'm very confused." The words fell in a rush, and she blushed as she glanced at Diana. "I'm sorry, that was wildly inappropriate."

"Why?" Diana asked with a shrug. "Gracious, you have been through a great deal in the past ten days. If anyone deserves all the confusion and uncertainty they feel, it is you. And since you and I are going to be great friends, I'm certain, you can talk to me about it. It might help."

"I was supposed to announce my engagement to someone else," Amelia said with a shake of her head. "And tomorrow I'm marrying Hugh. I'm spinning."

Diana nodded. "It would be impossible not to spin under those circumstances."

"And I hardly know Hugh," Amelia continued.

"Yes. It's a whirlwind." Diana sighed. "You know, I only married Lucas a little over a year ago, so Hugh is a recent friend to me. But he has been my husband's closest friend nearly all his life. I've watched him over the past year, observed who he is, what kind of man he is."

Amelia blinked. She was trying to determine that for herself, with little success. "What do you think of him?"

Diana took her hand and squeezed gently. "He is a good man, Amelia. A kind man. A decent man."

Amelia thought of how he'd bought her father's debts, how he'd used that to blackmail her into this wedding. It was hard to see him as all those wonderful things when that truth hung over her. And yet...

"Tonight he was kind," she whispered, almost more to herself than to Diana. "And yet he makes me...he makes me nervous. He is so dark, he is so unreadable, he is so...so..."

"Dangerous?" Diana offered.

Yes, that was the word for it. Hugh was dangerous.

Diana chuckled. "I have a feeling dangerous doesn't trouble you quite as much as you think it does. And that will ensure that you and I are fast friends. Dangerous can be very...stimulating."

Amelia felt the heat in her cheeks once more. "He—he kissed me."

Diana jerked her face toward Amelia. "Tonight?"

"Here in the garden before he was drawn away by some matter in the house."

"And how did you like it?"

Amelia covered her cheeks with her hands. There was something about Diana that made her feel she could be honest. And she needed to say what she felt out loud, to have someone scold her and tell her that it wasn't right. That would bring her back in line to propriety, certainly.

"It was wonderful," Amelia whispered. "I have never been kissed, you know. But he was gentle at first and then it just…spiraled out of control, and suddenly I was being dragged out to sea. I knew I would drown and I didn't care at all."

"You wanted to drown," Diana whispered.

"I know it's wrong."

"Wrong?" Diana shook her head. "That is called passion, my dear, and it is not wrong. You *should* feel passion for the man you will marry. You should feel that delicious warmth low in your belly when he watches you from across a room. You should feel the tingle when his hand brushes your skin."

Amelia blinked. "But—"

"But nothing!" Diana interrupted. "I know your mother is no longer with you. Has anyone talked to you about such things?"

Heat burned Amelia's cheeks "Not really. My maid mentioned just a few bare-bones details about what a man might want. It sounded somewhat terrifying."

Diana laughed softly. "Oh, that will not do! You are to be married tomorrow, and so I must share with you a few things about passion. If you would like to hear them."

Amelia thought of the feel of Hugh's hands skimming her body. Of his mouth on hers and the way her body had felt boneless and hot. About how she wanted so much more even if she couldn't define what *more* was.

"Yes," she said, perhaps a bit more strenuously than was required. "I will take any advice on that count that I can get."

"Excellent," Diana said. "Firstly, on the subject of kissing…"

CHAPTER TEN

Hugh had always known he would marry. It was his duty, after all, to do so and produce heirs and spares to carry on his family name and legacy. He'd been studious as a boy, thinking on every problem, planning it out. He'd believed he would marry before thirty-five and produce a child every two years after until he had enough sons to guarantee his line would carry on.

It had been a plan of necessity. No heart required.

As the years went by, though, as he watched James, Simon, Graham, Ewan, Baldwin, Lucas and Matthew each find true love…his view on marriage had shifted. Love seemed to make them all so very happy. He'd been jealous of that happiness from time to time. And so he had begun to wonder if he could experience the same emotion.

But now, as he stared across the room filled with his friends toward the woman he had pledged his life to not an hour ago, he was torn.

Amelia was his wife. And it was not the cold, emotionless bond that he had accepted would be right as a young man. Nor was it the glorious, loving relationship he had come to covet in the past few years.

He wanted her. God, how he wanted her. But he also knew she despised him and the lie that had been told to force her to the altar. He knew she loved someone else, his greatest enemy.

Their future was set, but it was not clear. She was accepted by his friends, of course. Not one of the dukes or duchesses had been anything but kind to her. Even now Robert danced with her, and there was no hint of the hesitations he had expressed previously as he smiled down at her.

But what did that mean for them? That she would be comfortable in his group of friends, but never in his arms? Would she always hesitate, as she had when the minister had asked her to pledge her life to him? She had looked up into his eyes in that moment and he'd seen all she felt she was losing by agreeing to the terms forced upon her.

"My friend, congratulations."

He turned at the sound of Kit's voice and found both him and Lucas approaching. Hugh slung an arm around Kit, and together the three watched Robert and Amelia dance.

"She is beautiful," Kit said softly. "Is that why the rush after our last discussion about the lady?"

Lucas exchanged a brief look with Hugh, but remained silent.

"It's complicated," Hugh muttered. "I don't want to get into it. At least not right now."

Kit didn't press. Instead he said, "Will you stay in London?"

"I think not. If it is agreeable to her, I would like to depart for Brighthollow tomorrow. I know Lizzie will want to meet her. And it will help us escape the whispers about our rushed union and—"

He broke off. He wasn't about to add the other thing he felt they needed to escape from: Aaron Walters. He didn't like the idea of the man being so close to Amelia. Of her being tempted by him. Every day that concept grew less and less acceptable.

"It looks as though Robert has finished his turn," Kit said. "If you don't mind, I will ask the lady for the next."

"By all means," Hugh said with a smile.

Kit nodded to his friends and then slipped off to charm Amelia just as all his friends were working to charm her.

"You're worried about Walters?" Lucas asked softly.

Hugh watched his wife smile up at Kit. She was so at ease

with his friends. She was never so at ease with him. "Yes," he choked out. "I will have to determine what to do with him when I return to London. He clearly has every intention of pursuing a dowry by any means necessary, and since I cannot be marrying every woman he threatens, there must be a more permanent way to keep him from damaging those around him."

Lucas scowled. "The bastard has to be involved in more than just seducing unsuspecting young women. Let me use my resources to investigate while you're gone. We'll figure this out."

"Thank you." Hugh let out a breath and turned toward his friend. "For everything. You and Diana have been very kind, and I appreciate you not spreading Lizzie's secret across the group."

"I understand," Lucas said. "But may I give you one piece of advice?"

Hugh nodded. "Of course."

"She is a lovely young woman," Lucas said softly. "But more—and better—than that, she seems intelligent and kind. Don't let yourself destroy what could be…good just because of this bad beginning. I nearly did that with Diana and if I had lost her—"

He cut himself off, but Hugh heard the desperation in his voice. The very idea of losing Diana was almost physically painful to his friend.

"I will try," Hugh promised. "But it won't be easy. Diana didn't hate you as Amelia hates me. And she didn't love someone else."

"She won't always love him, nor hate you," Lucas reassured him. "If you allow her to see your true self. No matter how painful that is. Let her in, mate."

Lucas clapped a hand against his arm, not waiting for an answer before he strode away toward his own wife and swung her up for a kiss. Hugh watched them with that burning jealousy still deep in his heart.

Then he shifted his gaze to Amelia. He wasn't as certain as Lucas seemed to be that showing her his heart would change anything about how she felt. But he was still drawn to her, despite everything that kept them apart. Despite everything that could bring their new marriage to a sudden and painful halt.

Amelia stood, hands shaking as Theresa unbuttoned her gown. Her *wedding* gown, which had been hastily prepared in the past few days. It wasn't the beautiful silver dress she had pictured when Aaron had proposed, nor had the brief, proper ceremony in Hugh's garden been the one of her dreams.

Of course, it had been lovely. And when Hugh took her hand, she had felt that shiver of awareness and thought quite hard about the things Diana had told her about passion and wedding nights and all the things that happened between a man and a woman.

But now the party was over, the night was long and she was the Duchess of Brighthollow. Through that door and an antechamber, the *Duke* of Brighthollow waited for her. And her heart would not stop throbbing until the rush of blood blocked out almost every other sound.

"Your Grace?"

She jumped as she realized Theresa was speaking to her. She was Her Grace. "Y-yes, I'm sorry, Theresa. What did you say?"

Her maid's face gentled. "You needn't apologize, Your Grace. I'm certain your nerves must be frayed to their ends! I only asked if you'd like to put on your regular nightdress or the new one."

Amelia glanced over at the two gowns laid across her bed. One was her serviceable cotton gown, comfortable and plain. The other had been gifted to her that very morning by the duchesses. It was a beautiful nude silk with a lacy bodice that left very little beneath to the imagination. It was scandalous beyond measure and yet, based on what Diana had told her the night before, it was perhaps the perfect outfit for what was about to happen.

"The new," she said, the words sounding slow and far away to her ears.

Theresa blushed as she picked it up, then helped Amelia out of the rest of her clothes and into the nightdress. She brushed out Amelia's hair and arranged it prettily, then sighed. "Well, you are ready. I should leave you to your husband."

Her husband. Amelia jolted at the thought. Hugh Margolis, Duke of Brighthollow, was her husband. Forever. She didn't know whether to laugh or cry.

"Thank you," she whispered.

Theresa cast her one last look as she stepped to the door. Then she said, "Just think of England, my dear. Good night."

Then she was gone, and Amelia stood alone in the great, beautiful chamber that would be hers for the rest of her days. Her head spun. Diana had described powerful pleasure and deep connection when she talked about what would happen in the next bedroom.

Theresa spoke of thinking of England and looked horrified on Amelia's behalf. And right now Amelia had no idea what to think of any of it.

She did not get a chance to think on it further, though, for there was a light knock at the door that led to the adjoining chamber. She jumped and pivoted to the entryway, trying to gather her nerves as she said, "C-come in."

The door opened and she caught her breath. It was Hugh, of course, but not the same formal, stern Hugh who had taken her hand and changed her name and future a few hours ago. No, this man was different. He no longer wore a jacket or a waistcoat. His cravat had long been discarded and a few buttons on his shirt were undone. He wore no boots.

This was...her husband, without formality to stand as a wall between them. And she could hardly breathe as she pondered how handsome he was.

"My God," he whispered as he took a step into the room.

"You are...you are magnificent."

She glanced down at herself and blushed. "I feel exposed, I admit."

His expression gentled and he stopped walking toward her. "Amelia, I...I wanted to talk to you about tonight."

Here it was. The moment when her innocence would belong to him, her body, perhaps her pleasure, if Diana was right.

She nodded. "Yes?"

He shifted, and discomfort filled his face. "I realize this was never your choice. I understand if there are regrets in your heart right now. You have had your future determined for you in the last few days, and I am a fiend in your eyes because of it. So I would not...force you to consummate the marriage tonight. We can take our time, get to know each other better, before you give me such intimacy."

She stared in disbelief. Here was a man she could never decipher, one who always seemed in command. And yet he actually looked nervous in that moment where he told her that her body was hers to control.

What was more surprising was her own reaction to that declaration. After everything that had happened in the past ten days, she should have felt relieved that he would not expect her to give herself to him.

And yet she didn't. Not even in the slightest.

She moved forward one hesitant step. "Do you know what I've been thinking about since last night?"

He shook his head slowly.

"That kiss," she admitted, heat filling her cheeks as she ducked her gaze from his. It was too hard to say these things when she had to see his expression. "All I keep thinking about is that kiss."

"But what will happen once I touch you is so much more than a kiss," he said.

She nodded, still staring at the floor. "I know. Diana...explained things to me. But she didn't make what would happen sound unpleasant."

"If I do my job right, it won't be," he said, his voice very rough now. And closer. She glanced up to see he had moved toward her. Not quite near enough to touch, but edging there.

"She said it could be…wonderful," she whispered.

He reached out and his fingers skimmed her cheek. It was like fire to her sensitive skin, and she sucked in her breath in surprise. His pupils dilated, and in that moment she would have given him anything, everything, just so he would keep touching her.

"I would very much like to make it wonderful." His hand dropped away. "But I don't want to force more from you than has already been taken."

"What if I offer it?" she asked. "Unless you don't want me."

He laughed under his breath. "That is patently ridiculous. In truth, I have not stopped wanting you likely from the first moment I saw you."

Her mouth dropped open in shock. "You did? But you were so stoic."

"Stoic," he repeated. "That is one way to describe it. But beneath that is a great deal more, Amelia. And I would very much like to touch you."

She didn't respond in words. She couldn't, for there were none left. All she could do was step forward on shaking legs. She lifted her hands to his chest, jolting as her palms met hard muscle beneath his fine linen shirt. She looked up at him, knowing all her wanton need was plain on her face, not caring in that moment. She lifted up on her tiptoes and he dropped his head, meeting her halfway.

And instantly, they were right back where they'd stopped the night before. His mouth devoured, tasting her, exploring her, and the world spun down to this one place and time. She gripped her hands into fists against his chest, as if she could anchor herself by clinging to him.

She couldn't. Her legs had begun to shake and her body pulse with an insistent need she had no idea how to slake. Touching him didn't help—it only built this fire inside of her even higher. Until it felt like she would explode.

Her knees gave out, but he didn't let her fall. He caught her, sweeping her into his arms as he continued to kiss her. She felt him set her on the bed, the pillows soft beneath her head, him hard as he pressed himself down over her, letting his full length cover her.

She arched beneath him, wanting more. Wanting all the things Diana had so scandalously described. Amelia had no idea what this would feel like, but she wanted it regardless. Wanted him regardless.

Regardless of it all.

Later she would have to analyze that. Try to determine what it said about her that she could be so ready to marry one man and just days later be willing to give herself completely to another.

But for now, there was only this. Only him. Only the way his mouth dragged away from hers and down to her throat where he sucked gently and made starbursts explode in front of her eyes. She dragged her fingers into his hair and shivered. It was long and fell from the queue when she tugged at the coarse, curly locks. He grunted as if satisfied by that response, and his mouth moved lower, tracing a shocking line along the bodice of her new night-rail.

How could every single touch feel so damned good? How could none of them be enough?

She had no idea, but Hugh seemed to be in no mood to stop touching her. His hand drifted along the neckline, then lower over the lacy fabric that just barely covered her breasts. His thumb skimmed one of her hard nipples, and any pleasure that had come before seemed like nothing in comparison. She cried out without meaning to and blushed at how foolish it was.

He glanced up and smiled. "You needn't blush, Amelia. When you feel pleasure, I want to know. When I learn your body, I can much easier give you more…" He leaned down and kissed her shoulder next to the strap of her nightgown. "…and more…" he whispered, tugging the strap down and exposing one breast. "…and more…"

His voice was muffled as he dropped his lips to her naked breast. He traced the shape and his mouth closed around the nipple that felt so sensitive she might burst. He sucked and her hips lifted hard against him. She shouted out again, but this time she was far too lost in sensation to feel embarrassed by the noise. He was made of magic and she was lost to it all.

He sucked hard, harder, swirling his tongue around her, and she found her sex pulsing in time, slick with wanting and hot with need. And just when she felt she might actually die from waiting, he switched his attention to the opposite breast and repeated his licks and sucks and tugs there.

"Please," she murmured, uncertain what she was begging for, but praying he knew.

He glanced up, all the teasing gone from his expression. All the sternness and coolness gone too. This was a new man, one driven by desire that glittered in his stare, driven by a need to pleasure her and take her and claim her. She let out a little gasp of displeasure as he pushed from the bed and got to his feet.

"I'm not leaving," he panted, his voice unsteady. "I just want to be rid of these."

He tugged his shirt over his head. She sat up with a gasp and stared at the half-naked man before her. He was…beautiful. There was no other way to describe him. His chest was thick with muscle, peppered with curly chest hair that made a trail into the waist of his trousers. The trousers he was currently unfastening. She swallowed hard as he stripped the pants away too.

Diana had described what he would look like, but Amelia had been unable to picture it. The thrust of his sex looked hard as steel and curled against his lower stomach like a divining rod or a sword ready for battle. She could surely not take that thing inside of her. Not take it and feel pleasure, no matter how much she was promised that her body would stretch to accommodate him.

"You'll be ready," he whispered, as if he read her mind.

She shook away her thoughts and stared at him. "How?"

He smiled and dropped back on the bed beside her. He caught her hand, lifting it to his lips where he brushed a kiss against her flesh. Then he pressed her hand to the breast he had just been lavishing with attention.

"When I touch you here," he whispered as he stroked her fingers over her own body. He glided her hand lower, down her stomach. "When I give you that pleasure that makes you lift against me and want something you may not even understand, that readies you."

She stared at his face as he pressed her hand between her legs. She was wet, hot, she felt the slickness against her fingertips.

"What you feel is your body's invitation to be taken," he said, leaning in to nuzzle her neck as he flexed her fingers against her sex.

She shivered at the sensations that jolted from the point of contact. She had never touched herself. She'd wanted to sometimes, but a lady wasn't meant to do such things...was she? It was hard to remember when she was grinding her body against her own fingers and feeling a building pressure unlike any she'd ever known.

His gaze locked with hers and she could not look away. She was his captive, and escape felt impossible, undesirable. He pushed her fingers harder and she lifted against them. Harder, faster, until her breath left her lungs and sudden sensation flooded her body. Waves of pleasure rolled through her as she bucked against her hand, his hand.

"Oh," she sighed as the pleasure slowly faded, leaving a warm satisfaction in its wake. "Oh."

He smiled down at her. "*That* is what will happen when we do this. That pleasure that is just for you, it belongs to no one else. You can take it whenever you like."

She swallowed. Here she had been distancing herself from him, bound to believe that he would take and take and take. But he kept giving now that they were alone.

It was very confusing.

He leaned in and swept her thoughts away with another deep kiss. She wrapped her arms around his neck, relaxing into the pillows as he kissed her slowly, languidly, like they had all night. And she supposed they did. They were bound now, after all. Which meant they could do this any time they liked without censure or shock.

She shivered at the thought and at the way he slowly pushed her legs apart with his knees. He lowered at her night-rail, smoothing it past her stomach, her hips, and finally lifted up just enough to remove it. Now she was naked. Naked, pinned beneath him, her legs splayed and the hardness of his cock— Diana had called it a cock—positioned just at the entry to her body.

She should have been afraid, and there *was* a small fissure of fear that shot through her. But there was more than that. There was anticipation. Readiness. Need and want and desire. All those things came together, pulsed between her legs as he brushed the head of him against her.

She lifted at the touch, digging her fingers into his bare shoulders at the shock. He pulled his head back. "Slow," he promised. Or perhaps it was a reminder to himself. Either way, the one word calmed her a fraction and she stopped bracing so hard against him, relaxing as he gently pressed into her body.

She shut her eyes, focusing her attention between her legs. As he moved slowly inside of her, there was pain, yes. A twinge of sensation as he breached her. But it wasn't unbearable, perhaps because it was joined by another sensation: pleasure. Oh yes, there was that. A delicious and wicked pleasure that came from the slick heat of their bodies coming together. That came from the realization that he was taking her, claiming her, marking her in a way that she could never undo.

And she didn't want to. Not when he filled her completely and then leaned in to rest his forehead against hers with a ragged sigh.

"How do you feel?" he asked, voice strained.

"Full," she moaned. "How does it feel to you?"

He leaned away, and he seemed surprised by the question. He swallowed hard before he answered, "Tight," he whispered. "Like a glove meant to fit me perfectly. Warm and wet and very, very, tight. It makes me want to..."

He ground against her, and she gasped as his hips found that same place where he'd put her fingers. The center of her pleasure. It returned now, a blast of tingling sensation that caused her pelvis to meet his again.

He cursed beneath his breath and then began to move. He withdrew and thrust, setting a slow, steady rhythm. She lifted to meet it, reaching for the release she had found when she touched herself. Reaching for more, because this joining made the feelings more intense. More powerful. More desperate.

His mouth covered hers and she held tight to him as they moved together like one body, one person. Wanting the same thing, needing it more than breath. And then it was there, and she cried out against his lips as he dragged her through release a second time. His thrusts grew faster, harder, and she felt him shake as he took her, his fingers bruising her skin with the intensity of his passion, sucking her tongue before he cried out a primal sound and she felt his heat pump into her.

He collapsed down over her, gathering her closer in the dark, and for that moment, nothing else mattered.

Although Hugh had never been a libertine like Robert or even Simon before his marriage to Meg, he had certainly had his share of lovers. Sex was a natural desire—he felt no shame in it and had always tended to the needs of the women he bedded. But he'd maintained control.

Tonight was different. As he looked down at the woman in his arms, the one who had a look of sleepy contentment on her beautiful face, he felt no control whatsoever. In fact, he felt quite the opposite. Tonight he was an animal, a slave to his baser desires. He'd come less than fifteen minutes before and he was already raring to take her again. And again. And again.

She shifted and her hand lifted to his chest. She smoothed the skin there just over his heart, and there was an ache that followed the motion. One he didn't want to name, one he didn't want to feel. Especially not with Amelia, who loved someone else. Who hated him, even if she felt desire when he touched her.

He shifted and slid from beneath her, getting up to find his trousers on the floor. When he turned, she was watching him in confusion and perhaps a little hurt.

"Did I...do something wrong?" she asked.

He shook his head. "Not at all. I just thought you might want to sleep alone in your own bed tonight. You must be exhausted after all the excitement of the past few days."

She worried her lip and he wanted to do the same, nip her skin with his teeth, soothe it with his tongue, explore every inch of her. He felt his cock rising and turned away.

"I suppose," she said softly.

He swallowed and picked up his shirt. As he put it on, he said, "It might be the last night you spend alone for a few, in truth. I was thinking we might leave London tomorrow and go to my estate in the country."

She sat up, and he couldn't help but stare as she covered herself with the sheets. "I see. So soon?"

He pondered the question a moment. He could be cagey, but there had already been so many lies. Telling one more felt so heavy.

"I'm sure my sister will be upset by missing the wedding and want to meet you."

Amelia seemed to ponder that, and then she nodded. "I suppose there would be no harm in getting out of London and letting the talk settle down around our marriage, as you said before."

"Talk?"

"Of course you know there is talk," she said. "I was far beneath you and we rushed to the altar. Half the city believes I am already with your child, the other that I'm a social climber who trapped you some other way."

She frowned as she said those words, and he sighed. He hated how this entire fiasco had played out. Hated it with every fiber of his being. Just like when he'd made love to her, their wedding had felt out of control.

He needed to get that back, and quickly.

"Soon enough another scandal will push ours away," he reassured her. "But for now I leave you to your sleep. Tomorrow we can leave in the morning and we'll be to Brighthollow in just two days' time."

She nodded as he moved to the door of his adjoining room. There, he turned. She was staring at him, silent, beautiful. Tempting.

But he walked away regardless, because she wasn't really his. And he certainly wasn't hers.

CHAPTER ELEVEN

Amelia looked out the window of the carriage, watching as the hustle and noise of the city transformed into the green of the pastoral countryside. The effect might have been calming under normal circumstances, but these were anything but. Her morning had begun early and in a rush, with servants loading carriages, and Theresa both trying to ready her and oversee the packing of her gowns and other things.

It left her feeling out of sorts. As did the man she rode with in the carriage. Hugh sat across from her, reviewing some paperwork. Like he hadn't touched her last night. Like nothing had changed, when everything had in that instant he fit his body into hers and turned her world on its head.

Even now, she wanted that again as she stared at him with that serious frown and his hair pulled back in a queue that tamed its curly wildness.

"Do you have something to say?" he asked, lifting his eyes. The tone was teasing, and she blushed at being caught staring at him.

"No," she said. He chuckled and lowered his eyes back to his papers. She was left unsatisfied, and so she folded her arms as a shield across her chest and said, "Well, yes."

Those dark eyes lifted again, and he slowly set his papers aside and nodded. "Do say it. You have my full attention."

She swallowed hard. Having this man's full attention was a rather terrifying idea. Whenever he looked at her, it was like he could see far under the surface. With full attention, it wouldn't take him long to understand every tiny thing about her while she knew nothing in return.

"Amelia?"

She blinked, realizing she'd been sitting in silence for a far too long. "I'm sorry. I was just wondering if this is how it will always be for me. For us?"

"This?" he repeated. "Riding in a carriage?"

"No." She glared at him a little. "I mean, this morning was nothing but commotion. Everything was rushed. And it's been that way from the first moment you declared you would marry me to absolve my father of his debts. There has been upheaval and upset and...and..."

"Chaos," he finished softly, all the teasing now gone from his face. "Yes, I understand. It must make you wonder about the whims of the man you married, and if I am the kind of person who makes these sorts of quick decisions that throw all into disarray. That would certainly affect you."

She nodded and tried not to think of her own past, of pains that she had long ago put away, accepted. "Yes."

He shook his head. "I have always been a measured person. I am careful in what I do and say. The last ten days of my life have been out of character in that way. And perhaps we could have made our trip to Brighthollow tomorrow or the next day to avoid some of the chaos, but in truth I am seeking the same normalcy as you are. The place where I feel most calm, most like myself, is at my home. With my sister. Perhaps I traded chaos for normalcy and it wasn't fair to you."

She caught her breath at that...well, it was almost an apology. It was also wrapped in a good deal of candor. If she was learning anything, it was that this man was incredibly honest and forthright. Which was a good quality. The best of qualities.

"Do you think our lives will settle down once we reach your estate?" she asked.

He smiled. "Indeed, I do. They will settle down once we reach our stop at the inn tonight, that is why I sent the servants ahead, including your Theresa, to ready the place for us. So that we can relax and cut through some of the tension that has been a daily part of both our lives lately."

She gave a small laugh. "I'm not sure I remember what it is like not to feel some anxiety hanging over my head."

"No?" His tone was soft, but there was a different timber to it now. She lifted her gaze and found his expression had changed. She recognized the desire that had flowed between them last night, and she shivered at that recognition.

"You look like a wolf ready to eat me," she said, locking gazes with him.

"A very good suggestion on how to make some of that anxiety go away," he murmured, and dropped to his knees in the space between their carriage seats.

She gasped in surprise, but said nothing, for he caught the back of her head and guided her lips to his. The moment they touched, it was electric. Sensation flowed through her, settling in all the places where he had touched her, but most especially between her legs. That place where she still ached, and yet longed to repeat all the pleasures they had begun the previous night.

What a wanton she'd turned out to be. But Hugh didn't seem to mind. In fact, if the way he drove his tongue into her mouth was any indication, he approved with all his heart. She wrapped her arms around his neck and sank into the kiss, forgetting everything except for the desire he woke in her.

He made some rough, animal sound deep in his chest, and then he drew his mouth away and stared at her, panting, pupils dilated and expression hard and hungry.

He held that gaze as he slid his hands down the length of her body, touching her breasts, her stomach, her thighs, her calves through her silky gown. Finally he reached the hemline, and she gasped as he began to slide it up. Up and up her body, baring her stocking-clad legs right there in what felt like an almost public space.

He pushed higher, leaving the bulk of the fabric against her stomach. He held her gaze as he pressed a hand on either of her knees and pushed her legs apart. She let him, for she was so heated and needy that she could not have denied him anything. She wore drawers, and he tugged the opening in them wide so that her sex was revealed. She turned her face, breaking their gaze at last, and shivered. When she peeked back, she found him looking at her body intently. He licked his lips, and she felt a tug of heat at the apex of her thighs. He leaned in, and she realized what he would do just a moment before his tongue swept over her sex.

She arched as he gripped her hips and slid her farther down the carriage seat, opening her even wider with his shoulders before he swept over her with his tongue again. The sensation was like nothing she'd felt before. Not when he touched her, not when he took her. This was…magic. His tongue was magic, and he licked her over and over again, tasting every inch of her flesh and smiling against her when she began to lift her hips in time to his ministrations.

Like the night before, she felt the pleasure and the pressure building, a dam that would strain and then break. As her mewls and gasps grew louder, he began to focus his tongue on the little bundle of nerves just at the top of her slit. He increased the pressure of his tongue bit by bit, and then he began to suck.

She twisted in the carriage seat, fisting her hands against the leather, jamming them into his hair to keep him close, to push him away as the sensation grew sharp as a knife.

Then she was jolted by release. But it wasn't like the previous night. These were shallow waves of pleasure, but infinitely intense and seemingly never-ending. She jerked against his mouth, her breath gone, her mind gone, everything gone but the wonderful pleasure that filled every part of her until there was nothing left but him and this.

Finally, he released her from the prison of pleasure, pressing one last kiss to her sensitive body, and then lifted his head to look at her. She knew what he saw. A wanton, sprawled across his carriage seat, her legs open, her dress cockeyed, her face flushed, panting like a dog in heat. She should have felt embarrassed by that, but she wasn't. And he didn't look shocked and horrified by it either. His smile was wicked as he smoothed her dress down gently, then leaned up and kissed her.

She pulled him in, tasting her pleasure on his tongue, sweet and earthy. He made a dark rumble in the deepest part of his chest as he braced one hand on either side of her head and pushed his tongue deeper into her mouth.

It was obvious what he wanted. She felt it in the hunger of his touch. When he pulled away, it was even more obvious in the outline of his thick erection against his trouser front. But he settled into his seat and smiled at her, making no effort to take or claim.

"Better?" he asked, all the wickedness in the world in that one word.

She blinked, trying to regain some purchase on her tingling, throbbing, dizzy body and mind. "Y-yes," she whispered. "If that is the way a wolf hunts, I do not mind being the rabbit."

He chuckled and moved to pick up his papers again. She stared in shock. Could he really go back to whatever he was working on as if *that* hadn't just happened? As if he wasn't still hard beneath his trousers?

"And what can the rabbit do in return, Mr. Wolf?" she asked.

He had been about to turn one of the pages in his hand over, and he froze mid-act and lifted his gaze back to her. "I beg your pardon?"

"It seems very unfair to leave you…" She motioned at his erection. "Thusly. Does the wolf not want something in return?"

"Seeing you come was an excellent reward, Your Grace," he said, but he pushed the papers away and the corner of his lip turned up in a half-smile. "I can take care of my needs once we reach a very comfortable bed at the inn."

"In how long?" she asked, shocked by how forward she was being with him. How easy this charged conversation was, despite her innocence. Something in this man brought it out.

Woke it up in her. "Five hours, six, seven?"

He shrugged. "Probably seven. We'll get there just at supper."

She shook her head. "Well, that seems an unfair amount of time for you to wait."

"You are kind to think of me, and I promise you that one day I will claim your body fully in that very carriage seat while you scream out my name and rake patterns on my back with your nails."

Her mouth dropped open at the description and the heated desire that flowed right to her sex when he said those words. "But not today?"

"You must still be sore from last night," he said, his tone gentling.

She shrugged. "Only a little."

"A little is enough to make me wait so that you can be most comfortable," he said. "Didn't you enjoy what we did?"

She nodded. "I think you know I did. I made it clear enough, I'm sure."

"I was fairly certain," he teased. "Pleasure shouldn't be tit for tat, Amelia. I can enjoy giving you release and not find my own, at least not right away."

She wrinkled her brow. Somehow she doubted most men would feel the same. She'd heard too many stories from friends and from whispers of women who merely endured their husband's affection. The very opposite from her experience, at least so far.

"Isn't there something I can do for you?" she asked. "You, er…licked me." Heat flooded her cheeks. "Can a woman do the same for a man?"

His eyes grew very wide. Very, very wide, indeed. She had shocked him. Apparently that was not something one did.

"I'm sorry," she said, ducking her head. "I don't know what is considered right or wrong."

He reached out to tuck a finger beneath her chin so she couldn't look away. "What is right is what feels good to you.

Nothing else. Yes, a woman can take a man in her mouth. But many ladies do not like to do it."

She glanced down his body at that thick line of his cock. She had certainly liked the feel of it inside of her. The concept of licking him, sucking him…that did not sound unpleasant. Not in the least. Especially if she could steal even an ounce of his restraint.

She slid forward on the seat and reached out, resting her hands on his thick, muscular thighs. When she touched him, he let out a ragged, needy sigh, and she smiled. Oh yes, she very much wanted to do this and take all that control.

"Please," she whispered.

Hugh's head was spinning. There was a war going on inside of him and he had no idea how to win it. What winning would even looked like.

Part of him, the gentlemanly part, said that Amelia was still so innocent. That it wasn't fair to her. That ladies didn't like such things. Did they?

And the other part, the animal part, looked at her full lips and wanted nothing more than to watch them close over his cock and suck him until he exploded. He wanted that more than anything.

But it seemed he didn't get to decide which would happen. Amelia reached out and caught up his papers, tossing them on the bench next to her. She slid onto his seat, her fingers massaging his inner thigh. He was hard as stone and his mind was addled by desire, both caused by the way she was tracing his leg with her fingernails, and also by watching her come a few moments before.

He wanted her so very badly, and she leaned up to kiss him as she slowly unfastened the buttons on his fall front. Her hand brushed him as she folded it away and broke the kiss. Together they looked at his hard cock, thrusting straight up in full attention.

She smiled as she reached out and dragged one finger along his length. She gasped and glanced at him. "The skin is so soft," she whispered. "What do I do?"

Jesus, but she tested him. He could barely breathe, but somehow he choked out, "Last night, when I took you…that is what you should do with your hand or your mouth. That's what feels…good."

Her face was serious, like she was studying French literature or mathematics and was trying to pass some kind of test. "I see. Let me try and you tell me if I'm doing it right, yes?"

He nodded, silent because his voice was gone. He watched, shaking, as she caught him in her palm. She stroked him from tip to base, and he couldn't help but lift up into her.

"Tighter," he gasped out. "A little faster."

She adjusted, and when she stroked a second time, everything was perfect. Her soft hand held him exactly right, she glided down his length and he couldn't hold back a long, low moan of pleasure.

Her face lit up, and for a little while she simply stroked, working his shaft as she looked into his eyes, her lips slightly parted and her own breath short. He realized that touching him was exciting her, that whatever need he had slaked by licking her was returning.

And her responsiveness excited him even more. Whatever else was between them, whatever she thought of him or accused him of in her mind, the physical connection was stronger than any he'd ever had before. And he wanted more and more and more of it. He wanted to teach her wicked things. He wanted to do things to her that most men wouldn't even consider sharing with a blushing bride.

He wanted to ruin her in the best possible ways, because he sensed that she would respond to it. Like it.

"I want to taste you," she whispered.

Her dark head lowered and he rested a hand gently on the

back of her chignon as he watched her pink tongue dart out. She was hesitant as she licked the head of him. Slowly at first, unartfully due to her lack of experience. She glanced up, and the sight of her watching him as her tongue swirled around him almost unmanned him right there.

"Take it into your mouth," he grunted.

She drew in a long breath and then did so. She sucked gently, then withdrew. Her eyes widened, and it was clear she now understood what he wanted. She shifted, balancing herself differently so she could grip the base. She worked him with her hand as she began to slowly thrust her mouth over him. Her tongue stroked the underside of his cock.

It was…spectacular. No, she wasn't practiced in the art, but she was a quick study, a natural at pleasure. He dipped his head back against the carriage seat and drowned in the sensations that shot from her mouth through his cock, through his entire body. Waves of pleasure, hitting hard against the shores as he surrendered himself to her entirely.

His balls tightened and he knew the end was near. He looked down, picturing the day when she would drain him entirely. But not today. That would be too much.

As his seed began to move, he caught her arms, dragging her up his body to kiss her. Her hand continued to pump over him and he spent, grunting her name against her lips as he did so.

Their breathing matched, hard panting, as the pleasure slowly subsided and he dared to open his eyes again. He was ready for her to look shocked or unhappy, but instead she had a sleepy, proud smile on her face. She tucked herself against his shoulder, resting her head there as he pulled the handkerchief from his pocket and tidied himself.

"Was that right?" she asked at last.

He laughed and tilted her face to look at him. "If it wasn't clear, I will certainly show you how right it was later."

"Why later?" she asked, eyes wide and just a tiny bit wicked.

He shook his head. "Because even a man who wants you as much as I do needs a break after something like that. But it was most definitely right. And now my mind is as clear as I hope yours is."

She smiled before she pressed a quick kiss to his cheek and moved back to her own seat. After he fixed himself, she handed over his papers and pulled a book from her reticule. Before she began to read, she said, "If that is the way you want to clear our minds, I will never object to chaos again."

He smiled at the light she naturally brought to everything. He had felt so dark for so long that it was almost blinding. But he couldn't be blinded. In the end, there was still much between them. Including the fact that she believed herself to be in love with his worst enemy. Including the fact that Hugh had lied to get her into this marriage. Into his bed.

And right now that felt worse than ever.

CHAPTER TWELVE

Hours later, Hugh glanced up from the supper that had been laid out for them at the inn and looked across the table toward Amelia. She was staring intently at her plate, moving the food around with her fork. Passion had bonded them in the carriage, but in the hours since that encounter, he had felt her begin to slip away. The walls between them couldn't be surmounted through orgasms alone.

And he had no idea how to connect with her otherwise. Or even if he should. After all, he had not married her because he wanted her. Loved her. Even knew her.

It had been to save her. To thwart Walters.

She sighed, as if the silence between them made her just as uncomfortable as it did him, and glanced up from her venison. "Do you only have one sibling?" she asked.

He blinked at the sudden question. The one about Lizzie. The one that made him tense and want to throw up even more walls to protect himself and to protect his sister.

"Yes," he said, and gave no more information.

Amelia pursed her lips. "She is much younger than you are, isn't she?"

"Seventeen this year," he grunted, and took a long, bracing sip of red wine.

Amelia let out her breath. "Will you tell me nothing else about her?"

"Why do you want to know?" he asked, still tense, still

guarded, though he had to admit it was likely unfair.

Her brow knitted, and she set her fork down against the side of the plate and folded her arms. "Great God, Hugh, you are difficult. I have no idea what you want from me."

He arched a brow. Deflection. He needed deflection. "Don't you?" he drawled, taking a page from Robert's book. The Duke of Roseford used passion as a weapon, and it seemed to work for him. "Even after last night and today, you don't know?"

He got the response he desired. For a moment Amelia's gaze widened and her cheeks grew pink. She shifted in her chair and glanced around, as if to be sure that the other patrons in the room hadn't heard his wicked words. He thought perhaps he had succeeded in distracting her, but then her gaze narrowed. Refocused.

He saw the steel in her return, the strength that she somehow had running through her veins. He admired it, in truth. Admired her singular dedication, her loyalty, the way her jaw set and she kept going forward even when she was deterred.

"*That* part of what we share is…wonderful. I couldn't have expected I would—" She cut herself off and took a few breaths to regain her composure. Her bright gaze lifted to his again, and she said, "But it is only one part of what one would call a marriage. You put up walls between us and you will not take them down."

He tilted his head. "I disagree."

"You disagree—does that end the subject?" she asked.

Hugh wanted to snap out the affirmative and close the topic at that. He did not share with people, not unless he knew and trusted them completely. Hell, he hardly shared with those he did know and trust to that level. And this woman, she wanted more.

His wife wanted more. He scowled.

"I am simply stating my opinion," he grumbled.

"This isn't a matter of opinion, but fact," she insisted. "Today in the carriage, for example. We spent an hour connecting on a purely physical level, yes. But the moment that was over, you focused on your paperwork the rest of the ride. I read my book. We might as well have been strangers in a post coach. So what in the world do you want from me, Hugh?"

He pressed his lips together. "I want *you*. Isn't that enough?"

He could see the frustration on her face. "Not for a lifetime, I don't think. Are you saying you want a purely physical connection until you are bored with it?"

"Bored with it," he repeated, wrinkling his brow at the thought. Right now he could not picture becoming bored with exploring her body and all the ways to make her shudder and moan and scream.

She shook her head. "Of course you will become bored with it. All men do, eventually. I'm a novelty to you at present, nothing more. And when that happens, then what? Nothing at all? Do you expect we will lead separate lives where I raise your heirs and spares and we pass each other in the hallways like ghosts?"

He frowned at the description. That was not what he wanted, no. His friends had so much more, and he'd seen the value of it. But how could he get there from the beginning they'd made?

Overcoming the walls he built, the very ones he was trying to deny to her, was not easy.

"Please, I just want to know a *little* about your life," she pressed, and her hand trembled as she reached out. She hesitated, her fingers hovering over his. Then she covered his hand for a brief moment before she snatched hers away. "I am not asking for the secrets of the kingdom."

He took in a long breath. She *was* asking for just that in a way. The topic of Lizzie was one fraught with secrets and lies that affected Amelia and could bring down the already tenuous connection they'd begun to build.

And yet he couldn't deny her. Not when she was looking at him with those wide, impossibly gray-blue eyes that spoke of peace and light. Things he'd almost forgotten in the cloud of the last decade.

Things that made him feel so very vulnerable as he said, "I love my sister very much. I raised Lizzie. She was only eight when our parents died."

Amelia's expression softened with both relief and empathy. "Yes, Diana said something about that."

He tensed, longing to slam the door he had opened a fraction. "You spoke to her about me?"

She flinched at his snappish tone. "I-I needed to know a little, at least," she whispered. "You would hardly speak to me at all at that point."

That was fair. The first few days they'd been acquainted, he hadn't spoken much. The situation was so complicated and dire that he hadn't been able to find the right words. He could imagine how frustrating that must have been to her. How frightening to think of a life with a stranger who stole her future and offered her no glimpse of himself.

He'd played the whole situation very wrong, he could see that now that he knew her better. Only he still hardly knew her at all.

"What about you?" he asked. "I know just as little about you, perhaps even less since at least you spoke to our friends about me."

She worried her lip between her teeth gently and then nodded. "I suppose that is a fair statement. The circumstances you and my father created for our engagement didn't exactly offer us time to get to know each other."

"Tell me about your childhood," he offered. "As much or as little as you would like."

He tensed as her breath exited her lungs in a shaky sigh. The topic he'd chosen was not a happy one. But she spoke regardless of whatever pain he had unearthed. In that way, it seemed, she was far braver than he was.

"When I speak to you about a marriage between ghosts, it is because I witnessed one," she said. "My mother and father did not love each other. Theirs was a union of coldness and distance.

She married for his title, he for her money. They each held it over the other's head for years."

"In front of you?"

She nodded. "Indeed, often. I was a byproduct, a tool, a weapon to use against each other. My father was kinder to me than my mother."

"Your mother was not kind?" Hugh pressed, horrified by that idea.

She set her jaw. "She was not present. She did not care a whit about my life. And then she died. Truth be told, my world hardly changed at all. At least my father actually seemed to have plans for my future. I think—I *hope*—he loves me in his own way."

Hugh turned his head slightly as he thought of the viscount's cruel assessment of Amelia's engagement to Walters. This man she so desperately wanted to love her had been willing to trade her to a bastard just to get what he wanted. And it was Quinton's bargaining and lies that had placed her where she was.

If that was love, Hugh wanted no part of it. Amelia deserved more.

"And you are close to him," he encouraged her.

She bent her head, and a sad, knowing smile crossed her face. "Close is a relative term, isn't it? Closer to him than to the woman who birthed me and hardly looked at me again. But that might not be called close. I would want to protect him, obviously."

Her gaze dashed away from Hugh's face, and shame filled him. He could judge Quinton all he wanted, but he had been part of her father's manipulation. Trading on Amelia's love for her father in order to get what Hugh wanted.

"Obviously," he repeated.

"It isn't that I don't recognize the shortcomings of our relationship. He wanted a son and he got me," she said. "I don't think he's happy about it, but he used me when he needed me. I was his tool." She shrugged like that meant nothing when it so obviously meant everything. "That is the world of women in our day and age. He used me. You used me. I know that."

Hugh shut his eyes. She lumped him in with a man like her father, and he deserved that. He deserved her censure, her hate, her fear…and yet she gave him something more than that.

"I don't want you to be miserable, Amelia," he said.

She lifted her gaze to his. "I know. And I'm…not. I thought I would be. I was taken away from the future I wanted and yet…I'm not miserable."

"How?" he asked, genuinely curious. He had always had a hard time adjusting when things went wrong. The planning nature in him chafed at the unexpected twists and turns in his life.

Amelia, on the other hand, flowed like the streams around his home. She could twist and turn and make the best of it all. That was something worthy of study.

"I accept that this isn't what I wanted," she said, and for a moment he saw the sparkle of tears in her eyes. She blinked them back and continued, "But it *is* what I am experiencing. And there are other things it seems I want a great deal. Things I never understood until you…taught me."

She was talking about *him*. Wanting him, needing him. Desire was what she clung to now as a raft to close the distance between them.

Just as he did. For now, that would be enough. It had to be enough.

He reached out and took her hand. Her breath caught as he wound his fingers through hers and then lifted them to his lips. He kissed her knuckles, lingering to taste her skin before he said, "Are you finished eating?"

She didn't break her stare as she nodded. "I am."

"Then may I take you up to bed, Your Grace?" he whispered. "And perhaps we can both explore those things we both want. All night."

Her throat worked as she swallowed and her pupils dilated in the candlelight. She nodded. "Yes."

He got up, tugging her to her feet, and they moved together

to the narrow stair that led to the bedroom they would share. All night, this time, no escaping to a connecting chamber. But he didn't want escape. He wanted her.

And he was going to have her until they both had their fill.

CHAPTER THIRTEEN

Amelia peeked out the carriage window into the rapidly gathering darkness outside. Her third day of being the Duchess of Brighthollow had been very different from the first two.

First of all, she had woken in her husband's arms. Woken to his mouth on her skin, his hands roving over her in sensual exploration. One exquisite release later and she had been a much more chipper morning person than ever before.

The day in the carriage had also been different. Unlike yesterday, when Hugh seemed determined to keep his distance through work, today he had talked to her. About nothing profound, of course. Deeper topics like his past, like hers, were not discussed. If she even edged near them, he grew tense and guarded.

Instead, they had talked about music and books, riding and details of his estate and staff that she might need to know in the coming ten days. And he had also touched her, finding new ways to bring her pleasure in the hot, close carriage. She shivered as she thought of them. She shivered as she thought of how easy it all was with him. Should it have been so easy and so quickly?

The idea seemed outrageous, and yet here she was.

But now they rounded a corner through a gate and up a long and winding lane. Hugh sat up, leaning in to look out the window over her shoulder. She felt his presence there, warm and strong, and just resisted leaning back into him.

"There it is!" he said, motioning out the window.

She caught her breath. Even in the gathering dark, there was no mistaking the huge manor house, which was perfectly situated at the top of a slight hill. Light flowed from the windows, making it a beacon for weary travelers.

She glanced over her shoulder and caught Hugh's expression in the dimness. His face was lit with excitement and anticipation and joy. He was truly coming home, and in that moment her heart leapt into her throat. He looked so very young and carefree. What she wanted, more than anything, was to turn into him, to kiss him until neither had breath left.

She couldn't, though. The carriage reached the top of the hill and came to a stop. He pushed the door open before any servant could come to do the duty and stepped out. As he pivoted to help her out, he grinned.

Once she had reached the drive, he leaned down to whisper, "Do you approve?"

She blinked at the unexpected question and the nervousness on his face as he asked it. Did her opinion of his beloved home truly matter to him?

"I don't think anyone could not approve," she said, looking up and up at the massive house. "It is truly magnificent."

"And wait until you see the grounds. The lake is perfection—we could boat there or fish if you're of a mind to try it. The woods, the rolling hills, everything is just as it should be here."

She squeezed his hand. "Including you."

"I suppose so. I am more myself here than anywhere in the world."

"Then I look forward to seeing you come out of your shell," she teased. Then she glanced up at the house again. "I do worry I won't be up to the task of managing such a place, though. A duchess has duties when it comes to the household, and I was never trained to such lofty heights."

He stared down at her. "I had not thought that the place might be overwhelming to you. Don't fear, my staff is wonderful and will help you in every way. I'm certain you will take to your role immediately."

She smiled at his reassurance, but before she could thank him for it, the door at the top of the stair opened. Amelia expected a butler to greet them, but instead a willowy girl with blonde hair done up in a loose chignon and wearing a stunning evening dress stepped out. She made a little cry and then ran down the stairs.

Hugh met her halfway, swinging her up in his arms and around in a circle. Amelia stared. She had always seen Hugh as so controlled, so unemotional, but here he left nothing back. His love for this woman, obviously his younger sister, was as evident as anything else about him. Clearly, he was quite capable of the emotion.

"Lizzie!" he laughed as he set her down and pressed a kiss to her cheek. "Great God, you've grown while I was in London."

"Oh, stop," Lizzie laughed as she swatted his arm lightly. "You tease me mercilessly, Hugh, and you know I have not wit enough to match with you."

"You sell yourself short, as always," he said, taking her arm and steering her toward Amelia. "May I present my wife, Amelia. Amelia, this is my sister, Elizabeth."

Amelia stepped forward, uncertain of what to expect from this young woman. She had no idea what Hugh had told her of their engagement and whirlwind wedding.

Lizzie reached out and took both her hands. "Oh, I am so pleased to meet you. We only received Hugh's letter a few days ago, but I have been awash in joy ever since. Welcome to our home and to our family. I have always longed for a sister."

Relief flooded Amelia at the kind words. "As have I," she said, squeezing Lizzie's hands. "I am an only child and it has been quite a lonely existence. But I can tell you and I will be fast friends."

"I'm so sorry to hear that you did not have the pleasure of a sibling as a child." Lizzie glanced over at Hugh with a smile. "I was blessed with the best brother in the world. The kindest and most patient brother."

Hugh was red as a beet, and Amelia couldn't help but laugh. "You go too far, Lizzie," he said, his tone suddenly gruff. "Don't lie to the poor woman."

"It isn't a lie," Lizzie said with all earnestness. "As I'm sure you already know, Amelia."

Amelia blushed. She felt as if she knew hardly anything about the man she married. Even more so seeing him here. "I'm learning, Elizabeth."

"Lizzie—all my family calls me that."

"Then I'd be proud to do the same." Amelia glanced at Hugh and found him smiling at the pair. She returned the gesture and linked arms with her new sister-in-law.

Lizzie began to guide them up the stairs toward the house. "Amelia, you do not know how happy I was to hear my brother had found a bride. I've long told him he needed to settle down and be as happy as all his friends. But I was sorry not to be able to be part of the wedding. Was there a reason for the great rush?"

Amelia looked over her shoulder. Hugh had gone tense, his face lined with worry. She realized he didn't want his sister, who obviously worshipped him, to know that he'd blackmailed her into wedding him. That their marriage had been one of cold calculation, not some kind of whirlwind romance that had swept her off her feet.

She supposed if she were cruel, she could use that fact. Hurt him by telling the truth. But that seemed pointless. It would only create disillusion in his sweet, kind sister and would not change what had happened.

"I did not expect such a quick marriage either," she said, treading carefully so that nothing she said was a lie. "But the moment Hugh came into my life, it was clear that there was no other option but to wed him. He made me an offer I could not refuse, after all. Once you know your future, there is no point in waiting."

Lizzie released her arm as they entered the foyer and turned to her with a dreamy smile. "Oh, how very romantic," she cooed, and for a moment there was a flash of sadness on her sweet face.

"How lucky for you both—I'm so happy for you."

"Thank you, my dear." Amelia said. She glanced up the stairs to see Theresa coming down. She'd not seen her maid since earlier in the morning, when she'd come in to help Amelia dress before the servants rode ahead to the estate.

Hugh turned toward the butler, who had been standing by quietly in the shadows. "Masters, good to see you. May I present the Duchess of Brighthollow."

Masters executed a low bow. "A very hearty welcome to you, Your Grace. We are so very pleased to meet you. The household staff will greet you tomorrow, as to give you time to rest yourself before you are overwhelmed."

Amelia stepped toward the man with a smile. "That is very kind, Masters. I look forward to meeting them all in the morning when I am more prepared."

The butler looked toward Hugh. "Supper will be served in half an hour, Your Grace. All your favorites, of course."

Hugh's smile was genuine as he came closer and patted the butler's shoulder. "Tell Mrs. Masters how grateful I am for that. I have missed your wife's cooking."

Masters puffed up a little at the compliment before he returned to proper butlerly coolness. "I shall. The bags arrived an hour ago, so all should be settled for Her Grace upstairs."

"Excellent. I see that her lady's maid is already here," Hugh said, inclining his head toward Theresa. "Good evening, Theresa. We have a little time, Amelia, if you'd like to go up and change for supper."

Amelia stared. She'd been so wrapped up in watching him interact with his servant and his sister that she hadn't been prepared to speak. "Er, yes," she said. "I wouldn't mind changing out of my travel clothes. Half an hour you said, Masters?"

The butler nodded.

"Very good. I shall see you all then."

She turned toward Theresa and followed her upstairs toward the duchess's chamber awaiting her. But she wasn't wondering about the room she would inhabit or thinking about supper or anything else.

All she could think about was Hugh, even as she walked away from him. She had thought him an ogre in London, a beast who would rip her away from a future she had so carefully planned and so deeply desired. But along the road to his estate, her thoughts about him had shifted somewhat. She'd seen his kindness and his passion. She'd even watched some of his walls lower.

Here, there was even more change to take in. He obviously loved his sister fiercely. And she loved him in return. He was kind to his servants and relaxed in the walls of this estate.

So who was the true man she had married? The ogre? The passionate lover? The loving brother? The kind duke? Who was he?

And with their bad beginning, would she *ever* really know?

Hugh watched as Amelia laughed at something his sister had said to her. It warmed his heart to watch the two women interact through supper and now as they stood in the parlor together, giggling like old friends. Lizzie could be so reserved, but it was evident she liked Amelia. They would be good for each other.

Amelia's gaze slid to him, and his body went on alert. She was good for him, too. At least when it came to wanting. He hadn't let himself feel that for a long time. Oh, he'd taken women to bed, of course. Robert refused to let him be a monk. But that longing, that tug of insistent desire?

That he only felt with her.

She smiled at him, but then she reached up and covered a yawn with the back of her hand. He shook his head. Perhaps tonight she didn't need overwhelming passion. After a whirlwind wedding, two days on the road and one night where he kept her up making love, perhaps the best gift he could give her was to let her sleep.

"Lizzie, I know it's early, but I think it might be time for me to turn in," he said.

Lizzie pivoted and her eyes went wide. "Oh, goodness, I wasn't thinking of your very long drive. I know I am exhausted every time I make the ride from London. Of course you two must need to rest."

Amelia smiled at her and then stepped forward to embrace her. "Thank you for understanding. And we have all the time in the world to spend together during my time here and then later in London."

Hugh frowned as Lizzie flinched ever so slightly. She had refused to go to Town since the incident with Aaron Walters. Refused to do anything except stay in the country and hide.

He had no idea how to change that. But at least Amelia's company seemed to cheer her.

"Good night," Lizzie said, kissing her cheek before she stepped toward Hugh. Her smile was wide and genuine as she hugged him. She whispered, "I like her so much."

Hugh squeezed her a little tighter and smiled as she left the room with a little wave. He turned toward Amelia. "What do you think?"

"Of Lizzie?" Amelia asked with a smile. "Oh, she's lovely, Hugh, truly. So sweet and kind and so welcoming. A delight. You should be so proud of her."

"I am," he said slowly. "She is the light of my world. I only want her to be happy."

"I can see that," Amelia said, stepping toward him but stopping just short of touching him.

He closed the distance she had not and reached to take her hand. "Thank you for not...for not telling her what I did in London," he said, feeling heat in his cheeks.

Amelia tilted her head. "The circumstances of our marriage, you mean?"

He nodded. "She wouldn't understand. And it would have

caused her grief."

Amelia searched his face, and for a moment he felt like she could see all the way through him. All the way to his soul. He shifted beneath the intensity of her look.

"Hugh," she said at last. "Whatever difficulties are between us are our business, no one else's. Certainly, I would not hurt your sister just to bring you pain or get some kind of strange revenge for what you did in London."

"Thank you," he repeated softly.

She edged closer. "Do you truly want to sleep?" she asked.

He shook his head. "Not at all. I want to take you to my room and make love to you in the biggest bed in the county."

She laughed, her cheeks growing pink at the frank words. "And yet there is a *but* in your tone."

"But," he said with a smile, "I see how tired you are. It's been a trying week for you, in more ways than one. So tonight, as much as it pains me, perhaps we should sleep alone. And tomorrow we'll be more refreshed to…to enjoy my estate and all its pleasures."

She tilted her head, and once again her look was probing. She lifted her hand to his cheek and stroked the skin there gently. He found himself leaning into her fingers.

"You are so impossible to read, Brighthollow," she whispered. "I hope to one day understand you. But I appreciate the offer of a night's sleep. I think I will be better equipped for everything if I take you up on that offer."

"Good night," he whispered.

She smiled and then lifted up on her tiptoes. She cupped his cheeks and drew him down, bringing his mouth to hers. Her lips parted and she traced his with her tongue. He was lost, swirling down into the sensation as she tasted his mouth and drew herself up flush against him.

He had no idea how long they stood that way. He was too lost to count the time. But finally she stepped away, her gaze bleary and her smile shaky.

"I look forward to seeing the biggest bed in the county

tomorrow. Good night." She squeezed his hand and slipped away, leaving him alone with his confusion, his thoughts and his erection.

CHAPTER FOURTEEN

Hugh stood on the terrace, watching down into his garden below where Amelia was picking flowers and placing them in a big basket draped over her arm. She was not wearing a bonnet and the early morning sun glinted off her sleek, black hair. She had not noticed him standing above her and moved through the garden at ease.

He was brought back to the first time he saw her, in her father's garden. She hadn't realized he was watching her then either as she picked flowers for her father's hall. She'd been engaged to Aaron Walters, and now he wondered if she'd been thinking of him that afternoon.

Was she thinking of Walters now? Or was she thinking of Hugh as she leaned in to smell a rose here and there? It seemed like a lifetime ago since that day when he'd looked down and pondered if he could marry a stranger in order to save her from his worst enemy.

Now he had. Now she was his.

Only she wasn't. Not completely.

"She truly is lovely."

Hugh turned to find his sister coming to the terrace wall to stand beside him. They watched Amelia for a moment, and then he sighed, "She is that. Beauty personified."

Lizzie shot him a look. "You would never be interested in mere beauty personified, but with no depth. So I know she is more than that."

Hugh nodded. There was no denying her words. Amelia was far more than her exquisitely beautiful face. She was light and intelligence. Kindness and frankness. She was everything. And he didn't like acknowledging that. It felt so damned dangerous to let himself feel it after such a short time. After all the lies.

"She told a pretty story of being swept away by you," Lizzie pressed. "Very romantic. But I know you, brother dear. I know you are not the kind of man who is carried away by heated emotion."

Hugh shifted. It seemed every woman in his life was determined to look through his hard shell and poke at the hidden soft spots beneath. "You make me sound cold as ice."

Lizzie's lips parted and she grabbed for his hand. "You know I think you nothing of the sort. I know your warmth and caring, your deep capacity for love and patience. I only meant that you ponder, you consider, you weigh options."

Hugh couldn't argue with that. His sister knew him far too well. "And so?"

Lizzie's gaze shifted back to Amelia below them. "I cannot believe that you simply saw this woman across a crowded room and decided to leap into a lifelong commitment within days."

Hugh almost laughed, though her description gave him no pleasure in the slightest. Nor did the truth, at present. "It wasn't a room. I looked at her from a terrace much like this one and knew what my future would hold."

She wrinkled her brow. "Why?"

"I wanted to..." He sighed. "Protect her. Be near her. Save her."

"Save her?" Lizzie repeated. "What did she need saving from?"

Hugh glanced at her. He could see Lizzie's worry clear on her face. And if she knew the truth...oh, how it would devastate her. It had been over a year since her ill-conceived escape with Walters, and he sometimes still caught a shadow of grief, pain, fear, regret on her face. She held herself utterly responsible for her decision, to the point that he suspected it kept her up nights.

If she knew Amelia had been engaged to Walters, herself? If she found Hugh's new marriage had been undertaken merely to thwart that bastard's cruel intentions?

He had a feeling his sister would spiral back into a deep and powerful sadness that had terrified him for months. And he feared it would damage her budding relationship with Amelia, who his sister seemed to like so much right away.

So she could not know the truth. Just as Amelia could not know the truth. The lies were difficult—they went against what he'd always believed to be his nature. But that was how it had to be.

"You worry too much," he said with a smile as he took her arm. "I appreciate it more than you know, but it is unnecessary. Amelia is my bride and I am…" He trailed off and glanced down at her again. "I am discovering every day what that means to me."

His words didn't seem to fully appease Lizzie, but she rested her head briefly against his shoulder. "I only want you to be happy."

He leaned down to kiss the crown of her head and barely held back a sigh. "I am doing my best to be just that. Come now, let's join Amelia in the garden, shall we? I'm certain no one could give her a better tour of this estate than you."

Lizzie worried her lip, and he could see she had a hundred questions, a thousand fears. Only she said none of them. She shrugged and said, "Very well."

She had surrendered, because it was in her sweet nature to do so, to trust and believe in him even if he didn't deserve it at present. So as he took her down the flight of stairs that would lead them to Amelia, he felt worse than ever. For deceiving her, for deceiving his wife.

And perhaps, if he looked close enough, too close, deceiving himself, too.

Amelia sat on the settee in the parlor, slippers off and legs tucked up beneath her, and laughed as Hugh and Lizzie put on a shadow puppet show of epic proportions on the wall across from the dancing fire. It was clearly something they had done many times before, for they were truly wonderful at it, twisting their hands into fish, fowl and animal alike. They even had characters and laughed together as they made them interact in funny voices.

It was yet another side to Hugh that Amelia had never expected to find when he stormed into her parlor and made his devil's bargain with her father. She'd tried so hard to harden her heart to any of his good qualities in London, despite the desire he engendered deep within her.

But now…here in his home with his sister near him, there was no denying that the man she'd reluctantly married had much more depth to him than the stern surface she'd been so frightened of when they first met.

All day she'd seen his many faces. He'd been quiet as Lizzie took her on the grand tour of the estate, smiling as his sister waxed poetic about the library and the music room and chiming in here and there as tales were told of their childhood in this place. Sometimes she caught him watching her, a look of anticipation on his face, and she was drawn back to the moment the night before when they had looked up at this beautiful manor house and he'd asked if she approved.

He wanted her to love this place as much as he and Lizzie clearly did. Even though it didn't really matter what Amelia's opinion was. This was her home—circumstances dictated that to be true. But he still wanted her to connect to it.

And she did. How could one not? It was beautiful, sophisticated, but still somehow warm and welcoming. The servants were kind and seemed happy and well taken care of. The grounds were vast and beautiful. She had never dreamed of such a lofty situation when she dreamed of her future as a girl, but somehow she didn't feel out of place here.

"Won't you join us, Amelia?" Lizzie laughed as she made her shadow fox run after Hugh's shadow rabbit along the wall.

Amelia shook off her musings and got up to join them. "I've never been very good at this. I only know one animal," she laughed as she wedged herself between the siblings. Immediately she was keenly aware of Hugh's presence at her left. The warmth of him. The brush of his knee against hers.

"I'm sure you are as proficient at this as you seem to be at everything else," Hugh teased, his tone suddenly thick with double entendre.

She shot him a look and then locked her fingers together carefully. On the wall a clumsy bird appeared and all three laughed as she swooped it toward Hugh's rabbit and Lizzie made her fox flee.

"You two have made a meal of me, I think," Hugh said with a smile.

Lizzie giggled as she leaned back against her palms on the carpet. "Oh, this was a wonderful day."

Amelia glanced at Hugh and found him looking at her in return. She blushed as she said, "It was. Thank you for making your home so welcoming to me."

"It's your home now," Hugh said softly. Those four words hit Amelia in the gut. Home. Could this be her home? Could this man become her home in some way? Was it possible to believe that after so short an acquaintance? After so difficult a beginning?

Lizzie nodded with enthusiasm, unaware of Amelia's torn heart. "Indeed, it is. And you fit here so perfectly—soon it will be impossible to remember a time when you didn't belong to our family." She let out a happy sigh that turned to a yawn. With a shake of her head, she looked at the clock. "Oh goodness, it's getting late. I should go to bed."

All three got to their feet, and Amelia smiled as Lizzie stepped into Hugh's arms and gave him a hug. Their bond was so lovely and pure, it warmed Amelia's heart to see it.

"Goodnight," Lizzie said, and turned to Amelia. They both smiled and then Lizzie grabbed her and tugged her in for a hug of her own. Amelia was stiff in surprise at first, but swiftly relaxed. There was no denying her new sister's sweetness and kindness.

"Goodnight, my dear," Amelia whispered.

"I'm so glad you are here," Lizzie said in return, then drew back to smile at her. "I'll see you both tomorrow. And I think we should go fishing if the weather is fine."

"An excellent notion," Hugh said as she moved to the parlor door. "Until tomorrow."

Lizzie gave a last wave and left the room. For the first time that day, Hugh and Amelia were alone. Immediately, her heart began to pound just a little harder and all the ease she'd felt faded, replaced by anticipation and a flare of heat she could now identify as pure desire.

It must have reflected on her face, she knew it did, she could feel it there, for Hugh's body shifted, his pupils dilated and he gave her one of those wicked half smiles before he strode to the door and quietly closed it. She heard him turn the key in the lock and shivered.

They were alone at last. No interruptions to come.

She faced him and watched as he tossed the key onto the sideboard.

"Drink?" he asked, motioning to the decanter.

She swallowed. "No," she whispered. "I don't need a drink."

His eyebrows lifted. "What do you need, Your Grace?"

Her body tingled as she stepped toward him. He didn't move, though she could see his hands twitch at his sides, his gaze track her like a bird of prey she had so clumsily created earlier in the shadows on the wall.

"I had a nice day," she whispered. "But…"

She trailed off. She had been raised to be a lady, raised to squash down those twinges in her body that she had not been able to name. Now she was driven to speak them. To claim them, and it was still an awkward endeavor.

"But?" he encouraged as she reached him. They were inches apart now, so close to perfection.

"But I missed you," she admitted with a shake of her head.

He smiled. "I was with you the whole day."

He would make her say it, clarify it, and she glared at him. "I meant I missed…touching you. There were so many times today when I looked at you and all I could think about was…was…"

He stepped in and caught her waist, dragging her flush against him. His mouth lowered, inch by painful inch, and he whispered, "This," before he claimed her.

Claimed was the right word. His mouth crushed down on hers with a passion that had been bubbling between them all day. Immediately the tone in the room shifted. There was no more playful teasing or friendly games. The powerful physical connection between them took over, and she wrapped her arms around his neck to lift against him as he drove his tongue hard into her mouth.

His hands slipped around her back, and she felt him slide two buttons of her gown open in rapid succession. She broke her mouth from his and stared up at him in shock and wonder.

"What…here?" she whispered.

"The door is locked and I can't wait to take you upstairs," he said. "Isn't it so much more wicked to think that we could take our pleasure here? And then every time you come into this room, you'll look at that settee…" He motioned across the room to the pretty upholstered couch near the fire. "…you'll know you rode me there until we were both spent with pleasure."

Her eyes went wide at the highly descriptive and specific nature of that statement. "Ride you?" she repeated, her hands shaking as she opened his jacket.

He chuckled and returned his hands to her buttons, stripping them open as he backed her across the room toward the settee he'd indicated. He tugged her dress and it fell forward, drooping at her arms. She expected him to remove it, to do all those wicked things she'd been dreaming about all day.

Instead, he stepped away. Holding eye contact with her, he shrugged off the jacket and waistcoat she had been tugging on, then removed his shirt. He sat on the settee, wrenched off his boots and slouched down, watching up at her through a hooded gaze.

"Can you imagine what in the world you might want to do with me, Your Grace?" he whispered.

She wet her lips nervously. A dozen possibilities filled her mind as she stared down at him, in the dominant position for the first time since he'd touched her the night of their engagement ball. Torn between uncertainty and a deep well of desire that told her to touch and lick and take like he would.

"I'm still figuring out what I can and cannot do in general," she admitted as she tugged the gown from her arms and shimmied out of it. She stood before him in her chemise and drawers and felt the heat of a blush fill her cheeks.

He leaned forward and slid his hand under the hem of her drawers, gliding his rough fingers over the smooth expanse of her thigh. She shivered at the sensation, at the answering tug she felt deep in her sex.

"You can do anything you like, Amelia," he said, lifting his gaze to hers. "Whatever feels good to us is what is right. You can't make a mistake in this, I promise you that."

There was something hypnotic to his low, seductive tone. Something that convinced her, more than any words, that he wanted her and she wanted him, and that would be enough.

She drew in a shuddering breath and then slid the thin straps of her chemise away from her shoulders. Slowly, she let the fabric roll away from her breasts and down her stomach, crumpling it at her feet so all that was left were the drawers.

He muttered something under his breath. She wasn't sure if it was a curse or a benediction. Both, perhaps, rolled up into one. He flopped back against the settee, hands gripped against his muscular thighs, and watched her with a hungry gaze.

She felt answering hunger in her chest, in her limbs, in the slick heat that pooled between her legs. She swallowed hard, emboldened by the shared madness of this never-ending desire. Slowly she edged forward, nudging herself between his legs until her stomach was right in front of him.

"Untie me," she ordered, her voice shaking at how powerful she felt.

He glanced up at her, that wicked half-smile cocking his lips once more. "Yes, Your Grace," he murmured, and reached out to tug the silky tie on her drawers. He moved purposefully, teasing her as he let his fingers trace the waistline of the last thing she wore.

Finally, he loosened the knot and looked up at her as he let his fingers move beneath the fabric and pull them down her legs. She kicked them away, moaning as he let his hands travel back up her hips, cupping her backside as he tugged her in to press a searing kiss against the flat plane of her belly.

"Yes," she whispered, dropping her hands into his hair and pulling it from the queue. "Yes, yes, yes."

There was no other word but that one, and he listened to its every meaning. His mouth traced down to her hip, he sucked on her thigh and his fingers slid along the path until he rested his palm on her sex and teased her open.

She knew she was already wet, already hot and waiting. When his fingers slid inside of her, there was no resistance. She'd been waiting for this since the previous day in the carriage, and now he was touching her and she wanted nothing more than to give herself to him all night.

He was watching her as he filled her with one finger, then two. She bore down on him as he pressed a thumb to her clitoris and ground it gently. Her breath became short as the pleasure she had been denied for more than twenty-four hours returned in a heated rush.

He stroked her for a while—she had no idea how long, for time had lost all meaning. It was clear he was in no rush to bring her release. He wanted to tease, to draw out her need, to make her take it or beg for it.

And she was ready to do both. Especially when he withdrew his fingers from her clenching sheath and lifted them to his lips, where he licked them clean with a smile.

"Come down here," he said, catching the back of her knee and gently guiding her to place it on one side of his thighs. She lowered herself to straddle over him, feeling the thick outline of his cock as she moved into position. Her hips flexed of their own accord and she ground over him.

Her eyes widened. *Ride him.* This was what he meant. Once he unfastened his trousers and freed his cock, she could take him inside and do just that. Ride until she was spent, until she had milked every ounce of pleasure from them both.

She thrilled at the idea. But once again, he seemed in no hurry. He slid his fingers into her hair, tugging her chignon loose so waves fell around her shoulders, her back, their faces. He slid his hands into the locks, cupping her scalp as he angled her head for a deep, probing kiss.

She melted against him, tasting his desire as their tongues tangled in languid, unrushed passion. There was no need to go too quickly, even if her needy body disagreed. They had all night—and after tonight, the rest of their days—to explore each other.

And that was far more comforting a notion than perhaps it should have been.

He cupped her backside and tugged her flush against him, rocking her and stealing her breath as she dropped her head back with a gasp of pleasure. One that increased when he caught one nipple between his lips and began to suck gently.

She flexed her hips against him in time to those glorious sucks and licks and nips, feeling pleasure rise in her, push her toward release, toward madness. And it affected him, too. He was already hard, but every rolling flex of her hips made him even harder.

She reached between them, hands shaking, and traced the line of his cock. He lifted his gaze and met hers, and in that moment she knew they were both ready. No more teasing or preparing. She lifted slightly and he tore the buttons of his trousers open. His cock pushed on the loose fabric and cast the front fall away, revealing him in all his naked, hard glory.

She couldn't find words as she lowered herself back into place. He slid a hand between them, positioning himself at her entrance, and then she was taking him inside as they let out a moan in unison that echoed in the quiet chamber.

Once he was fully seated, he reached out and dragged her down to his lips again, kissing her as he flexed his hips up, thrusting from below as she dug her fingernails into his bare chest. She met his stokes, grinding her hips down to his. It took her a moment to find the rhythm, but once she did, she let out a soft cry at how very good he felt.

And how right their joining always was. Like their bodies were made for each other, made for these illicit pleasures. She wanted them, wanted him, wanted to learn all the ways he liked to be touched, all the ways they could make each other shudder like they shuddered together now. And that wasn't just a general desire, an ache that needed to be filled by any person in her orbit who could do so.

She wanted *this* man. No other. It was shocking, but it was true. Long gone were thoughts of Aaron or of some fairytale ideal she'd spun for herself as a naïve girl. All that was left was Hugh, and as the first flutters of release ripped through her, he was all that mattered.

She dropped her head back, gasping out pleasure. She gripped him through the crisis, continuing to ride, continuing to grind as the sensations rolled higher and higher.

He pounded faster, his neck straining, and then he let out a low groan of his own and she felt the heat of his release joining hers. She collapsed against his chest with a sigh of pleasure and his arms came around her, tucking her tightly against him as he slid kisses along her neck and her shoulders.

"And now you're truly home," he murmured.

She opened her eyes at that statement. Perhaps he meant it that their marriage was fully consummated, or that she truly belonged because she had been claimed in his house at last.

But there was something deeper to the words. Something that rang so true that it was terrifying. She felt like she was home. In his house, certainly. In his family, yes.

But mostly in his arms. Yet she had no idea what he wanted for their future, so it made his words terrifying, because they could lead her to heartbreak that could change her life forever.

CHAPTER FIFTEEN

Hugh could not believe how swiftly a week had passed since he and Amelia had arrived in Brighthollow. But the days had rolled away, filled with laughter and relaxation. The nights with unbridled and thus far unrelenting passion. In three days they would return to London, for he had things to attend to in the city and he found himself preoccupied over whether they could bring the charmed nature of their time on his estate with them.

It wasn't that it had been perfect. There had been times when being with Amelia was almost painful. She was so lovely, and when he caught her looking off into the distance with a troubled expression, he was obsessed with her thoughts. Was she thinking of Walters? Wishing that her life were different? She was owed that desire, of course, but it still tore his heart to shreds.

He'd tried to run from it. Distance himself. But somehow Amelia always found him and drew him back, like a beacon in the darkness.

He shook his head as he pushed back from his desk and paced out of his study. He'd been working all morning, but now he wanted to see his wife. His *wife*, which was still a foreign and shocking concept.

He prowled the halls, searching for her like a lost dog seeking its master. But she seemed to be in no parlor, not in the library, not the music room. As he turned every corner, the keen desire just to look at her face grew sharper and more desperate.

"Good afternoon, Your Grace," his housekeeper, Mrs. Williams, said as he poked his head into yet another room. She straightened from her work and tilted her head with a friendly smile.

Hugh focused on maintaining even a fraction of decorum and returned the expression. "Good afternoon, Mrs. Williams."

"May I help you with anything?" she asked, watching as he looked around the room in what felt like lost distraction.

"Er, my wife," he admitted, and hated how heat flooded his cheeks. "I cannot seem to find her. Do you know if she went for a walk?"

"She didn't, sir," the housekeeper said with a knowing expression, like she could see what he didn't want to admit. "I think she and Lady Elizabeth were going to the ballroom."

Hugh wrinkled his brow. "The—the ballroom?" he repeated in confusion. "Why would they do that?"

"Her Grace said something about practicing," Mrs. Williams said. "I don't know much more about their plans."

Hugh's warm desire to see Amelia faded a little at that statement. Practice. In the ballroom. His wife didn't know his sister very well. Certainly, Lizzie had not shared her painful past. What Amelia was doing might trigger Lizzie's bad memories. Her uncertainties.

"Thank you," he muttered as he exited the room and strode down the long hall to the back of the house, where the massive ballroom was situated. The door was cracked as he approached and behind it, he heard the echoing voices of the two women. They were…laughing.

He stopped in his place, stunned by that realization. Lizzie *hated* the ballroom—she avoided it at all costs—and yet he heard her giggles coming from behind the big, carved door. He hesitated, then pushed the door open just enough that he could see inside.

In the middle of the big, empty room, Amelia and Lizzie were facing each other. As he watched, Amelia executed a stiff, formal bow and Lizzie curtsied. Then Amelia held out her hand

and they began the intricate steps of the quadrille, spinning round the room as they tried to maintain serious expressions.

It was a failure. Halfway through the sequence, Lizzie let out a laugh that echoed in the room, and Amelia followed suit until both of them were bent over at the waist.

After a moment, Amelia straightened, wiping tears of mirth from her eyes. Lizzie clutched her stomach and Hugh could tell she was trying to control her laughter.

He was...stunned. Despite her warm welcome of Amelia, Lizzie had been shy, even before Aaron Walters had destroyed her world. She had chafed at the idea of dancing and had begged him to dismiss her dance teacher years ago. His presence made her nervous, she said. He had agreed, thinking he could hire someone new in time. But every time he brought up the subject, Lizzie blushed and demurred and pleaded with him not to make her exhibit so publicly.

But here she was, actually enjoying the lesson Amelia was teaching.

The two women regathered some tiny shred of composure, and Amelia smoothed an errant curl from her cheek before she said, "What about a waltz, Lizzie? It's a bit slower? Certainly more romantic."

Lizzie's smile fell and she backed up a step. "Oh, no. Not the waltz. That is not...I don't wish to..."

Amelia moved forward and caught her hand. "You are a lovely dancer, Lizzie. Very naturally graceful. You needn't be nervous. A waltz can be very enjoyable."

Lizzie ducked her head. "I cannot be a very good dancer. I haven't had much practice."

Hugh could see the confusion on Amelia's face, and he knew why. Most young ladies, especially the ladies of Lizzie's rank, were trained almost from the time they could walk to dance. They knew every song and turn of foot by heart by the time they were Elizabeth's age and ready to come out to Society.

"I assure you," Amelia said carefully. "When you come back to London with Hugh and me, you will be the belle of any ball. You needn't worry yourself."

All the color drained from Lizzie's face, and Hugh could stand by no longer. He rushed into the room with a wide smile he hoped would distract Amelia from this topic of questioning.

"Good afternoon, ladies. I did not know there was a ball here today."

Lizzie's face brightened a little at the sight of him, and she rushed forward to take Hugh's arm. He felt the slightest tremble to her grip as she curled her fingers around his bicep.

"Amelia was just teaching me a few dances," she explained.

Amelia was watching them closely, and he could still see the troubled expression on her face. "Yes," she said slowly. "Lizzie seemed so enraptured of my description of the first time you and I danced that I thought it might be fun for both of us. But I'm not very good at leading."

Hugh caught her eye. "You seem very well equipped at doing so."

She blushed immediately and he stifled a smile. At least distracting her was enjoyable. And it seemed to have worked, for she didn't press further on the subject of why Lizzie didn't like the dance.

"You are a very good dancer, Your Grace," she said instead. "Perhaps I could play the pianoforte and you could help Lizzie with the steps yourself."

Hugh blinked as he looked down at his sister. That was an option he hadn't considered before. He'd simply did as she asked and sent her dance teacher away, but he'd never thought to teach her himself. It wasn't the worst idea. He could go slowly if she required time and patience.

"Would you like to try?" he asked her softly.

Lizzie's hesitation was plain on her face, but then she glanced over at Amelia. Clearly, she wanted to please her new sister-in-law. That drive seemed more powerful than her nervousness. With a tiny sigh, she nodded. "If you have the time."

"I do," he said, and smiled at Amelia as she walked to the

pianoforte that was in the corner of the room. She settled into place and began to play.

For a moment he was stunned into silence. Ladies were taught so many skills. His sister, herself, was a fine musician and singer, though she had to be coaxed to show off her talents. He supposed he'd guessed that Amelia would be a proficient in some of those arts, too, but he hadn't expected her playing to be so...beautiful. So passionate.

She stopped playing and laughed. "Is this a concert or a dance lesson? Go on, you two, *spin!*"

Hugh shook off his surprise and took Lizzie's hand. They stepped out together, and as Amelia began the song over again, he spun his sister around the floor, taking his time as he walked her through the steps. At first, Lizzie was hesitant. She looked at her feet regularly and muttered beneath her breath with every missed step.

But as the song continued, he watched her confidence grow. It was a beautiful thing to behold, for so much of it had been crushed under Aaron Walter's boot. To watch Lizzie flower, smile as she figured out the timing of a step...it warmed Hugh's heart. *That* was the gift Amelia had given to him. To them.

As the song ended, Lizzie curtsied and then turned to Amelia with a nervous laugh. "How did I do?"

Amelia got up and came around the pianoforte to embrace his sister gently. "That was wonderful. A little more practice and no one will ever know that you didn't feel comfortable." She glanced at Hugh as she continued, "I have no idea why you didn't learn to dance years ago, but you are a natural."

Lizzie tensed, and Hugh smiled down at her. "Lizzie, I have a hankering for Mrs. Masters' bread pudding before I leave. Do you think you might ask her very sweetly to put it on the menu for tonight or tomorrow? You know she'll never refuse you."

Lizzie nodded and hurried from the room. After she'd gone, Amelia turned to Hugh, her gaze narrowed. There was a beat of silence before she said, "You don't want me to know anything, do you?"

He wrinkled his brow, feigning innocence when he knew exactly what she meant. "Don't be foolish."

Her glare darkened. "Don't try to make me think I don't see what is right in front of me." Her voice shook with the power of her emotions. "I am only in this family of yours as far as you desire. That much is very clear."

He folded his arms. "What are you talking about?"

Her expression transformed from one of just anger to a mixture of hurt. Seeing that there, knowing it was caused by him, he felt like an ass of the highest order.

"You will make me spell it out? Very well. The more I come to know Lizzie, the more I realize she is *afraid* of coming out. Afraid of London. I haven't pressed her on that topic because I know she will tell me in time if she trusts me enough. But *you* don't want me to know the truth. Not ever."

Hugh stared at her a long moment. He had come to realize over the past few weeks just how wonderfully kind and accepting Amelia was. Under any other circumstance, he might have encouraged his sister to confide in her. Lizzie needed a friend.

But it wasn't that simple. Amelia had been involved with the same young man who had crushed Lizzie. Once she knew that, Amelia was too clever not to put the pieces together of why Hugh had pursued her. Why he had said that Walters was a bastard.

He had no idea how she would react to that. How she would feel if his lies came out now, when they were still feeling out their relationship, their future.

Perhaps someday he would feel comfortable enough to tell her. But now? Now it felt like he could lose her if she knew.

Lose everything that had come to mean so much to him.

"She is my sister," he said softly.

Amelia shook her head. "She wishes to be mine, as well. And if you don't want that, then it makes me wonder, yet again, why I am here."

"Because you are my wife," he said, rushing forward, hands

153

outstretched.

"Am I?" she whispered, her voice trembling once again. "I don't feel like it."

Her face crumpled as she turned and walked away. As she exited the room, Hugh had a flash of desire to call after her. To make her come back, to fall on his knees and tell her every painful part of his story from beginning to end. To give her what he had spent a lifetime trying to push away, not share.

But he wasn't strong enough. So all he could do was stand in the middle of his ballroom and wish things were different.

CHAPTER SIXTEEN

Amelia sat at the desk in her study, writing a letter to her father. Well, that wasn't exactly true. She'd said that was what she was doing, she had a piece of paper in front of her with *Dear Father* scribbled across the top, but she was not writing. She was fuming, staring at the window toward the garden below and reliving her last conversation with Hugh.

Just as she had been doing since the previous afternoon.

Why his behavior bothered her, she could not say. After all, she had never wanted a marriage to this man. This frustrating, utterly handsome, completely irresistible man. If he wanted to lock her out and have a marriage that involved no true connection, why did it matter?

Except that it did. It mattered a great deal. Nothing had changed that. Not a feigned headache. Not a night alone in her chamber. Her emotions still bubbled inside her.

She pushed the letter aside and put her elbows on the desktop and her head in her hands. The walls in this house were driving her mad, that was all. She was too close to the problem, too close to the attraction. Perhaps when they returned to London, she would be able to detangle herself and gain some perspective.

There was a light knock on her door that adjoined their chambers, and she turned slightly. She frowned. Hugh stood in the entryway, watching her closely.

"Come in," she said after what felt like an eternity had passed between them.

He did so and slowly closed the door behind himself. She tracked the movement, hating how her body warmed at the idea of being alone with him.

Traitor.

"I wanted to talk to you," he said.

She arched a brow. "Why? It seems we have little to say."

His expression tightened and she saw a flash of both frustration and pain in his gaze. He drew a long breath. "I missed you in my bed last night, Amelia."

She rose and took a step toward him. "Then you do not wish to talk—this is about my body. I would not deny you. It seems I cannot, at any rate. I am a slave to the desires you have awakened in me. So take it."

His gaze flowed over her, heated and focused, but then he shocked her by shaking his head. "No. No, that isn't what I came for."

"What did you come for, Hugh?" she whispered.

"To talk," he said, moving forward. "To try to make you see."

She backed away with a shake of her head. "But I already see." Her anger made her voice tart, and it was bubbling up stronger and stronger in her chest. Emotions she had never been allowed to feel or express. "You are going to keep me on the outside, and that is where I've always been. My lot, it seems, is to *almost* be part of a family. To *almost* be loved and cared for. I thought I could have that with—"

She broke off and turned away, blinking at the tears that swelled in her eyes. She gripped her fists against the desk and tried to control the weakness that seemed to dictate everything in her body and soul.

"You thought you could have what you wanted with Aaron Walters," he said, finishing her thought in a dull, empty tone.

She faced him slowly. "Yes," she admitted softly. "And your hatred for him, for whatever reason you had it, took that away from me. Now you refuse to give me that desire here. So…I'm alone. In a house full of servants and people, I will *always* be alone."

He held her gaze, nostrils flaring, hands shaking at his sides. At first, she thought he was angry, pushed too far by her refusal of him, by her bluntness when she addressed their circumstance. But when he spoke, his voice wasn't angry.

It was broken, laced with the same pain she felt.

"I know how that feels," he said. "I know."

"How could you?" she asked with a shuddering sigh that she couldn't hold back for a moment more. The weight on her shoulders was too heavy to even try.

He hesitated, and then he reached out. "Will you come with me?"

She blinked at the hand, that hand that had brought her so much pleasure in the past. Attached to a man she did not fully trust or know.

"Why?"

He bent his head. "If you want to know me, if you want to be let in to my world, as you say, then *please* come with me."

Her heart stuttered. Was he truly offering her a way into his mind or his soul? And did she really want that? To be connected with the man who had destroyed her hopes and dreams, who confused her and made her want to laugh and cry and surrender and scream all at once?

It seemed she did, at some base level, for she nodded slowly and took the proffered hand. "Very well. Lead the way, Your Grace."

Hugh felt the weight of Amelia's hand in his like it was a boulder. Her soft fingers pressed into his palm, and it made him question his plan with every step as they walked across the large estate together.

He didn't want to do this. And yet he did. It was utterly confusing.

"The woods here are a bit thick, watch your footing." It was the first thing he'd said in the past twenty minutes they'd been walking. Amelia hadn't pressed, just moved beside him in silence, as if she understood he needed that silence to calm himself.

They exited the path and he slowly picked his way along what had once been a trail into the deepest part of the woods. He knew it like the back of his hand, despite the fact that it had been years, a decade, since he last came here.

"There," he said, stopping and pointing across the tangle of branches.

Amelia caught her breath, and together they stared at the little building standing dilapidated in a clearing not ten feet away. He smiled despite the strange ache in his chest.

"What is it?" she asked.

"The place where I came to escape," he explained. "I built it—rather poorly, as you can see from its condition—when I was ten or eleven, during a summer my father insisted we come to Brighthollow so he could start teaching me how to manage the estate."

"But you built a playhouse for yourself instead," Amelia said softly.

He nodded as he released her hand and crossed the steps to the worn-out little house. It was so very badly built out of warped branches and rusty nails. Had he stolen them from somewhere? He could hardly recall. He did remember crying some afternoons as he banged away at the thing.

"Looking at it now, I think I'm lucky it didn't collapse down on me and kill me," he said with a laugh as he touched a wall and felt it buckle slightly.

"Why did you need to hide?" she whispered.

He didn't turn toward her. He'd been thinking about telling her this story all night, but he couldn't look at her. Not yet. Not yet.

"He needed me to be perfect," Hugh said.

"Your father." Her voice barely carried.

He nodded, still staring at the shabby house. "My father. Hugh the first, Hugh the greatest, for I have likely never lived up to his name, at least not in his eyes. I'm sure he rolls in his grave regularly when I make the wrong decision."

"That sounds like a great deal of pressure for a boy."

"It was," he said, thickness entering his throat. "I could not make a mistake. If I didn't know how to do something immediately, I had failed and that was unacceptable."

"But failure is how we learn," Amelia said. "Did he not know that?"

Hugh glanced at her over his shoulder and saw the pain on her face. Empathy for him. He wanted to reach for her, but turned away instead. "Apparently not. He required that I hide my emotion. Anger was not to be accepted. Certainly not fear or pain. I had to hide any lack of understanding. Any need for more. If I didn't he would—"

He broke off. He didn't want to say what *he* would do. How the crack of a switch felt against his skin. How the fear of worse to come felt.

"Hugh," she whispered, and then her hand touched his arm. Once again he felt the weight of her fingers on his skin, but this time it didn't feel like pressure. It felt like relief.

He looked down, lost in gray-blue eyes. Her soothing, safe gaze felt like a cocoon that he could wrap around that broken part of him. Perhaps even heal, which had never felt possible before.

Now she offered that, and in that striking moment he realized one fundamental fact. He loved her.

He nearly staggered beneath the weight of that realization. Love was something he hadn't truly believed in for a very long time. He had slowly been a convert to its existence as he watched his friends find it. But when it came to himself? He hadn't dared to dream there would be love in his future. Certainly he'd never thought he'd find it in such a short time, after such an intense and troubled exchange of lies and passion.

And yet here it was, in the form of the utterly beautiful, completely perfect woman who held his hand. A woman who in no way felt the same about him. Yesterday she had declared it once more, lamenting all she'd lost when they wed.

The pain of that fact, combined with the other, was almost unbearable.

She reached up and touched his cheek. "I see all those hurts, still alive in your eyes," she whispered. "And I wish there was some way to take it all away."

He leaned into her palm. Old hurts stung, yes. But it was the new one that burned. Boiled. Sliced like a knife.

"You are taking it away right now," he whispered.

"You and I are more alike than perhaps I ever knew," she said, her fingers stroking his jawline and sending shivers through him. "We have fought our whole lives to earn the love that should have been freely given. We have *both* felt like outsiders to our own existence."

He pressed his lips together. Yes, there was that. That common bond that now flowered between them. She was here with him now, after all. Looking up at him with sweetness and gentleness, with true caring.

Wasn't it possible that she could love him? Given time, if he worked at doing exactly what she suggested, earning her love...couldn't she?

"You are looking at me so closely," she said, her fingers dropping from his face. "I'm becoming a little nervous."

He pushed aside the thoughts in his mind. He would not share them. He would simply start today, now, to show her that he was worthy of her heart. That was all he could do. Woo his wife and try to make up for what he'd done in the past.

Even if she didn't know about it.

"You shouldn't be," he said, hoping his voice sounded calmer than he felt. "I was only pondering that despite our shared pains in our past, we handle them so differently."

"How so?" she asked, stepping away from him toward the

little playhouse. She leaned down and smiled as she peered into the window at the chair that sat half-broken in the middle of the dirty, rundown room.

"You flow with change," he said. "As elegantly as you dance or walk or move at all."

She blushed as she faced him. "You think I do?"

"I know you do. I've watched you. I stole everything you ever wanted." He bent his head. "And you glided into the future you didn't want with a grace and kindness that I certainly have not earned."

"It was a difficult situation," she said slowly. "For both of us. I will admit that I hated you at first, but you are quite frustrating, Hugh, for you make it impossible to hate you for long. And since I cannot hate you, and since this *is* the life I will lead, I feel the best choice is to make it a life I want. There are a good many things about it...about you...that make that easy."

He frowned. "I have not found that talent of optimism in the face of unwanted change. Where you are light, I seem to be dark."

Her expression softened, and she moved closer once more. She lifted her chin, examining his face closely. "Not always," she whispered.

His breath came short now, a combination of high emotion and a desire for her that never seemed to fade. He realized now that it never would. Touching her wasn't just about pleasure— in some ways it never had been. His body had craved what his mind would not accept until it was forced.

He wanted to be near her. He wanted to be connected with her. And when they made love, he was able to have that connection. She allowed it, and so he fed on it like he was starved.

Perhaps he had been. Until her.

"I need your light, Amelia," he murmured. "I never knew how much."

She was silent as she wound her arms around his neck, lifting up so her lips were close to his. "Then take it," she whispered in the moment before she kissed him.

His mind emptied of his troubles and his fears, replaced by his desire and his passion and the love that now flowed like a river through it all. He gathered her closer, pressing their bodies until it felt like they were one. That she was truly his, at least in the fantasy world they would now enter.

"I need—" he panted, unable to finish the sentence.

She nodded because she understood. It was all the acquiescence he required. He lifted her feet off the ground, continuing to kiss her as he placed her back to the smooth bark of a nearby sweet chestnut tree. Leaning against the hard surface, he cupped her backside, grinding her against him as he kissed her like it was the last time.

Or the first time. And it almost was. This was the first time he'd kissed her when he knew he loved her. That made it different. Sweet and special and desperate and needy.

She moaned against his mouth, lifting into him with as much hunger as what was stoked in his body. His hands shook as he pushed her skirt up, his breath caught as he slid his fingers along her skin. She opened her legs, her mouth dragging along his jaw as he unfastened the placard of his trousers.

He lifted, she opened and he slid inside. Home, because it was her, and now he understood how much that meant. Would always mean, even if she never felt the same way. He thrust into her, their foreheads touching as he took and took and took, marking her, marking himself, claiming even if he did not yet say it out loud, that he would be hers until his last breath left his lungs.

She began to moan her pleasure, her hands digging into his shoulders, and then her pussy rippled around him as she orgasmed. He thrust harder, dragging them both through her pleasure, but he had no control left. Not after today. He grunted as heated sensation ricocheted through him, and then he cried out as his seed pumped hard and hot into her clenching body.

Her mouth found his again and he drowned in her taste, never wanting to part himself from her. Knowing that he had to.

And knowing that once he did, the real work to win her would begin.

CHAPTER SEVENTEEN

Something had changed in Hugh. Amelia couldn't place it as she sat in the library, staring with unseeing eyes at the book in hand, but she felt it as strongly as if it were something palpable.

It had been two days since he took her to the playhouse in the woods and confessed the details of his childhood to her. And he had not been the same since. No, he wasn't entirely open with her, she knew he held back, but he was trying. He shared his thoughts, asked her about hers. He told her more and more about his life, including how he'd come to be in his large group of friends and what that meant to him. About his mother, his father, their loss, and the weight of carrying a title and of becoming what amounted to a father at such a young age.

She was beginning to know him, *truly* know him, and it encouraged her to be more open, herself. Passionate nights would give over to hours of whispered confidences and private jokes.

And her feelings for the man grew with every day they spent together. The life she led with him, which had seemed like such a horror a month ago, was now something…well, she didn't want to lose it. And she wondered what would change once they left for London the next morning.

The door to the library opened, and Amelia forced a smile as Lizzie entered the chamber.

"Hello, dearest," she said, tossing her novel aside. "Coming to find a book?"

Lizzie shook her head. "Return one," she said, and held up a slim volume in her hand. "I finished it last night." She placed it on the shelf and then came to sit beside Amelia. "I cannot believe how quickly ten days has flown by."

Amelia took her hands and squeezed them gently. "I know. It seems only yesterday that we arrived. I have adored my time here. I love that I get to return here again and again."

Lizzie frowned slightly. "But tomorrow you'll go. I hate that part."

"Then why not come with us?" Amelia pressed. "Oh, Lizzie, how I'd love to have you in London. We could have such fun, and I know Hugh would adore having you near. The Season is coming to an end, but we could introduce you in a small way and then you could join us for parties and balls. I would love having my dear sister at my side."

Lizzie turned her head, and Amelia saw the sparkle of tears in her bright eyes. She had pushed too hard, though she still had no idea why Lizzie was so opposed to taking her place in Society.

"I don't want you to think it's because of you or my brother," Lizzie whispered. "It isn't."

Amelia put an arm around her. "I know. I never thought that. But I cannot help but wonder why it is that London and Society in general are so frightening to you. I know you are shy and reserved, but we would be with you. And Hugh's friends have wonderful wives. You'd not be alone or forced to navigate your way without so many friends at your side."

"I *am* shy," Lizzie admitted. "I've never liked being out and about very much. But I always knew that I'd have to come out at some point. Have to overcome the failing that makes me want to hide from others. No, it's something…else that makes me hesitate."

Amelia searched her face. Lizzie was not good at hiding her feelings, not like Hugh. Now her emotions were very clear and very painful. Amelia could almost taste them, they hung so heavy in the air.

"What happened?" she whispered. "Won't you tell me if it might help?"

Lizzie worried her lip gently and then sighed. "You truly have become like a sister to me in the short time we've been acquainted," she began. "There is so much of me that wants to tell you the truth. Only—only I worry you will...not...not..."

"Not what? Understand?" Amelia encouraged.

Lizzie placed her head in her hands and her shoulders began to shake. "I fear you won't love me anymore if you knew. That you'll never look at me the same way again."

Amelia drew back at that statement. She had assumed Lizzie's reticence came from something minor, but this breakdown implied something far deeper and bigger and more painful than she'd ever guessed.

Something Lizzie really did need to talk about.

"Look at me," Amelia whispered. When Lizzie dared to do so, Amelia gently wiped tears from her cheeks. "I could *never* not love you, no matter what you tell me. I promise you that."

Lizzie smiled through her tears. "You make me believe you."

"Because it's true. Oh, Lizzie, I can see what a weight you've carried. If you would like to let me shoulder some small part of the load, I'm happy to do so. And if you're not ready, I respect that, as well."

Lizzie got up and walked across the room, her expressive face filled with pensive worry. Amelia forced herself to remain in her place, allowing her friend to work through her feelings on her own.

At last, Lizzie turned and said, "There was...a man."

Amelia caught her breath. Lizzie was so sweet, so innocent, it was hard to believe she would have involved herself with someone. But she kept the shock from her face and nodded. "I see."

"He lived in the village," Lizzie continued. "He seemed so kind. We met at a little soiree at the meeting hall and he asked me to dance. When I said I didn't like to dance, he took me for a walk instead, and it was…"

"Very romantic," Amelia said when Lizzie did not seem capable of continuing.

Lizzie nodded. "When I look back now, I suppose I can see that it was part of some trap he was setting. He had studied me, I think, determining my personality so he would know how to best s-seduce me."

Lizzie's cheeks flamed and Amelia got up, wanting desperately to comfort her. But she stayed in place and did not push, not yet. "That is what he did?"

"Well, he asked me to marry him. Hugh had been gone and I was hesitant. I knew this man had so little to recommend him, at least in my brother's eyes. And he said the same, that the great Duke of Brighthollow would never accept him or allow him the chance to prove his worth."

Amelia wrinkled her brow. "That does not sound like a man with your best interest at heart."

"No. But I thought myself in love with him by then. Foolishly, it seems. He convinced me that if we ran away, Hugh would have to agree to our union and that one day this man would prove his worth."

"Oh dear," Amelia breathed.

"I was so silly." Lizzie balled her hands into fists at her sides. "Sixteen and wanting so much to be loved that I agreed. I convinced myself that he would love me and that Hugh would understand some day."

"You ran away with him?" Amelia gasped, thinking of Hugh and his deep love for his sister. He must have been terrified when he found out.

"I did, expecting we would marry within hours and make it proper, or at least less scandalous. But we didn't. Hours passed and he started talking to me about Scotland, Gretna Green."

"Four days from here?" Amelia said, her mouth dropped open in shock.

"Yes. I was horrified, for I knew what people would say if

they discovered I'd spent three nights alone with the man before I married him. But he insisted it was best."

"And it was too late to escape," Amelia said.

A nod was her reply. "I felt increasingly that it was. The first night we stopped along the road, he only kissed me. I...liked it enough, I suppose. He was forceful and didn't seem to care that I didn't know what I was doing." She shuddered. "By the second night we stopped, he told me we were practically married already. That we would be soon enough. He convinced me to—"

Lizzie's face was almost purple with humiliation now, and Amelia caught her hand at last. "I understand. I understand what you did."

"I had such romantic notions," Lizzie sighed after she had gathered herself enough to speak. "He wasn't cruel, but I didn't...like it. And when it was done, he wouldn't even hold me."

Amelia shut her eyes, thinking back to her own wedding night. To how gentle Hugh had been, how giving and caring. And how he had been just the same every night since. What they shared in their bed was not cheap, it was not cruel. It had bonded them physically and helped her see him as more than some ogre who had stolen the life she thought she wanted.

And Lizzie had not experienced that same care. Amelia had never hated someone more, despite not knowing this man's identity.

"I'm so sorry," Amelia whispered.

"I knew I'd done the wrong thing and I wanted so badly for Hugh to come." Lizzie covered her face. "But I couldn't leave. I'd surrendered my innocence, I *had* to marry him. On the third night he stopped just before the border of Scotland. And then...Hugh was there. He swept in like a knight in shining armor, and I don't know what he ultimately did to make that man go away, but he did it. And Hugh took me home."

Amelia's eyes filled with tears, not just for what Lizzie had been through and how it had changed her, but for Hugh, as well.

She knew, both from observation and through their conversations, how important his sister was to him. His heart must have broken to know what she had endured. It certainly explained his protectiveness of her.

"He was so kind," Lizzie mused. "He could have railed at me all the way home, for I deserved it after the trouble I caused. I almost wanted him to. But he never did. Not even once. He comforted me and allowed me space to grieve what I'd done. When I tried to apologize, he wouldn't hear it, even though I know in my heart that he must have sacrificed a great deal of money to protect me."

"But then, I know you wouldn't expect anything less of him," Amelia said. "He's Hugh, after all."

"Yes. He is that. So now you know why I am so opposed to coming out. And London terrifies me. What if that man is there? Or what if there is another man like him and my nature is to be so foolish? Or what if people find out what I did?"

"Oh, darling, listen to yourself," Amelia said gently, in order to stop the wildness that was building in Lizzie's voice. "What if, what if, what if…you could run yourself ragged with all those worst possibilities. And *what if* something wonderful happens to you instead?"

"I can't even picture something wonderful anymore," Lizzie whispered.

Amelia wiped at a tear, hurt by the idea that this sweet, lovely girl was so traumatized that only horrible futures could exist in her head. She and Hugh would have to work on that together, ease her back into the world and protect her as she got her confidence back.

She blinked. Together. It was so easy to see them as a unit now. Two halves of a whole, with the same desires and goals.

She shook off those thoughts. "If you cannot picture it, let me," she said. "*What if* you make new friends? Hugh's club members have married and their wives are the sweetest, most wonderful women I have ever met. I assure you, they will greet you with open arms."

Lizzie shifted. "I hadn't thought of that. I do know Meg and Charlotte. They were always so kind to me when I was a little girl."

"Of course they would be," Amelia said. "They're both divine. And the rest are just as welcoming and good. You'll have them as your base, and I'm certain you'll meet many other friends along with them."

Lizzie's face had brightened considerably, and she nodded. "Very well, that doesn't sound very bad."

Amelia took that as encouragement and continued, "And what if you meet some delightful man?" Lizzie caught her breath, and Amelia raised a hand to calm her. "I'm not talking about this Season or next. You're young and you should enjoy yourself before you settle yourself into whatever your future entails. But I'm talking about in a few years. What if you meet someone who is handsome and kind, someone who challenges you in the best ways and makes you feel...feel..."

She trailed off, for she realized she was talking about Hugh.

"Amelia, how will he make me feel?" Lizzie asked, dragging her back to the present.

Amelia stared at her, and then the words fell from her mouth. "Like you are home. Home wherever you are with him."

Lizzie blinked. "There could be such a man?"

"I know there is," Amelia said. "I know there is for you."

"I wish I knew so strongly," Lizzie said.

"You'll just have to trust me," Amelia replied, still unsteady from the depth of her feelings being revealed in this conversation. "One final thing to consider, my dear. *What if* your future is not written in stone, unless you choose to lock yourself up here forever in penance for what some heartless bastard did to you?"

Lizzie stared at her, shock on her face. "I-I hadn't thought of it that way. Hugh has never pushed me to do it."

"Of course he hasn't. He is your protector. He'll never make you do anything you don't want to do. Nor will I, but I want you to think about it. Come with us. Enjoy the end of the Season, not in an earthshattering way, but in a small way. It's a first step, you don't have to take any of the others just yet."

"A first step," Lizzie repeated. "I suppose that isn't as terrifying as when I think of everything that comes after that first step."

"And I'll be with you all the way," Amelia reminded her.

Lizzie clasped her hands together. "I'll think about it for an hour or two. And then I'll let you know."

"Good," Amelia said, leaning forward to press a kiss to her cheek. "Whatever you decide, I will support you."

Lizzie caught Amelia's hands as she began to move away, and her pale blue eyes were bright with tears. "I'm so glad you married my brother. I'm so happy you're my sister now and forever."

Amelia's throat was thick. She had never had a true family, and it had been a painful thing for her. But now, as she stroked a tear away from Lizzie's cheek, she felt exactly as she had described to her. Like she was home.

And that was not something she might have found if she had married Aaron Walters as she'd once thought she wanted.

"I'm glad, too," she said.

Lizzie squeezed her hand and slid from the room. Amelia stood alone for a moment, and then she hurried from the library and down the long, winding halls toward Hugh's study. Right now she needed to see him. Touch him. Comfort him and let herself be comforted.

She pushed the door open without knocking and found him seated at his large, mahogany desk. He had a quill in hand and he was bent over a ledger, ticking off boxes in a seemingly endless sea of columns. His gaze was very focused and his mouth drawn down in a stern frown.

She froze at the sight. He had smiled so little when she first met him, it had been easy to cast him as a villain. Cold and calculating. But now she understood him better. The man she had married was a serious person, yes. A past where he'd been forced to hide any imperfection and a youth stolen by sudden responsibility had made him so.

But that only made him stronger. He had been through so much and come out the kind of man who would do anything for those he loved. And since he didn't smile often, when she was able to coax a smile to his lips, that made it more of a triumph.

She saw her life laid out before her in an instant. A life where she would never want for anything, thanks to this man. A life where her mission would be to make his days and nights easier. To love who he loved with the same fierceness he did.

And that sounded like heaven.

"Did you come to gawk at me or talk?" he said, glancing up from the ledger with one of those rare and wicked smiles.

She laughed a little and then reached back to close the door. "I was distracted by gawking, I admit. There is much to gawk at."

He arched a brow and slowly pushed from the desk to his full height, tracking her every move as she came across the room to him. "I like where this is going," he drawled.

She reached him, looking up into his dark eyes. Seeing the pain he always carried with him and understanding it all the more after today. She let out her breath in a shuddering sigh and then wrapped her arms around him, holding him tight as she smoothed her hand over his back gently.

His arms came around her after a beat of hesitation and he rested his chin on the crown of her head. For a moment they stood like that, bound in a new way.

"Not that I'm complaining," he said, his voice muffled in her hair. "But what brought this on?"

She pulled away a fraction and looked up at him once more. "I know about Lizzie, Hugh. I know everything."

CHAPTER EIGHTEEN

Hugh jerked from the warm and comforting circle of Amelia's embrace and staggered back across the room in horror. "What?"

Her eyes went wide and confused at his powerful reaction. "All is well, Hugh—I do not judge her for it, nor you."

He stared. Did not judge him? How could that be possible when he had deceived her about this very subject?

And then he realized how. Lizzie might have told her something about what had happened to her...

But she hadn't given Amelia the name of her betrayer.

"She told you about *him*," he whispered, his voice sounding harsh in the quiet room.

"She did. Oh, Hugh, I have never hated another person so much in my life. Your sister is so sweet and so innocent...that some bastard would take advantage in order to access her fortune is beastly."

He nodded, hardly able to breathe. "Y-yes," he finally stammered. "She did not say his name to you?"

Amelia shook her head. "No, she did not."

Hugh caught his breath. He had been lying to this woman, his wife, his love for weeks now. And he'd never wanted to confess what he'd done more than in this unique opportunity.

"Amelia," he began, shaking from the raw power of his terror at how she would react.

She grabbed for his hand, her warmth seeping into every

part of him. "No, Hugh, don't. Don't tell me."

"Why?" he asked.

"Because the fact that she would trust me with such a devastating story means a great deal to me. One day she may wish to give me even more details, and I will be open to hearing them. But in the end, it is her story to share, not mine to investigate or yours to reveal on her behalf."

He shifted. She was right in one way. In another, he knew so much more than she did. If he told her now, it could destroy them. But he feared if he waited for the truth to come out on some distant day, it would guarantee she would be broken by it.

"Please," she repeated. "I see how much you want to tell me, but wait. Wait a while and let's see how she does. I came here not to talk about her experience, but yours. You must have been devastated."

He jerked out a nod. "Yes," he whispered, taken back to that horrible day when he'd discovered Lizzie had run off with a bastard of the highest order. "I was frantic."

"She told me you chased after her, rescued her like a knight in shining armor." She smiled.

He shook his head. "Not soon enough."

She held his hand tighter. "Yes, she told me that part, too. I hate that she was used in that way."

Hugh closed his eyes, conjuring the perfect image of Lizzie when he'd burst into the cottage along the road. Her glassy-eyed expression, her sadness that she had been compromised, was so obvious. So painful.

"I wanted to tear him apart," he growled, his rage renewed. "I wanted to destroy him down to his very elements. But I couldn't."

"I assume he had told others his plan. If he died, they would make sure everyone knew *why* you had torn him apart," Amelia said softly.

Hugh looked at her. She was staring at him with such understanding. He didn't deserve it. Not in the slightest. And yet she gave so freely. She had from the very beginning. Her body, her gentle spirit, her light into his darkness.

"Yes," he choked out. "If there is one thing that man knows, it is how to protect himself. If I moved on him, he would make sure everyone knew my sister was ruined. If I hurt him, the same. The only way out was to pay him. A horrible, ugly, obscene payment that then allowed him to look like he belonged in good Society. And I could do nothing." He dropped his head. "I hate myself for it and for the consequences it brought to bear."

She reached for him again, sliding her arms around his waist and resting her head on his chest. "You have suffered, I can see. And I assume alone."

He nodded. "There was no way to explain my upset without revealing Lizzie's secret. I couldn't tell anyone. It was only recently that I said something to Lucas and Diana."

She hugged him tighter. "And now me."

He smoothed his hands over the silky softness of her dark hair, and the feel of it soothed him a fraction. "Yes," he whispered. "And now you."

She gazed up at him. "Hugh, look at me. You are a good brother. She is lucky to have you."

"I had one job in this world and it was to protect her. I failed."

"*That* is your father talking," she said, her gaze soft and filled with empathy and understanding. "Telling you there is only one path to success. Lizzie is alive. She is here with you, not married off to some cruel bastard who would use her. And she still has a future laid out in front of her. You have *not* failed. What happened wasn't your fault."

She leaned up and he met her lips halfway. She was gentle, as if he was delicate or needed *her* protection. And he did. In that moment, it felt like this wonderful woman was all that held him up. So he let her, clinging to her as all those old fears and heartbreaks washed over him and tugged him into a hundred pieces.

At last she drew away and smiled up at him. And once again, he knew that he had to tell her the truth. When she offered him such respite, to lie would not be fair.

"Amelia," he began, holding her closer so that he would remember what her arms felt like if his confession made her flee.

"Yes?"

"I need to tell you—"

He didn't get to finish the sentence. Before he could, the door to the study opened and Lizzie stepped inside. She blushed as she saw them in each other's arms and turned away with a gasp. "Oh, I'm so sorry," she said, her gaze down. "I'm so sorry."

Amelia extracted herself from his embrace gently and moved to her. "No need to apologize, my dear. Your brother and I were just having a talk. What is it?"

"I know I said I needed an hour or two to consider your thoughts," Lizzie said, lifting her gaze to Amelia at last. "But I've come to a decision."

"A decision?" he repeated. "What were you deciding?"

Amelia turned on him with a warm smile. "Lizzie and I were talking earlier about her going back to London with us tomorrow, rather than staying here."

He could not control the shock that flowed over his face. Lizzie had been adamant about not wanting anything to do with a future that included London. Nothing he'd said had budged her from her position, and eventually he had given up, hoping time would soften her.

Instead, it was ten days in the company of Amelia that did it. It seemed she brought light to both their lives.

"Yes," Lizzie said, watching him carefully. "I realize I have been reticent."

He nodded. "You have, though I never judged you for that."

"Of course you didn't. You're Hugh." She exchanged a look with Amelia like that was some kind of private joke between them, and his wife smiled in return. "But I also realize how much it worries you that I will not go. So…" She drew a long breath. "I think I *will* accompany you."

Amelia rushed forward and hugged his sister as she gushed,

"Oh, that is wonderful, darling! I'm so pleased that you'll come with us. We'll have such a time together."

Hugh saw Lizzie's hesitance, but also her determination to overcome her fears. She had so much more strength than she believed. He could only hope she'd one day see it.

"I will go and start the arrangements," Amelia said, "and send word ahead of us so that your chamber in London is prepared." She glanced at the siblings with a bright smile. "I'm so very happy."

She darted from the room, calling out for Masters as her voice faded down the hallway. Hugh smiled at Lizzie now that they were alone.

"Are *you* happy?" he asked. "You aren't just doing this to please Amelia or to please me, are you?"

Lizzie sighed. "Wanting to please Amelia has become a very large drive for me."

It was the same for him, though perhaps in very different ways. "But?"

"But I know it's time," Lizzie said with a shrug. "And Amelia said some things that helped me see that I cannot live my life in fear, can I?"

"No, I would not like to see you do that," he said. "She says you told her about...about Walters."

Lizzie dropped her gaze before she nodded slowly. "I did. I hope you aren't angry. I just feel so close to her, and it was so nice to be able to tell a friend...a sister. Especially since she was so kind about it."

"I could never be angry with you about it, Lizzie. As Amelia said to me earlier, it is your story to tell or not tell as you see fit. That you trust and like my wife enough to share it warms my heart. It makes me think that our family could be stronger than ever now that Amelia is in it."

Lizzie nodded swiftly. "Oh yes, I feel the same way. I adore her, Hugh. And not just because she is kind and funny and so very smart. I like her because of what I see in you when you're together."

"And what is that?"

"It's hard to explain." Lizzie paced the room. "It's almost like a weight gets lifted from you when she comes into your orbit. You smile more and you watch her like she's the most important thing in the world. You're...*happy*."

He bent his head. That was the most apt description she could have said to describe how he felt when he looked at Amelia. "I *am* happy," he said. "I have much work to do. I have...things to tell her that may mar our happiness, but it must be done. It must be."

"Things?" Lizzie asked with concern. "Such as?"

He patted her hand. "Nothing to trouble yourself over, I promise. But I do want to ask you one thing."

She nodded. "Anything in the world, you know that."

"Yes, I do. When you told Amelia about Walters, you didn't tell her his name."

Lizzie tensed. "No. I hate to say it. It's like poison on my lips."

He frowned. "I'm sorry, so sorry. But will you...will you not tell her?"

She wrinkled her brow. "Wh-why?"

He sighed. If he said the truth to Lizzie, it would hurt her almost as much as it would hurt Amelia. And he owed his wife the truth first, at any rate. "I'll explain another time. For now, please just trust that it will be better if I tell her. I'll do it once we're settled back in London. I have so much to say once that day comes."

Lizzie seemed to consider the request for a moment, but then she nodded. "Of course, Hugh. If you think it would be better, I leave it to you to tell her whatever you think is important. I don't pretend to understand, but I trust you."

He flinched. Trust him? She'd done that and he had failed her. He was beginning to think Amelia might trust him, too, and he was going to have to tell her about all the lies. Ones that would tear her apart and maybe pull them away from each other in the process.

But he owed her the truth. About his heart, about his past, and about everything he had withheld in an attempt to save himself. And once all those things were on the table, then at least he would know he was the kind of man she deserved.

CHAPTER NINETEEN

Amelia had always liked London. Her father had insisted they spend most of their time in the city as she was growing up, so she enjoyed the hustle and bustle, the people and the noise. But as they turned into the drive of Hugh's city estate a few days later, she felt less enthusiastic to be in Town than she normally would have.

It wasn't that their trip had been unpleasant. With Lizzie in the carriage with them, their threesome had been jolly, indeed. She loved watching Hugh as he interacted with his sister. His gentleness and patience made her think about him as a father, and that idea thrilled her beyond measure, for she'd always wanted a large family.

They'd played games, read out loud to each other and had some good talks. And at night, at roadside inns? Well, Hugh had been happy to remind her how lovely it was to be alone together, too.

But now she thought of Brighthollow and the wonderful time she'd had on the estate. Things would change in London. Hugh would have matters to attend to and so would she. That bubble of privacy and contentment was gone, and she would have to navigate her way in her marriage here in this more complicated world.

Still, she smiled as the carriage stopped. Hugh helped his sister out first and then her. He held her hand a little too long as they faced the pretty brick façade of the estate.

"Welcome home, Your Grace," he murmured low. "I hope you will like this place a little more now than when we left it." She smiled, for it was like he'd read her mind and her worries. His low tone soothed her immediately. It was funny how he could do that.

"I already do," she reassured him as she slid her hand into the crook of his elbow and squeezed gently. "I cannot wait to see what pleasures London brings us."

They entered the foyer and he leaned in. "Neither can I." As he released her, he let his hand glide down her back and tap her backside very lightly. She jolted at the inappropriate and utterly intoxicating touch and glared at him. Damnable man and his easy seduction. Now all she could think about was that chamber upstairs, and she couldn't go up and drag him there until she finished with...

"Your Graces and Lady Elizabeth!" Murphy gushed as he took coats and motioned for servants to take them away. "How wonderful to have you home. You've several messages, and supper will be ready in less than an hour if you're of a mind to rest."

"Oh, I could certainly use a moment," Lizzie said with a girlish laugh. "And I cannot wait to see my old chamber. Is it just the same, Murphy?"

He smiled at her. "Just the same, my lady. We did not dare move a thing in the hopes you would return soon."

Lizzie's face lit up and she clapped her hands together. In that moment, there was no doubt of her youth, and Amelia smiled. She liked seeing Hugh's sister so bright and excited and carefree. This was what Amelia wanted for her and would fight to make sure she had during their time in London.

"Go on up then, Lizzie," Hugh said. "Reacquaint yourself with our home."

"I will. And I won't be late for supper. I want to plan every moment of our walk in the park tomorrow with Amelia." She leaned and kissed Amelia's cheek before she scrambled up the stairs, calling out her maid's name with every exuberant step.

"Being here looks to be good for her," Amelia mused as Murphy bowed away and left them alone a moment.

Hugh smiled as he reached out to cup her cheek. "Being with you is good for her. Thank you for being so kind to her. And to me. You've brought new life to us both."

Amelia's lips parted at those sweet words and the warm expression on his handsome face as he said them. "It's easy to be kind to her," she said with a shrug that belied how important this moment was to her.

"I may be more difficult, but I appreciate it nonetheless. I hope one day I will even deserve it." He ducked his head and brushed his lips to hers briefly. Far too briefly. Then he backed away. "Murphy will leave my messages in my study—I think I'll take the time before supper to review them. Yours will likely be in your chamber before we choose a room to transform into your own study. I'll see you later."

She watched him go, her heart throbbing a bit too hard, a bit too loud. Telling her things that she still struggled to hear. How could she feel so drawn to this man when she'd truly believed herself in love with another just over a month before? What did that say about her and her fickle nature?

"Perhaps it only says you *thought* you wanted boyish sweetness and in fact you needed something very different," she muttered as she moved up the stairs toward their chamber and whatever peace she might find there.

But she knew it might not be any peace at all, for her heart fluttered and thoughts of her husband would likely plague her until they met again at supper.

Amelia drew a deep breath of cleansing air as she and Lizzie walked through the park together the next day. Normally such exercise cleared her mind, but today she was distracted by thoughts of…well, of a great many things. Chief amongst them was her husband. Hugh was so changed. That struck her every time she spent a moment with him. Kinder, softer, sweeter and so much more seductive.

She shivered as she thought of how he'd made love to her last night and then held her in his arms. She'd never wanted to leave.

"You are woolgathering again," Lizzie giggled as they rounded a bend in the path.

Amelia shook off the troubling thoughts. "I am. It must be the travel that is making my mind wander."

"Are you *certain* that is all it is?"

Amelia faced her with a forced laugh. "Of course, what else would it be?"

"Nothing except for your mooning over my brother day and night." Lizzie blushed. "Perhaps I should have stayed back in Brighthollow to allow you two to be newlyweds."

"Don't be silly. We love that you are here with us."

"It's obvious you like being around him very much."

Amelia wrinkled her brow at the uncertain tone of Lizzie's voice. "Yes," she said, drawing out the word slightly. "He is good company."

"I mean you *like being around him*," Lizzie repeated, her gaze darting away.

Amelia jerked in surprise, for she understood the meaning that was meant in those innocuous words. "Ah, I see. Lizzie, though it would be very inappropriate to speak to you about my...private relationship with your brother, I do think that you should know what we share is something you can still have. I hope you won't judge your future by one bad experience from your past. With the right man everything can be...can be...perfect."

She said the last word in a whisper, for it struck her how right that word was. *Perfect* was how she would describe the physical connection between herself and Hugh. And as he let his walls come down and showed her more and more of his true self, their time outside the bedroom was also becoming more perfect.

"Amelia, Lizzie!"

The two turned, and Amelia couldn't help but smile. There, at the top of the hill, were Meg, the Duchess of Crestwood, and Charlotte, the Duchess of Donburrow. They'd stood from a picnic blanket where their young children were still playing, and were waving.

"You say you know both Meg and Charlotte, yes?" Amelia asked as they started up the hill together.

Lizzie nodded with enthusiasm. "Oh, yes. They are sisters of men in the duke club, just as I am. Though they were both so much older than I was, they both kindly included me in their circle back when I was a girl."

Amelia smiled. Of course they would, for she couldn't picture either lovely woman being anything but kind, no matter their age. "Good afternoon, ladies!" she said as they reached them.

Hugs were exchanged and Amelia laughed as both women cooed over how tall and beautiful Lizzie was becoming. It was clear she would have champions of the highest caliber as she made her way in Society, and that pleased Amelia greatly. Together they could all make her transition easy.

"And look at the bride," Charlotte said, reaching for Amelia's hand. "The country has done you wonders—you practically glow."

Amelia swallowed hard as Meg examined her more closely. "You do look wonderful, Amelia. I wonder *whatever* could be making you so happy?"

They laughed good-naturedly, and Amelia did the same, despite the heat that flooded her cheeks at their teasing. And at her own thoughts about Hugh, which rushed back, louder and more confusing and unbalancing as ever.

"Sit with us," Meg said, patting the blanket. "We so need to catch up, Lizzie—we have not seen you in an age."

Lizzie glanced at Amelia and, when she nodded, happily took a place on the blanket with the other two. Amelia remained standing, trying to calm her restless, throbbing heart.

"I could actually use a bit of air," she said. "A little walk to the edge of the lake and back. But then I will sit and we'll have a lovely, long chat together."

The three women glanced up, and she saw concern on all their faces. Meg was gentle as she said, "Of course. Travel can be quite overwhelming. Take a moment and we will be here waiting."

Amelia squeezed Lizzie's shoulder, then turned and made her way back to the path. Just over the next rise was the lake's edge, and she followed the lane there. She stood near the water, drawing deep breaths as she tried to control her wild emotions.

Emotions that were building up inside of her. Telling her one thing and one thing only: that she was in love with Hugh. And it was a much deeper and more powerful feeling than anything she had felt for Aaron Walters.

"Amelia?"

She froze as her name was said by the voice of the very man who had just come into her mind. She turned and found Walters standing before her, watching her intently.

She stared, still uncertain if this was some odd conjuring from her errant mind. And also taken aback by his appearance. He looked the same, of course, as he had when she'd left his home just two weeks before. He held a hat in his hand, but every hair on his head was perfectly in place. His bright eyes were the same. He was still tall and absolutely handsome.

But when she looked at him, she felt...nothing. He seemed a boy to her now, shifting around as he cast side glances at her. Not like Hugh, who had always held her gaze steady. Who always made her feel like he was certain at all times.

"M-Mr. Walters," she stammered at last when she realized she had not yet responded to his greeting. "What a surprise to see you here."

The shy smile that had been on his face faded and something harder set his jaw. "Mr. Walters," he repeated. "Is that what *he* would force you to call me?"

His poisonous tone should not have been surprising to her.

After all, her husband had destroyed Aaron's hopes weeks ago, and he believed that it had been done just to hurt him. Still, hearing that venom raised her hackles and made her wish to defend Hugh.

"No," she said. "I simply believe it would be inappropriate for me to be so familiar as to call you by your first name now."

He folded his arms. "Very well, *Your Grace.*"

He stared at her, unblinking, and she shifted with growing discomfort. What had Hugh said to her all those weeks ago? That Aaron was not a good person? She'd never pressed him on that topic since. At first because she had been determined not to believe him. Then because she had been separated from Walters. There had seemed no point to finding out why her husband didn't like him when she was trying to make the best of the situation.

Right now she wished she knew. Wished she'd pressed.

"You look well," she said, glancing past him up toward the hill where Charlotte and Meg were sitting with Lizzie. If she needed help, would they hear her cry? And why did she feel she needed to know that answer all of a sudden?

He looked down at himself and his lips thinned. "I am a survivor. It is how I am made." She frowned at that odd description, and the frown deepened when he stepped closer. The hard edge left his face and voice, and the boyishness returned, like it was a lever he could turn off and on. "You must be miserable."

Amelia was once again put off by his familiarity and drive to corner her into speaking ill of Hugh. Perhaps he meant it as a comfort, perhaps he was unhappy so he wanted to commiserate. But she had no desire to participate. Not right now when she was able to admit to herself that she had fallen in love with her husband.

"No," she said, trying to make her tone gentle but firm. "I'm not. Of course, our beginning was not ideal, but there is no misery. If you have worried about me during the time I was away, you needn't trouble yourself further on that score."

His eyebrows lifted. "I see." Once again boyishness was replaced by darker things. Anger. Rage. But not pain. "Does that mean you never loved me at all, *Amelia?*" He emphasized her given name, and it suddenly felt like a slur he hurled.

She took a step away from him. "It will only hurt us both to talk about this, Mr. Walters." His cheek twitched and she sighed. "Aaron. Whatever was in our past, it is over now. We must adapt and move forward. I'm certain there is much happiness to come for us both. Now I think I should go. Good day."

She turned to walk away, but to her shock, he caught her arm. His fingers dug into her flesh as he pivoted her back, dragging her closer.

"He will convince you he cares for you," he hissed, spittle flying from his mouth. "But he will discard you. *That* is his game. Be intelligent enough not to fall for it."

Amelia jerked her arm away and lifted her hand to rub the red marks he had left on the flesh. "You forget yourself, sir," she said. "Good day."

She marched away, and this time he allowed her retreat, but tears had leapt to her eyes at his words. They were so cold, so cruel and...and they reflected her own fears. What if Hugh's attention toward her *was* something that was fleeting? He had not declared any deeper feeling toward her, never even hinted at it. So even if she felt as she did, in the end there might be no future.

She started up the hill toward the others, but as she did, she saw Lizzie standing a few feet in front of her. She had been so upset by her encounter with Aaron, she hadn't even noticed Lizzie coming down.

Now she stared at Lizzie's face. It was pale, her lips trembling and her hands shaking at her sides as she gazed straight ahead. Amelia's stomach dropped. She hoped Lizzie had not seen her interaction with Aaron and misread the situation. It would be so difficult to explain to the girl, and Hugh would certainly not be happy if he knew she'd met with her former fiancé.

"Lizzie," she said as she got closer. "I didn't see you coming."

Lizzie never looked at her, just continued to stare at where Amelia and Aaron had been talking. Amelia glanced over her shoulder, but Aaron had left.

"Lizzie?" she repeated. "What is it?"

Lizzie finally looked at her, and her eyes were wide and wild. Tears gathered in her eyes. "Why?" she asked. "Why would you talk to him?"

Amelia swallowed hard and tried to remain calm in the face of Lizzie's deep upset. "Whatever you think you saw, it isn't what you believe," she began, hoping to convince her sister-in-law before the moment escalated into something worse.

"Hugh said you didn't know who he was," Lizzie said, seemingly oblivious to Amelia's words. "He said not to tell you his name. But you know it, obviously you know it."

Amelia blinked as her terror was replaced by confusion. "I-I don't understand, Lizzie. What are you talking about?"

Lizzie caught Amelia's hands, and the tears that had sparkled in her eyes began to stream down her cheeks. "That is the man who seduced me," she choked out.

Amelia's mouth dropped open in shock. "What? No, you must be mistaken. Perhaps he only looked like that other man."

"I would know Aaron Walters from a mile away," Lizzie sobbed. "He took my innocence and I never wanted to see him again."

CHAPTER TWENTY

Hugh lifted a glass and saluted Diana and Lucas as they sat in their parlor together. Once they'd all taken a sip, Diana smiled at him. A knowing smile.

"You seem very happy," she said with a sly look toward Lucas.

Hugh set his own drink aside with a shake of his head. "Ah, am I that obvious? Yes, I am happy. Not content, but happy."

"Not content?" Lucas repeated. "Why is that?"

Hugh let out a long breath. This would be the first time he said these words out loud and it seemed to require courage to do so. But it was good practice, at any rate, for his plans for later.

"I have…fallen in love with Amelia," he said. The words rang in the air around him and felt more true and right than even in his own mind.

Diana clasped her hands together and then pivoted to Lucas on the settee, where they sat together. "Oh, it is just as I told you. Isn't it? Isn't it?"

Lucas laughed as he settled a hand on her knee. "I never doubted you—you are ten times more clever than I am." He turned his attention to Hugh. "In love with her, eh? I cannot say I'm unhappy this has happened. She seems a lovely woman and you will make her very happy."

At that, Hugh's smile fell and the joy he felt at the confession of his heart faded. "That is the part that keeps me from being content."

"You don't know her heart?" Diana said softly.

He shook his head. "No, I don't. We are connected, I know that to be true. There is much between us that makes me thinks she could care. But when I forced her to be my bride, she believed herself in love with someone else. So that is one thing."

Lucas nodded. "I can imagine that would weigh on a man's heart."

Hugh sighed. "Worse than that, she has no idea the lengths I went to in order to secure our marriage. The lies I told. Or the connection between Walters and my own sister."

Diana's lips parted. "You haven't told her?"

"At first it was because I knew she wouldn't believe me," he explained. "She was determined to think the worst of me. And I didn't trust her. Lizzie's secrets are so delicate, I couldn't tell a stranger, even one who shared my bed and my title and my name. As I grew to know her better, to care for her more, I...was...afraid. I *am* afraid."

"That you'll lose her," Lucas said.

Hugh nodded. "Yes. The longer I wait, the more I fear that will be true. Lizzie even confessed her past to Amelia, who has become my sister's champion, but I was not able to tell her that *Walters* is the man she despises so deeply. Now that we're back in London, I intend to do so."

Diana let out her breath. "You should. And sooner rather than later. She may not be happy with you about what you withheld and the lies you told, but it will be better than if she were to discover the truth some other way."

He bent his head. "I imagine her reaction and it chills me to my very bones."

Lucas reached out and tangled his fingers with Diana's. He met Hugh's gaze evenly. "She may well react poorly. I think she's earned that, even. But at least you will have given her your whole heart along with the truth. She is your wife, Brighthollow. You'll have the rest of your life to make it up to her."

"That is my plan," Hugh sighed. "To win back her trust and earn her love with every day of the rest of my life."

"Well, if you love her, it will be worth it," Lucas said. "It seems you've already realized that, though."

Hugh pictured the past two weeks with Amelia. How she had so easily stepped into his life, changing him for the better with every touch and word and deed. He knew he needed that in his life as much as he needed food or breath.

"At any rate, that leads me to a far less pleasant subject. You sent word that you wanted to see me about Aaron Walters."

Lucas's expression hardened and he released Diana's hand as he got to his feet and paced away from them both. "Yes," he said. "I spent the time since you wed and left the city looking into this man. I still have contacts in the War Department, and Diana has been a great help."

Hugh glanced at her in thanks. It was a wonderful thing, really, what good partners his friends were. He longed to find a way to share the same trust and connection with Amelia someday.

"Was there anything to uncover?" he asked.

Lucas set his jaw. "He's involved in a great many things, I fear. I've followed trails that connect him with robbery and moving money from one bad debt to another to keep ahead of prison. But he's cunning—those trails implicate him, but might not be enough to make him go away. I was digging deeper and I…I found something that could."

Hugh stared in shock at his friends. He'd seen Walters as merely a mercenary bastard with a collection of bad friends. This was all far more serious, indeed. "What is that?"

Diana leaned closer. "Walters was not always called by that name," she said. "Three years ago he was called Stephen Monroe and he lived in a rookery in the West End. He was known for his card manipulations. His pickpocketing."

"And you think that might end him in prison?" Hugh asked.

"No." Diana's voice shook. "He married a girl above his station. He probably seduced her the same way he did your sister, the same way he did Amelia. He found her because she was vulnerable, wanted love, and he became what she desired. When they married, it became clear she had less money than he'd thought."

Hugh gritted his teeth. "Bigamy then, that would be the charge? Since he intended to marry my sister and Amelia when he was still wed?"

"He wasn't still wed," Lucas said. "He killed his first wife."

Hugh pushed to his feet and staggered back in horror. "Killed?"

"Steady." Diana got up and reached out to catch his hand. "Yes, there is a great deal of evidence that he murdered her when she was no longer of use to him. He was about to be arrested when he disappeared. Soon after that, he became Walters."

Hugh's stomach turned as he thought of his sister alone with the bastard for days, in more mortal danger than he had even believed. And Amelia—Amelia who had wished to marry the man. Would he have cut her down eventually too?

"Why would he go so far?" he whispered.

Lucas shook his head. "Because he has no scruples. People are tools to him. They provide what he needs and he discards them. He's left a trail of associates to pay for their crimes, a large number of broken-hearted women he has seduced and stolen from. And then…this poor young woman."

"He wanted my sister." Hugh trembled with every word. "He wanted my wife. For their fortunes. I thwarted him both times. I must protect them, in case he decides to keep his eye on them, or exact some kind of revenge."

"I agree," Lucas said. "I am ready to arrange a guard for both women immediately. I have good men for the position. They can be at your home as early as tomorrow morning."

"Do it," Hugh said, his mind reeling. "In the meantime, I must go to them. Now, to determine they are safe. And I must tell Amelia the truth. It is about more than my betrayal now. This is about her safety."

Lucas nodded, and he and Diana followed Hugh to the door. "I'll come call later tonight," Lucas said. "I can provide more information if Amelia requires it. And Diana can be a shoulder to lean on if she's upset."

"Thank you for your help. I'll need it all before this is done."

Hugh tipped his head and then rushed out to his waiting horse. As he thundered through the gate and onto the busy street, his mind reeled and his heart throbbed. After weeks avoiding the pain the truth would cause, now there was even more at stake.

And losing Amelia's heart was not the worst that could come of it. He only hoped he could find a way to protect her and keep her.

Hugh burst through the front door and called out, "Amelia! Lizzie! Where are you?"

There was no answer, but Masters rushed into the foyer. Hugh's heart dropped, for the butler's expression was pale and lined with worry. Something had happened. Hugh knew it like he knew his own name.

"Where are they?" he whispered.

"Lady Elizabeth is in her room," he began.

Hugh didn't wait for the rest. He bounded up the stairs two at a time and raced to his sister's door. He knocked and did not wait for her response to burst inside. Lizzie was seated by the fire, wrapped in a blanket. When he stepped into her room, she looked over at him. Her cheeks were streaked with tears and her eyes were wide and frightened.

"What is it?" he asked, trying to keep his tone gentle when what he wanted to do was catch her by the shoulders and make her tell him everything. "What's happened?"

Lizzie stared at him, almost unseeing, then mumbled, "In the park."

Hugh drew a breath and dropped to his knees before her. "In the park? What happened in the park?"

His sister shook her head. "It was fine. It was lovely. Amelia and I were walking, giggling like girls. Meg and

Charlotte were on the hill. Amelia stepped away a moment..."
She trailed off and ducked her head.

Hugh cupped her cheeks and gently lifted so she had to look
at him. "What happened?"

"I saw h-him," she sobbed, leaning in to rest her head on his
shoulder, where she began to shake. "Aaron Walters was there,
talking to Amelia like they knew each other. I got upset, I asked
why she was talking to him when you told me not to give her his
name."

Hugh's stomach dropped. "*That's* what you asked her?"

When Lizzie nodded against his shoulder, he scrubbed a
hand through his hair. That was all. It was over. Amelia had
found out the truth in exactly the worst way possible. The way
he had hoped she would never know.

"What did she say? What did she do? What did he do?"

"H-he was gone by then," Lizzie croaked out, lifting her
head. "But Amelia went so pale. I thought she might faint. She
rushed me to the carriage—we didn't even say goodbye to Meg
and Charlotte. And she kept asking me if it was true. If Aaron
Walters was the man who had...hurt me. If you knew. I was so
overwrought, all I could do was say yes."

Hugh was shaking now, and he tried with all his might not
to shout at her in his upset. This was not her fault. It was his.
Only his. Forever his. For not being honest. For not trusting
Amelia, even long after he knew he could.

"Is she here?" he asked. "Is she home?"

"No," his sister whispered. "She took me here and told them
to help me upstairs, then she left in the carriage again. I cried out
after her to find out where and she said...she said..."

"Where did she go?"

"To confront him. She said she was going to confront *him*,"
Lizzie sobbed.

Hugh rocked back and fell onto on the floor in front of her.
Of course that is what she would do. Amelia had such strength,
and she loved his sister quite like her own flesh and blood. She'd
been enraged when she discovered Lizzie had been used by

some nameless bastard she'd created into a monster in her beautiful head. He'd loved her for that.

But she had no reason to fear Walters. She didn't know what Hugh did. So she would go to him, face off with him. Give him a set down. Never realizing that it would put her on the trail of a madman who might destroy her to keep her quiet, or to hurt Hugh, or just to please himself.

He pushed to his feet. "Stay here, Elizabeth, you must stay here. Do you understand?"

"Is it my fault?" she whispered.

He shook his head. "No. And I will explain everything to you, I promise you. But you *must* stay here where I know you will be safe."

He ran from the room, ignoring how she called after him, and nearly crashed headlong into Masters. The butler straightened his back. "We are all very worried, Your Grace. What can we do?"

"Get a message to the Duke of Willowby straight away," he said. "Tell him that Amelia has gone to Walters. That is exactly what it must say, and then the address of Aaron Walters' home here in London. It's in my book in my desk drawer."

"Yes, Your Grace," Masters said. "And what about Lady Elizabeth? She has been overwrought."

"I know. In the same message, ask the Duchess of Willowby to come here and comfort her until we return."

Masters nodded. "Where are you going, Your Grace?"

"After my wife. Get me a gun."

CHAPTER TWENTY-ONE

Amelia glared up at the little townhouse as the driver helped her from the carriage. Her hands shook and her stomach turned as she looked at that façade and knew what awaited her behind it.

Something false. Something untrue.

But then, she could say that about her husband, too. Later. Later, she would say it. Right now she had something else to deal with.

"Your Grace, I do not like leaving you without a chaperone," the driver said.

She touched his arm gently. "I will be but a moment, I assure you. Please don't worry yourself."

He looked less than convinced, but what could he say? She was the Duchess of Brighthollow. His employer. Hugh's wife. How ridiculous that felt at present, when she reflected on all that had happened.

Hugh had *known* the connection between Walters and his sister all along. It had been why he came to her. Why he bought her father's debts, if there had actually been debts to purchase. He'd known all of it and never told her. Kept it from her willfully and well past the point where he should have known he could trust her.

It made Aaron's words from earlier in the day, cruel as they were, ring with more truth in her ears. *He will convince you he cares for you. But he will discard you.*

Was that what had happened? Hugh had taken her to hurt the man who had hurt his sister? Pretended to care because it made her more pliable? Because it made it easier? Would he walk away when he recalled that he'd only wed her to thwart Aaron's plans?

She shook her head, pushing away the thoughts she would confront later, and rang the bell at Walters' door. In a moment, it opened and Aaron stood there, just as he had the last time she'd come. Now she wondered if he truly had a servant at all, or if that was just another mask he wore: Gentleman.

"Your Grace," he said, and sounded genuinely surprised to see her. "What are you doing here?"

"I know what you did," she whispered, hating how her voice broke with emotions she didn't want to reveal. "I know."

His lips thinned and he stepped back to usher her into the foyer. "This does not seem the kind of conversation one should have on the doorstep."

She looked past him into the house and then back at her driver. The other man would come for her if she didn't return quickly, and she didn't believe Aaron would hurt her physically. No, the pain he caused was something else entirely.

She moved past him into the house. Even more of the pictures on the walls were gone than the last time she'd been here, and some of the furniture was missing, too. She shook her head as she followed him to the parlor where they'd talked before. It was evident to her now that Walters was selling off the items. They probably weren't even his, but had come with the property he was letting.

She folded her arms as she moved to stand before the fire that could not penetrate the chill in her entire body. "Are you running out of the money my husband paid you?" she asked. "Have you spent it all already?"

Walters had still had that sweet, boyish expression as he led her inside, but now she watched it shift. Vanish. Harden. There was no more kindness in his eyes now, no more gentleness. Now she saw the true man behind all the lies.

The monster.

Her heart leapt at that sudden, easy shift, and for the first time she wondered if she had made a foolish mistake by coming here.

"I had other plans, Amelia," he said. "I *should* have refilled my coffers with your dowry, only that husband of yours ruined everything, didn't he?"

"I've never been so happy that he did so." She shook her head. "Here you are, practically admitting that you were only after me for my money. Based on everything else I know, I must believe our entire relationship was a cruel machination designed to manipulate me to your side."

"Indeed," he said with a little bow. "You have uncovered the truth at last. I'd tell you good show, but you were stupidly convinced of my character for far too long to congratulate you on finally seeing the light."

"Are you *proud* of this?" she asked, stunned by his attitude. There was no remorse to him whatsoever.

He smiled. "I am. Why would I not be? I have played the role of a lifetime, many times. Do you know how easy it is to convince silly little girls like you or Elizabeth or…or others that love is right in front of them? Stupid, desperate girls who want love so badly? You wanted a prince. I provided him. That there was a price shouldn't surprise you—that is the way of our world."

Amelia flinched, but she couldn't deny that what he said was true. She had recognized that fundamental truth about herself more and more over the last few weeks. That her past made her crave the kind of belonging Hugh had so easily provided. Only what he offered had been real. Even though he'd lied to her in the beginning, in the end, the feeling between them was true.

She had to have faith in that or else she would collapse.

"You bastard," she said, pulling herself back to the problem at hand. "You exploited the hurt and the naivety of young women who cared for you."

He shrugged. "Exploit or be exploited, my dear. There is no other option in this ugly world we live in."

"Of course there is," she said. "There were a hundred other options than to use me, to harm Lizzie so deeply."

He nodded slowly. "Ah yes, Lizzie. Sweet, little Lizzie with all her shyness and uncertainty. She was fun. And very lucrative, in the end. His money, the money you came here to confront me about, it gave me the opportunity to look more gentlemanly for the next catch."

"Me," she whispered.

"Do you ever wonder why I bedded her and not you?"

She turned her face. "You are disgusting."

"She was uncertain," he explained. "And I knew that if I claimed her innocence, she would not run. But you...*you* were panting for it. That night I proposed, you leaned so far into me, just begging for that kiss, I could hardly breathe. I didn't have to seduce you—you were aching for a wedding night and would have done anything to get there."

She pivoted, but like in the park earlier that day, he caught her. His fingers dug in, just as they had then, and terror filled her. Hours ago, she had been in a public place where her screams would have brought assistance.

Here they were alone. She had no idea if her driver would hear her if she cried out, or even if he could get inside.

This had been a terrible, emotional mistake. One she regretted down to her toes.

"How was it in the end?" he asked, his face closer to hers. "To be bedded by a man you despised?"

"I do not despise Hugh," she spat, yanking at her arm.

He lifted his eyebrows. "You don't, do you? He must have been very satisfactory, because I'm seeing it all so clearly now. You've convinced yourself you're in love with him, haven't you?"

"Let me go!" she snapped. "I'm leaving."

"No, you aren't," he insisted, his tone almost bored. Like this attack on her person was nothing out of the ordinary, nothing that mattered at all. "You are such a little fool. You've traded one liar for another."

She stopped jerking to escape and stared at him evenly. "Don't you dare compare yourself to my husband. You are not half the man Hugh is. Not a tenth."

Walters didn't blink or flinch. Without warning or preamble, he simply threw his free hand back and hit her hard across the left cheek. She staggered, stunned as pain roared through her face and up into her ears. His grip on her arm tightened, as if to keep her upright, and he smiled at her.

"I would expect his whore to say nothing less. You are a loyal little lapdog, aren't you?" He reached into his coat pocket and withdrew a pistol. He lifted it to point it at her as he slowly let her go and backed away.

She stared at the barrel of the gun, pointed at her face, then back up to him. "What are you going to do?" she whispered.

"Ask him," Walters said, motioning his head to a spot behind her.

She turned and caught her breath. Hugh was standing in the door to the parlor, staring at the scene before him. His face was drained of all color, and in his hand he held a pistol of his own.

"Let her go," Hugh said, looking at Amelia, not at Walters. Her face was swollen already from where the bastard had struck her, and she was watching him with terror and faith on her face. She might hate him, but she was happy to see him.

And he had to save her.

"Let her go," he repeated, this time stronger. "Your quarrel is with me."

Walters chuckled. "You think we are in a quarrel? This is far beyond that, Your Grace. You have damaged me, hurt me and my prospects in Society. I want to return the favor. And what better way to do that than to hurt *her*?"

He shook the gun toward Amelia, and she made a soft sound of fear deep in her throat that cut Hugh down to his very core.

"That was *always* your weakness, you know," Walters continued. "Caring about others. Had you simply exposed me after your sister, this wouldn't be happening. But you wanted to protect her. You were so desperate to protect her. And I can see that same desperation now. It will get me whatever I want, won't it?"

"Yes," Hugh said, hating that word and clinging to it at the same time. "Whatever you want."

"More money?" Walters taunted.

"Yes," he repeated. "And you'll need it. You must know that the War Department has looked into your past. They know about Stephen Monroe. They know about the girl you married and murdered."

For the first time, Walters' smug expression wavered and the gun in his hand trembled slightly. Amelia squeezed her eyes shut, her fists clenched at her sides. Tears leaked from the corners of her eyes and Hugh couldn't even touch her, comfort her.

"You sent the War Department after me?" Walters growled.

"I have friends there. They took it upon themselves," Hugh said, recognizing the rage that was bubbling up in this dangerous, unhinged man. "They are circling, coming for you. But if you let Amelia go, you can run. I'll send money—you can go to the continent, you could go anywhere."

Of course he had no intention of doing any such thing, not this time. But if Walters would look at his past and think he would let him go, that could save Amelia, which was all that mattered.

"I *will* go," Walters said. "After."

Hugh edged toward Amelia. "Then shoot me. Don't shoot her, shoot me."

He positioned himself in front of her and set his gun on the ground.

"Hugh," she said softly, her hand coming up to curl against

his hip. "No. No."

"Shhh," he soothed her without looking away from Walters. "Shoot me, I'm the one you hate. I'm the one who ruined everything. You want me to plead for you? I'll do it. Do not murder the woman I love. Take me and let her live."

Walters' face brightened with a little pleasure. "A very nice request. One filled with heartfelt emotion, even. But I think I'll kill you both. You both deserve it. You first, Your Grace, so that Amelia can see you make your noble sacrifice. And then her, so that she bleeds out next to you on my floor."

His finger slid to the trigger of the gun, and Hugh reached behind himself, taking Amelia's hand as he waited for the moment when his world would become pain and then darkness.

But before Walters could shoot, there was a crash in the foyer and Lucas jumped into the room, firing off a shot that dropped Walters where he stood.

Hugh pivoted, diving on top of Amelia and dragging her to the ground where he covered her trembling body with his own just in case Walters had any fight in him. But there was nothing, only the ring of Lucas's shot in the air and the acrid smell of gunpowder.

"Are you two well?" Lucas said, crouching next to them as half a dozen men filed into the room, guns drawn and at the ready.

Hugh lifted his head and looked down at Amelia. She was staring up at him, her hands cupping his cheeks, her body shaking beneath him.

"Amelia?" he asked. "Amelia, are you hurt?"

"No," she gasped out. "No, are you?"

"No," he whispered, then dropped his mouth to hers. She let him kiss her, didn't pull away, though she had every right to do so. He kissed her, not with passion, but with utter relief. With terror at what he had so nearly lost.

But when he pulled away and rolled off of her, getting up to help her back to her feet, he knew this wasn't over. Not even close. And losing his wife might still be a very strong possibility.

CHAPTER TWENTY-TWO

"What will happen now?" Amelia asked as their carriage turned back into the drive at the London estate an hour later. It was the first thing she had said to Hugh since they got into the vehicle.

He jolted in surprise, like he hadn't thought she would speak to him ever again. "Lucas says the department has enough evidence to mark the case as a justifiable end to a bad criminal. Our names will be kept out of the report, it seems."

She dropped her chin. "Like it never happened."

He let out his breath. "I suppose."

"Only it did," she whispered, glancing up at him and flinching as she flashed back to the moment Hugh had stepped in front of her, ready to take a bullet to save her life, and said that he loved her. She would never forget it.

"Yes, it did," he said, reaching for her hand. She let him hold it for a moment, then slid it away. He sighed again. "I want to talk to you about this, Amelia. I want to talk to you about everything."

She nodded. "You owe me an explanation. But you also owe your sister the same. She will want to know about Walters, too. And his end."

He turned his head. "It will hurt her."

"Yes," Amelia agreed. "But the alternative is to lie and I think you've done more than enough of that. The truth is what this situation requires, Hugh. I suggest you start telling it."

The carriage door opened and she took the footman's waiting hand and stepped out. Stepped away from Hugh and up into the house. She knew he was trailing behind her, she felt his presence, just as she always felt his presence. It was unavoidable. Looming.

Comforting.

But today she couldn't get lost in that. Today she deserved more than his comfort. She deserved to know the answers to her questions. She deserved the anger she felt in her chest.

She had earned it.

As she stepped inside, Diana and Lizzie rushed into the foyer. Lizzie's face was pale as she hurried to embrace her brother. Diana came to Amelia, and her fingers reached out to gently trace the bruise on Amelia's cheek.

"I'm so glad you weren't permanently harmed," she whispered as she hugged Amelia. Amelia almost buckled at the embrace, but managed to keep herself upright.

"It is thanks to your husband," she whispered, and then glanced back at where Lizzie and her brother were still hugging.

Diana's eyebrows lifted. "How bad?" she asked.

"Bad," Amelia said. "Lucas is unharmed. He saved our lives."

Diana nodded slowly. "He is good at that."

"He stayed behind to finish up with the reporting. He said he would see you at home."

"Then I'll leave you now, for it seems your family has much to process together. But I hope you'll let me see you again, perhaps tomorrow or the next day."

"Of course," Amelia said, leaning up to kiss her cheek. "Thank you."

She moved into the parlor as she heard Diana say her goodbyes. Her hands shook as she tried to pour herself tea, sloshing hot liquid onto the saucer before she managed to get the cup filled. As she took the first sip, Lizzie and Hugh entered the room.

And again, she felt his eyes on her. It was like the beginning of their relationship, when he'd sometimes just watched her. Reading her. At the time, that had made her nervous. She didn't understand it or him.

Now she did and it took everything in her not to rush into his arms and let him comfort her.

Lizzie moved over to her, and Amelia set her teacup down as she was pulled in for a hug. When she backed away at last, Lizzie stared at her face in horror. "Oh, Amelia," she breathed. "Did he do that to you?"

Amelia reached up to touch the bruise, which now ached dully. "He did," she said, determined not to lie, if only to set a good example for Hugh. "He wanted to do worse, but...but he cannot any longer."

Lizzie shook her head and looked at Hugh in question. "What?"

He cleared his throat. "Aaron Walters is dead, Lizzie," he said, gently but firmly. As she lifted her hand to her mouth in shock, he continued, "He attacked Amelia, with the intention of killing her. Luckily the authorities came in and he was struck down. He cannot hurt you, hurt *us*, any longer."

Lizzie staggered to the settee and sat down hard. She stared at the floor in front of her, shaking her head in silence. Amelia pushed aside her own upset and took the place beside her.

"What are you feeling?" she asked. "There is no wrong answer."

"Sad," Lizzie admitted. "And relieved."

Amelia nodded as she took her hand. "I feel the same."

"Why did he attack you?" Lizzie asked. "Because you confronted him about me? Is this my fault?"

Amelia glanced up at Hugh. His face was positively crumpled, broken. She understood why he wanted to protect Lizzie from the truth. Protect himself from the consequences. She met his stare and held it, hoping he would find strength.

He sighed and took a place in one of the chairs across from the settee. "I have lied to you, Lizzie," he said after what felt like forever. "I've lied to you and I've lied to Amelia. And I need to be honest now."

"Lied to me?" Lizzie sounded utterly confused. "No, Hugh. You are the most honorable man I know."

He shut his eyes, and the pain that flowed over his expression was heartbreaking. "I am not, Elizabeth. Not in the slightest."

"Just start at the beginning," Amelia encouraged softly.

He opened his eyes and his dark gaze snared hers. "The beginning," he repeated. "Yes. Lizzie, after I found you with Walters, I paid him to keep the secret of what had happened between you."

"Yes," she said. "He said you would have to and I thought you must have in the end. I'm so sorry."

"No," he said, leaning forward in his chair as if he could draw her closer. "No, *I'm* sorry. I hated giving that bastard money for his silence. I wanted to call him out, destroy him in every way. Not provide for his comfort."

"You could have if I hadn't been so foolish," Lizzie whispered.

Amelia squeezed her hand. "You are not to blame for a villain's cruelty, Lizzie. You must let that guilt go. Hugh was trying to protect you as best he could. If you could protect him, you would have done the same."

She nodded. "I would," she said on a sigh.

Hugh glanced at Amelia, and she saw his gratitude for her interjection. The one that absolved both him and Lizzie of some of their pain. Then he shook his head and continued, "Letting him go, it didn't just pain me. I knew the bastard might go back to his evil ways. I had men tracking him. Watching to see if he was going to do something wicked again."

"And he did?" Lizzie asked.

"Yes," Amelia said when Hugh seemed to struggle. "He did."

"Lizzie, Aaron became engaged to…to Amelia," Hugh said at last.

Lizzie jolted, jerking her hand from Amelia's and getting

up from the couch to back away. "What?"

"I didn't know about what had happened with you, of course," Amelia said. "Aaron made me a victim. Just like he did with you, he became the vision of what I wanted." She glanced at Hugh. "What I *thought* I wanted."

"Oh no," Lizzie said, her whisper filled with the deepest pain.

Hugh nodded. "When I found out, I intervened, but I…I was still hesitant to give details as to why Amelia shouldn't marry this man. So I…I lied to force her to marry me instead."

Amelia caught her breath and focused only on her husband. "You told me that you owned my father's debts," she said. "Was that true? Did you buy them in order to manipulate me or were there ever any debts at all?"

"I lied," he admitted softly. "Your father's idea. He said you would protect him at any cost. He made up the story about the debts, knowing it would turn you against me but also force your hand. I went along with it, despite how distasteful I found it. I lied, Amelia."

The gravity of all that had happened hit Amelia with the force of a tidal wave. She heard a sound in the air and realized with a start that it was her own moan of pain, of heartbreak. And in that moment, she felt like it would never stop hurting again.

Nausea washed over Hugh as he stared at Amelia, her body bent over, her shoulders shaking as she made a sound of anguish that felt like it shattered his very soul. He had done this to her. Not Walters, not her father…*him*. And he wanted to rush to her, to comfort her, to erase what he'd done.

But he couldn't. The best he could do was sit with the consequences and *feel* them. He owed her that.

Lizzie moved to him, and her hand came to rest on his shoulder. He started, for he had almost forgotten she was in the room, so focused was he on Amelia. He glanced up and saw her pain, but also her sweetness. Her love for him. Her forgiveness and understanding.

He reached up to cover her hand gently.

"I love you, Hugh," she whispered. "You know that."

"I do, though whether I deserve that is a debatable topic."

She shook her head and leaned down to kiss his temple. "Not debatable at all. But I need to think about what has happened today. And I think you and Amelia need privacy to do the same." She glanced at Amelia, who was still hunched over in pain. Her concern was clear on her face as she whispered, "Do whatever you can, Hugh."

He smiled at her as she left the room and shut the door behind her. When the click echoed in the room, Amelia lifted her head and looked at him. She was crumpled, broken and he ached for his part in it.

"I need you to know I'm sorry," he said. She opened her mouth and he lifted a hand. "Oh, please, let me finish, and then I swear to you I will give you the floor for everything you want to say."

She shut her mouth and nodded.

"I'm sorry," he repeated. "I'm sorry I lied to you. I'm sorry I allowed your father's manipulation. I'm sorry I didn't tell you the truth in Brighthollow when I began to truly know your character and that you could be trusted with any secret. I wanted to tell you then, so very much. But mostly I'm sorry that my foolishness, my cowardice, put you in danger today."

She did not respond, but simply watched him. Her expression was hooded, unreadable. He imagined much the same as his own when they had begun. Only she hid from him because she no longer trusted him.

And that crushed him.

"When I saw him with that gun on you…" he whispered, not even caring when his voice broke and tears filled his eyes. "When I thought he'd kill you, I was terrified. Terrified to lose you. Terrified I'd never get to tell you that I love you. I love you,

Amelia. It doesn't excuse what I've done, but I need you to know it because tomorrow is not guaranteed and I *never* want to leave it unsaid again."

Amelia's ears rang at that declaration. It was the second time Hugh had said he loved her today, but the first time without it being under deep duress. And the words sank into her skin, just as they had before, and brought a joy to her heart that was almost terrifying in its power.

Especially considering all the other things he'd told her.

"How can I believe you?" she whispered, getting to her feet and walking away because looking at him was too hard. "How can I have faith in you or in myself after everything that has happened? You may say this only to make my anger dissipate. It could very well be another manipulation."

"No," he said softly. She turned. He had risen, but did not follow her. "I am not manipulating you. I know those words mean nothing, but they are true. I don't *deserve* your forgiveness, Amelia. I don't even ask for it. I betrayed you. Whatever you need to do or hear or say to overcome that, I will give it to you."

She stared at him. This man she had come to love in their time together. Only she'd thought that of Aaron, too, hadn't she? Not as powerfully, perhaps. Not as completely. But...trusting herself was just as hard as trusting him.

So she couldn't launch herself into his arms as she wanted to do. She had to be measured. Careful.

"I want space," she said, watching his face for the reaction.

Pain washed over his features, but he pushed it away. Went calm again, cool. He nodded slowly. "That is understandable. I will give you that space, Amelia. For as long as you need it. But I'll be here, whether it's a day or a week or a month or ten years. I'll be here waiting."

His emotions were so plain on his face, quite a feat considering how he had been punished for just that as a child. Now he came to her, utterly open. Because she needed it.

"Thank you," she said, and then glanced toward the door. "It's been such a long day. I think I'll go up, have a bath and go to bed."

"Yes," he whispered. She turned and went to the door, but as she lifted her hand to open it, he said, "I love you, Amelia."

She froze there, hand shaking, body and mind screaming at her to accept those words. But she didn't turn. She left the room, left him behind and trudged up to her bed.

But there would be no sleep tonight. She knew there would be no sleep for a long time to come.

CHAPTER TWENTY-THREE

Amelia sat on the settee staring at the fire, a letter drooping from her hand. Hugh had left her be for three long days, but that didn't mean his presence in her life had been any less constant. Her favorite flowers appeared in her bedroom every afternoon when she came to prepare for tea. Her favorite foods were laid out for her at meals. The servants were extra gentle with her. Lizzie slipped in and out of rooms like she was trying to be a ghost so that Amelia could have her time.

And then there was this letter from her father, received not an hour before. She'd expected it. Certainly, he would have heard about the death of Aaron Walters by now, and she guessed he would have a reaction.

Just not this one. He'd written her a letter of apology. Her father. The man who had never looked at her and not seen how he could further himself. He had written her something heartfelt and warm, filled with what felt like true contrition about Walters' nature and what he had almost allowed her to do.

That was Hugh's work, she was certain. Her father had written something about her husband telling him the news, and she could well imagine the dressing down Hugh had given him on her behalf.

Yes, her husband was always there, even when he wasn't in the room with her, filling up all the space and making her want him. Heart and soul, body and mind.

There was a light knock on the parlor door, and she

straightened and faced it. "Enter."

Masters put his head into the room. "Your Grace, the Duchess of Willowby has arrived. Are you in residence?"

Amelia sighed. She had expected Diana far earlier, based on their conversation from a few days before. In fact, she had been expecting all the duchesses to descend upon her, driven to wheedle her forgiveness out of her.

"I'm home," she said. "Send Her Grace in, thank you."

Masters went to fetch her guest and Amelia took her time folding the letter from her father and putting it away. She stood, smoothing her skirts, and faced the door with something resembling a smile.

Diana swept in a moment later and immediately crossed the room to hug Amelia wordlessly. Amelia buckled against her friend, drawing deep breaths so she wouldn't humiliate herself by weeping.

She had done enough of that in private.

"Sit," Diana ordered gently, as if this was her parlor, not Amelia's.

But Amelia could not deny her, so she did as she was told and watched as Diana hustled to the sideboard. "Should I order more tea?"

Amelia chuckled. "It seems to be your house, Your Grace."

Diana turned with a smile. "I'm sorry, I'm being thoughtless and pushy. Lucas says it is in my nature to take care of others. The healer in me, you know." She came back to the settee and took a place next to Amelia. She searched her face. "The bruise has healed a great deal. It should be gone in a day or two."

"If only the rest was so easy," Amelia sighed.

"Yes, if I could patent a salve for a broken heart, I would double Lucas's fortune." Diana shook her head. "But that is not possible."

Amelia worried her lip. "I assume Hugh has gone to you two." Diana's silence was the answer. "Did he sent you as his agent?"

"No." Diana said immediately. "Quite the opposite. There have been many offers to come and talk to you by all the duchesses and half the dukes. He has asked everyone to leave you be, respect your wishes to be left alone. I'm certain he would be angry if he knew I was here."

Amelia ducked her head. "So everyone knows then?"

Diana smiled. "They're a family, Amelia. I was like you, alone most of my life, and in the beginning the idea that all the friends and their wives were so intertwined was unsettling. But you'll see, as you come to know everyone, that it is truly magical. You end up with a heart full of sisters and brothers to turn to. People who won't judge and who accept you for exactly who you are."

Amelia clenched her hands together. That sounded like heaven. "*If* I come to know everyone. I don't even know where my marriage stands at present."

"That's why I'm here," Diana said, patting her hand. "To help you through this, since I thought you might need a friend."

Amelia laughed, though she felt little humor. "Aren't you a little biased?"

Diana's laugh was heartier. "Oh yes, I am. But so are you."

Amelia let out her breath slowly. "I am." She glanced at Diana. "He lied to me. My father, I expected that from him, as much as it hurt. He always saw me as a tool to be wielded. But I hated it, and Hugh knew how much I did. I never expected *him* to…"

Diana nodded as Amelia trailed off, unable to continue. "I cannot imagine. Especially since it is so obvious that you care for him."

Amelia flinched. "Yes, that is true, too."

"Do you love him?" Diana's question was gentle, but Amelia felt her seeking gaze. She nodded without looking up. Diana retook her hand. "He made mistakes. Two very bad ones. The first was before he knew you. The second was when he was afraid to lose you."

Amelia bent her head. As she'd spent the days and nights

alone, she had come to much the same conclusion. "He should have told me," she said.

"Yes, he should have. But he didn't," Diana said.

Amelia shifted, feeling a swell of protectiveness toward Hugh. "But...he meant to. Didn't he?"

"He did. He has said as much to all of us, as he paces our halls, tormenting himself. He hates himself for not doing so, and for putting you in danger because of it."

"I've lost so much." Amelia got up and walked away, restless in her confusion and despair.

"I'm sure you have," Diana said after a moment's silence. "I have, too. I've been in the kind of pain where I was so afraid to move that I actually made it worse. I nearly lost everything. I would hate to see you do the same."

Amelia turned and speared her with a gaze. "You think I should forgive him."

Diana shrugged. "I think you shouldn't shut him out while you try. Amelia, he *does* love you. That much is plain."

"What's funny is that I've stopped questioning that," Amelia said, her voice trembling. "I think of all he did, all he said, all the ways we've been connected. I know, in my heart, that he does love me. But I can't trust...myself."

"Why?"

"I thought Walters was a good man!" She shook her head. "I couldn't have been more wrong. But I told myself I loved him. And now I tell myself the same about Hugh. What if I'm just a fool, like Walters said? What if I'm so desperate for any scrap of love that I'll find it in any corner?"

Diana got up and rushed to her. "There is a marked difference between a man who manipulated you to get your fortune and one who has truly fallen in love with you. And I assume the feelings you have for each man were different, too."

"Yes, of course. With Walters, I was always...slightly uncomfortable. Always reaching for something that I now understand he kept away from me in order to reel me in further. I was uncertain with him. With Hugh...even at the beginning when I tried to tell myself I hated him, there was something about him that drew me to him. He offered me kindness and gentleness. He offered me the truth about his past, even though I knew it was difficult, and he coaxed my own from me without judgment or lack of interest."

"You connected. Truly," Diana encouraged her.

"Yes," Amelia admitted. "Diana, when I am with him…I've always wanted a home. A real home. I pictured it as a place, but…"

"It's a person." Diana blinked at tears. "That, my dear, is love. And it's real, not some schoolgirl notion from a lonely mind. It is how every one of our duchess friends would describe her husband, and all of them are truly in love."

Amelia lowered her gaze, but not because she was upset or sad or confused or filled with self-recrimination. It was because the happiness and acceptance that filled her was so powerful that she had to steady herself.

"Talk to him," Diana said. "Give him that chance to be the home you've earned. And to be the same for him."

Amelia smiled at her. "I will. I must."

"Good," Diana said, and squeezed her tightly into a hug.

Amelia clung to her, a raft in a stormy sea, and shook with the power of what she felt, what she knew and what she would do. She only hoped that when she reached for Hugh, he would be there to take the hand she offered and the future they both deserved.

Hugh sat in his study, staring at a pile of correspondence that had gathered in the past few days. There were invitations and inquiries, some likely important, but how could he focus on such mundane things when all he could think about was Amelia? All he could want was Amelia. All he had lost that had ever mattered was Amelia.

He glanced up and jolted, for there she was, standing in the entryway like his errant, troubled mind had conjured her there. She was pale, with circles under her eyes like she hadn't slept, and she watched him closely.

"Amelia!" he cried, leaping to his feet and coming around the desk. He brought himself up short there, remembering her desire to be alone. She didn't want him crowding her, forcing her.

She stepped inside and shut the door behind her, leaning back on it like it was the only thing holding her up.

"I spent my life knowing I could trust no one," she said softly, without preamble, without hesitation. "My mother was uninvolved, my father unconnected. It made me who I am. That day when he tried to kill us, Aaron said I was so desperate for love that I was a good target. And he was right. I was desperate. And then there was you."

Hugh bent his head, feeling the accusation in her words. The one he deserved. "I took away what you wanted. I caused you pain."

"No." He lifted his gaze to hers and found her staring at him intently. "At first I thought you did that. At first I wanted to despise you for it. But as we grew closer, I came to a realization that has changed me as much as my past did."

He could hardly breathe, and forced himself to stay where he was rather than rush to her and take her into his arms. "What is that?"

She moved since he didn't, pushing from the door and crossing two steps closer. He could almost touch her now. God, how he wanted to touch her.

"I realized everything I have ever wanted was in your house. Your company." Her voice broke. "In your arms. I tried not to, because you are too intense and too strong and too...too *you*, but I fell in love with you."

A strangled sound came from Hugh's throat, and he couldn't move as he stared at this beautiful, remarkable woman he had hurt, who was standing before him confessing her heart regardless. This strong, powerful woman who could bring light to everything dark in him. Who could carry him when he felt weak. This woman he loved more than anything else on the earth. In the stars.

"I had only just accepted how I felt," she continued. "When I found out what you'd done. That you'd lied to me."

He stiffened, now wondering if she was describing her love in past tense. It was so hard not to try to explain himself, to argue his case. But he managed to simply nod. "Yes."

She shifted. "I've thought a lot about that in the time you've given me. And Hugh, I can understand why you lied. I know my father. And even if I didn't, he confessed to me in his letter—which I'm sure you had a part in—that he all but forced you to marry me to save me from Walters."

"I still could have told you why," he whispered.

She shook her head. "I was a stranger. Why would you have trusted me with Lizzie's darkest moment?"

He frowned. "I should have. It impacted your life and at least you would have been able to choose your own path. It was my pride that silenced me as much as her reputation."

She nodded slowly. "So you have said. And I have one question, Hugh."

"Anything."

"Once you knew me, once we grew close…why *didn't* you tell me right away?"

He froze, for the answer to that question was difficult. But he could only be truthful now. If he wanted her back, and he wanted her back more now than ever since he knew she loved him, he had to give her honesty as his first and most powerful gift.

"The more I fell in love with you, the more I feared what my deception would do. I convinced myself at first that I could simply wait, let our relationship blossom and then tell you. Once Lizzie confessed to you, I recognized how unfair that was. I wanted to tell you then, but we were going to London. I decided to tell you here. After things had settled. I didn't know how dangerous Walters truly was until the day he attacked you."

Her face relaxed a fraction. "But you would have told me."

"*Yes*," he declared with a passion that leapt to the surface with ease. "I don't expect you to believe that, but I would have. Perhaps even the day you found out yourself. I know I must prove myself to you. Prove that you can have faith in what I say again."

"How?" she asked.

"Any way you choose," he said. "Any way that will show you I am worthy. It may take a long time and I'm willing to do it. Every day in every way I can."

She moved closer once more, and her breath shuddered out as she reached for his hand. Her bare fingers closed around his hand and the warmth of her crept through his entire being. How he had missed that. Missed her.

She looked up at him, her eyes misty with tears. "I still love you," she whispered.

"You do?" he asked, barely able to believe it. Praying it wasn't a dream.

She nodded. "I do. I love you and being apart these past few days has been terrible for me. I can see it has been for you, too."

"I wanted to respect your wishes," he said, lifting her hand to his heart and knowing she could feel the throb, even through all his clothing. "You don't know how many nights I stood at your door and wanted to come in. Just to look at you. Just to touch you."

He lifted her hand higher, brushing his lips to her knuckles as a tear slid down her cheek. But she smiled. She smiled at him and in that moment, he saw his future in her eyes. A future that was not marred by pain, but filled with joy and beauty. Surrounded by love.

"You had good intentions," she whispered. "I know you did. You are incapable of anything else. And if you promise me today that those lies are the last you'll ever tell me, I will believe you. We can start fresh."

He cupped her cheeks, smoothing tears away with his

thumbs. He met her gaze and held there so she could see the truth in his eyes. "I will never lie to you again, Amelia. Never."

"And do you love me?" she asked, that little smile lifting her lips again.

He laughed. "Have I not said it? I swear, I've screamed it out a thousand times in my head since we got to London. I love you, Amelia. I love you with a power that frightens me. I thought I was fine and that my life was balanced. You came in, crashed in, and I realized I'd been in the dark all this time. I told you in Brighthollow that you were my light. I meant it."

"And you are mine," she whispered, her voice filled with joy again. Touched by laughter and happiness.

"I need you, I love you, I cannot live without you," he continued. "And if you can truly give me a chance, I won't squander it. I will spend all my life earning what you've given me. And I will never let you go."

She lifted up on her tiptoes and her lips found his. He pulled her flush against him, tasting her, drowning in her, surrendering to her fully, perhaps for the first time. And he felt the same in her. A kiss that was a vow, as much as any they had ever spoken. A kiss that gave them a future together that he couldn't wait to watch unfold around them.

She pulled back at last, her fingers tracing his cheeks as she whispered, "We'll never let each other go. Not ever."

"Not ever," he repeated, and then he kissed her again as his heart soared.

Enjoy an exciting excerpt from

The Duke of Desire

out October 2018

Fall 1812

Robert Smithton, Duke of Roseford, looked out over the ballroom floor with disinterest. He'd never enjoyed this exercise in exhibition, but as of late it had become almost unbearable. He felt his mouth turn down even lower as he looked at the couples bobbing about the floor. Friends of his, many of them with happy brides in their arms.

Once upon a time, he would have said those men had thrown away their freedom. But it was hard to feel that way now when their joy was so clear. So sharp. Like a knife to the gut.

"What are you brooding about?"

Robert jumped and turned to find three of those very friends standing at his elbow. The Dukes of Abernathe, Crestwood and Northfield. James, Simon and Graham respectively, because the titles were so damned tedious.

It was Graham who had spoken, and he handed over a drink for Robert with a grin. Robert refused to return the expression. "Who says I'm brooding?"

He took a slug of the drink and found it watered down, indeed. God, he would be happy when the Season was over. When his friends would retreat back to their estates and their frustrating contentment and he would be left to…to prowl and dive into all the darkness that kept the pain away.

"I'm an expert," Graham retorted, but then another grin brightened his face. Robert was warmed by it. Just two short years ago, his friend would not have smiled so easily. Love did that, it seemed. "Or I used to be."

"Ha," Robert grumbled, winking at the men so his ill humor would not be perceived as a slight. "As if any of you are experts in anything anymore. I am the last bachelor."

Simon let out a long laugh that turned more than one interested female head. Not that he noticed. He only had eyes for his wife, just as all the others did. "You are not the last bachelor."

"There's Kit," James said with a shake of his head. While he smiled, Robert felt his concern just below the surface. James had always been the King of the Dukes. Robert had always been his most troublesome subject.

"Kit?" he repeated with a snort of derision. "He is a saint— he hardly counts. No, it is left to me to sow all the wild oats for all of you old married men."

Now all three men looked concerned and Robert began to calculate how quickly he could make a run for it.

"Aren't you tired of it all?" James asked, his tone soft, all teasing departed.

Robert tensed and looked out at the glittering ball without answering. He couldn't answer, at least not without gathering himself first. He didn't want them to see, he didn't want them to know, to hear it in his voice that James was right. He was tired of all of it.

Once upon a time he used to take such pleasure in…well…pleasure. All the parts of it, anticipation to orgasm. But now, now he went through the motions. It was rote. Expected. He was never fully satisfied, even when the experiences were passionate. And if he stopped, he feared the reasons why would catch up to him, overtake him.

He certainly didn't want to face them. What his friends had found was not for him. It didn't exist and he didn't want it. That kind of intimacy was not something he wished to share with any other human being.

"You believe everyone's path must take them to where you are," he said at last, because it was clear they were waiting for some kind of answer. "Just because mine hasn't and won't doesn't mean I am tired of it."

James caught a breath like he was ready to argue that point, but before he could, another man approached. The Marquess of Berronburg was not a member of their duke club, and judging from the way James, Simon and Graham all recoiled slightly as he stepped into their midst, he was not about to be invited into the periphery. Robert couldn't blame them for it. Berronburg was often rude, he imbibed too much and his lechery for women was nearly as legendary as Robert's.

Of course, Berronburg was far less subtle in his advances. He was a lout. But he was Robert's lout. They often prowled together since he had no old friends to do that with anymore.

"Ah, look, four dukes, all in a row," Berronburg crowed loudly. "Do I get some kind of special prize if I find them all?"

James shook his head slightly. "I have no idea, Berronburg." He glanced at Robert. "Perhaps we can continue this conversation later. For now, I will find my wife."

He turned, and Simon and Graham excused themselves as well. Robert stared as they walked away. As the other men met and married the great loves of their lives, he had often wondered if he might one day be pushed from their ranks because of his refusal to do the same. If at some point his old friends would look at him and see someone no better than the marquess who was prattling at his side.

That would break his heart.

"I say, are you listening at all?"

Berronburg shook his arm and Robert blinked, coming back to the present and turning toward the man with a scowl. "Who would not hear you when you're practically shouting the ballroom down? A bit of discretion, if you please, my lord."

Berronburg pursed his lips. "Those dukes are a bad influence on you, Roseford, I swear to Christ. I was asking you if you'd heard the news."

Robert stifled a sigh and settled himself back into the role of rake, rogue, scoundrel. It settled onto his shoulders, but less readily than it once might have. "News?"

Berronburg was practically bouncing. "Yes, yes, yes."

"Well, you always do have the best gossip. What is it then?"

"The Countess of Gainsworth is returning to Society."

All of Robert's maudlin thoughts vanished in an instant at that unexpected information. He tilted his head. "The Countess of Gainsworth?"

Berronburg grinned. "The very one. The infamous lady whose sexual prowess was so great that she struck her husband dead while in flagrante delicto!" The marquess rubbed his hands together and his eyes lit up lewdly. "Can you imagine?"

Robert shook his head. Everyone knew the story. It had circulated through Society like wildfire about a year ago. The whispers had died down, of course, after the man was buried, but now that his wife was coming out of mourning, there was no doubt the world would go abuzz again.

He almost felt sorry for the lady.

"Can you?" Berronburg insisted, elbowing him.

Robert smiled. "I can, indeed. Who could not? She'll have her pick of lovers, of course."

Berronburg laughed. "I agree. There will be dozens who would be willing to risk the cost."

Robert snorted in derision. "Please. Her husband was an old bastard. Put her with a younger man of…talent? No one will suffer but the bed sheets. Are they taking wagers yet on who will win her to his bed?"

"Of course," Berronburg chuckled. "I assume you will be putting yourself into the mix."

Robert jolted at the suggestion. Had he been considering it? In truth, he could scarcely picture the countess. He rarely pursued married women. Too much complication. But certainly the rumors of her prowess interested him. As did the feather that winning her would put in his cap.

He glanced over to find Berronburg watching him closely. Intently, even. "Why are you waiting for my answer with such focus, my friend?"

Berronburg shook his head. "Half the men with interest will drop out if you enter the fray, Your Grace. Including me. That is too much rich competition for my blood."

Robert shrugged. "I have not yet decided what I will—"

He stopped midsentence because something had caught his eye. Someone, to be more specific. Two ladies had entered the ballroom. The one was slightly older, with dark hair and a kind expression. But it wasn't the elder who caught Robert's eye. No, it was the younger. She was stunning, truly beautiful, with thick brown hair and a face that could stop any man in his tracks. She shifted as she said something to the footman at the door and seemed to take a deep breath before she was announced.

"The Countess of Gainsworth," the footman said. "And Mrs. Sambrook."

The reaction of the crowd was immediate. There was a stunned silence that rippled through the entire room and then a low rumble as talk began. The countess stood, almost frozen, for a moment. Her companion said something to her, and Lady Gainsworth set her shoulders back and stepped into the ballroom. The women were greeted by the hostess of the ball, Lady Vinesmith, who looked around the crowd as if she regretted asking the countess here now that the room was reacting so strongly.

Robert watched it all unfold, this little drama, and couldn't take his eyes away. Couldn't shake a tiny niggle of...memory that itched in the back of his mind as he watched the exquisite countess edge to the wall and stand there, a blank expression on her face.

"Better tell the others to put their blunt away," he murmured.

"Why?" Berronburg asked, his own gaze fixated on the countess, just as Robert's was.

"Because the lady is mine. I guarantee it," Robert said with a grin.

Other Books by Jess Michaels

THE 1797 CLUB

For information about the upcoming series, go to www.1797club.com to join the club!

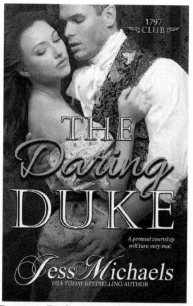

The Daring Duke (Available Now!)
Her Favorite Duke (Available Now!)
The Broken Duke (Available Now!)
The Silent Duke (Available Now!)
The Duke of Nothing (Available Now!)
The Undercover Duke (Available Now!)
The Duke Who Lied (Coming August 2018)
The Duke of Desire (Coming October 2018)
The Last Duke (Coming November 2018)

SEASONS

THE WICKED WOODLEYS

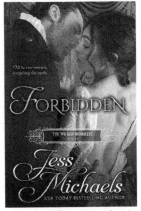

THE NOTORIOUS FLYNNS
The Other Duke (Book 1)
The Scoundrel's Lover (Book 2)
The Widow Wager (Book 3)
No Gentleman for Georgina (Book 4)
A Marquis for Mary (Book 5)

THE LADIES BOOK OF PLEASURES
A Matter of Sin
A Moment of Passion
A Measure of Deceit

THE PLEASURE WARS SERIES
Taken By the Duke
Pleasuring The Lady
Beauty and the Earl
Beautiful Distraction

About the Author

USA Today Bestselling author Jess Michaels likes geeky stuff, Vanilla Coke Zero, anything coconut, cheese, fluffy cats, smooth cats, any cats, many dogs and people who care about the welfare of their fellow humans. She watches too much daytime court shows, but just enough Star Wars. She is lucky enough to be married to her favorite person in the world and live in a beautiful home on a golf course lake in Northern Arizona.

When she's not obsessively checking her steps on Fitbit or trying out new flavors of Greek yogurt, she writes historical romances with smoking hot alpha males and sassy ladies who do anything but wait to get what they want. She has written for numerous publishers and is now fully indie and loving every moment of it (well, almost every moment).

Jess loves to hear from fans! So please feel free to contact her in any of the following ways (or carrier pigeon):

www.AuthorJessMichaels.com

Email: Jess@AuthorJessMichaels.com
Twitter www.twitter.com/JessMichaelsbks
Facebook: www.facebook.com/JessMichaelsBks

Jess Michaels raffles a gift certificate EVERY month to members of her newsletter, so sign up on her website: http://www.authorjessmichaels.com/

84935194R00146

Made in the USA
San Bernardino, CA
14 August 2018